THE TILTING HOUSE

ALSO BY IVONNE LAMAZARES

The Sugar Island

THE TILTING HOUSE

A NOVEL

Ivonne Lamazares

COUNTERPOINT / CALIFORNIA

THE TILTING HOUSE

This is a work of fiction. All of the characters, organizations, and events portrayed in this novel are either products of the author's imagination or are used fictitiously.

Copyright © 2025 by Ivonne Lamazares

All rights reserved under domestic and international copyright. Outside of fair use (such as quoting within a book review), no part of this publication may be reproduced, stored in a retrieval system, or transmitted in any form or by any means, electronic, mechanical, photocopying, recording, or otherwise, without the written permission of the publisher. For permissions, please contact the publisher.

First Counterpoint edition: 2025

Library of Congress Cataloging-in-Publication Data
Names: Lamazares, Ivonne author
Title: The tilting house : a novel / Ivonne Lamazares.
Description: First Counterpoint edition: 2025. | San Francisco : Counterpoint, 2025.
Identifiers: LCCN 2025005771 | ISBN 9781640097094 hardcover | ISBN 9781640097100 ebook
Subjects: LCSH: Cuba—Fiction | LCGFT: Domestic fiction | Novels
Classification: LCC PS3562.A42175 T55 2025 | DDC 813/.54—dc23/eng/20250303
LC record available at https://lccn.loc.gov/2025005771

Jacket design by Jaya Miceli
Jacket image © Luis Francisco Pizarro Ruiz / Alamy Stock Photo
Book design by Laura Berry

COUNTERPOINT
Los Angeles and San Francisco, CA
www.counterpointpress.com

Printed in the United States of America

10 9 8 7 6 5 4 3 2 1

For Steve and Sophie, always

For my mother

Immigrants . . . cannot escape their history any more than you yourself can lose your shadow.

—ZADIE SMITH,
White Teeth

Even if you had returned,
You'd only be a kind of ghost.

—A. E. STALLINGS,
"BURNED"

Freedom is destruction plus movement.

—KARL OVE KNAUSGAARD,
My Struggle: Book 1

CONTENTS

PART ONE
Visitors
1

PART TWO
Salons
69

PART THREE
El Focsa
165

PART FOUR
Return
239

Acknowledgments
291

PART ONE

Visitors

I

Paladero, Havana

In 1989, that desperate year, my aunt Ruth decided to unload me on my deadbeat father in *el norte*. I don't mean to be harsh about this now, decades into the future; after all, in those days of scarcity Aunt Ruth survived mostly by scheming and prophesying, especially when it came to me.

One evening in her Paladero house, in the front room she pompously called the parlor, Ruth delivered her masterstroke. She said to me, "*Niña*, the world's tilting the other way." She sat at her large mahogany desk, the dogs Lucho and Tigre asleep at her feet. "Maybe now," she said, "your father will come visit and bring us a few dollars. Or who's to say, maybe he'll send for you." She wrote my father's name across her elegant blue stationery. "We'll let him know that your mother's passed."

Ruth's voice was low and kindly. Out the window the light was thin, and Paladero Park across the street was filling with neighborhood couples, screaming children, and old people sitting on their benches.

I tried not to worry. On the subject of my father, Mamá had

been mercifully clear: "You can't find someone," she'd said, "who doesn't want to be found."

RUTH'S SCHEMES ABOUT my deadbeat father started in the fall after Mamá died, on the evening the banned VOA spoke of German youth on the other side of the world climbing to the top of the Berlin Wall and dangling their feet over the eleven-foot drop. Ruth sat up in her desk chair, stunned by the news. She turned off the radio. "Germans dancing," she said. "Now *there's* a sight to behold."

She, of course, beheld more. For one, she said, dust from the Berlin rubble would drift to us from across the Atlantic, and stones in Havana's seawall would crack and fissure and issue in the Last Flood. (Ruth, a Witness, saw Armageddon in every ripple of Havana Bay.) But before the world's ruin, Ruth said, the bankrupt, empireless Soviets would ditch us, and when they did, we'd starve. "Starve," she repeated, opening her eyes wide. This last prediction scared me. "Your father, *niña*, is our only hope."

My father, our "only hope," was one of the traitor worms, men and women who'd abandoned the revolution years before and fled to the enemy north (*la yuma*, *Una* *y* States). As a result they'd been banished, never allowed to return. But Ruth now swore that traitor *yumas* like my father would sweep back into Havana soon, cheered by all of us (*And—hah!—niña, by this government*) for their lifesaving dollars.

On this last point she wasn't wrong. A few *yuma* traitors had already shown up in the city center. They wore fancy sunglasses and spectacular new shoes, doled out money to teary-eyed relatives, and spread their *fula* in a few government-approved dollars-only bakeries and bodegas.

"In a twinkling, *niña*," Ruth said, "all has changed. You'll see. Our turn will come."

But nothing changed that year. The seawall held back the sea, my father didn't write, and Ruth each morning clomped out of the house with our ration book to the empty bodega and then to the bakery for our quarter loaf. Before I'd leave for school she was back, sweaty from the long, rowdy lines and dragging her polio-shriveled leg. "What can I do," she'd say to me, indignant, unbagging her few eggs and a gob of lard wrapped in brown paper, "if someone cuts in line and someone else starts punching or pulls a knife? Can I punch back? Run away?" She looked down at her leg. "A person can go out for bread in this city and end up on their deathbed in Calixto García Hospital."

By evening, after she'd managed to feed us, Ruth and I, along with everyone else on the block, spilled out into Paladero Park. At thirteen, I stood in a circle of girls in the small Milo rotunda, pretending to ignore the boys on the cement bridge—Hernando Malanga-head Pita leading his neighborhood gang over the arch, the group of them pelting stones at their empty beer bottles below. Ruth and her old friends sat on their wooden bench parsing out our "Special Period" of hunger after the German wall's collapse. Small children screamed from the fenced-in playground.

As Ruth had predicted, that world—Ruth's, mine, the neighborhood's—soon tumbled, but its undoing looked nothing like her visions of Fire and Flood. Even now I can't say exactly whose fault it was, though I suspect that a large part of the blame was mine.

As for the other part, it probably belonged to many—especially to the young *yuma* who showed up on Ruth's porch one day looking nothing like we'd expected, and who, in the end, whether I wished it or not, turned out to be one of us.

2

1993

It took four years for the first *yuma* savior to appear on our block, and to Ruth's bitter surprise this visitor appeared not to us (despite Ruth's unanswered letters to my father) but to the bedraggled Prietos next door.

Sonia Prieto—a cousin who'd gone to Miami as a skinny teenager—was back that summer as a swarthy thirty-year-old lawyer, fat like a goose and stuffed with crisp green *fula*. Within a few days Sonia had bought the Prietos two large kerosene lamps, a portable stereo, and a battery-operated fan from the Ultra Market, now dollars-only. Ruth, burning with jealousy, kept track of the empty boxes by their curb.

The kerosene lamps lit up the Prietos' house during the constant blackouts. Ruth and I watched neighbors bounce in and out of their bright door. Some neighbors, who for decades had shunned the Prietos for their counterrevolutionary past and their Virgin of Charity altar, now stopped by daily. (Ruth shunned the Prietos' altar too, but not because the government frowned on religious displays. As a Witness she considered the statue—the

Virgin's beautiful downcast face and the capsizing boat with the three saved fishermen—nothing more than pagan idolatry.)

Even the block's Revolutionary Defense Committee president, Dr. Cuevas, visited the Prietos now. He must have sipped coffee and turned over in his hands the new gadgets bought with the visitor's dollars. CDR President Cuevas, who'd shunned his long-gone *yuma* relatives as the Party had at one time required, was in this tilting world, cut off from the precious foreign currency that could buy him food in the dollars-only shops, his own stash of useless pesos flooding away as if through the hole in the Germans' wall. Without connections to relatives abroad, Defense Committee President Cuevas found himself defenseless in the Special Period. "How the wheels come round," Ruth had said of the Cuevases. But the large turning wheels had been rolling over many, including those who'd done nothing wrong in her long, watchful accounting.

Ruth refused to attend the Prietos' gatherings. "We used to live by a vipers' nest," she said to me, watching the spectacle from her rocking chair. "Now we live by the circus."

Whenever the Prietos' door opened, Beatles songs drifted to us on Ruth's porch. One evening in a fanfare of music, Sonia came out of the Prietos' front door, grabbed hold of their porch railing, and waved to us with her other hand. Ruth and I waved back. Sonia Prieto looked to the trees in Paladero Park across from our two houses, took off her shoes, set them on the Prietos' step, and sloshed barefoot through the muck of the street toward the park.

"Something's not right with that woman," Ruth said in a low voice.

Sonia walked past the park's Milo rotunda to the children's muddy playground. She squeezed her enormous grown-up butt onto a child's swing and went at it a long time, the metal chain squealing under her heft.

"Our turn will come," Ruth said again to me, but without the ring of triumph she'd summoned back in '89 when the Germans had first climbed up their wall. The sun went all the way down and the swing in the park squealed on, then stopped. Sonia must have walked back across the muddy street to the Prietos' house in the dark.

BUT, TO USE Ruth's words, our turn came.

A few days after Sonia Prieto swung her butt on a child's swing, a pale young woman crossed the street from the park toward Ruth's house. My friend Tere and I watched her from the porch.

The stranger came straight to Ruth's gate, stood on the sidewalk, and set down her knapsack. She took in the double doors, the windows, and the weather-worn brickwork of Ruth's house. She looked at the garage and up at the old servants' room above the garage (there were no servants after the revolution). A black yankee camera hung from her neck. She was small; her dark wavy hair went past her shoulders. She wore red sandals.

The young woman looked at Tere's round, guileless face, and she spoke to me instead. Whenever Tere and I were together—she was born with Down syndrome—I was responsible for what Tere did and what was done to her.

"Vilar residence?" the woman said.

Her formal wording surprised me, also her odd accent. She was clearly a *yuma*, and apparently foolish enough to have walked here alone from the bus stop with an impressive *de afuera* camera hanging from her neck. I said, "My aunt is inside, taking her siesta."

Tere opened the gate without permission, and the woman came up the porch steps and set her blue knapsack on the tiles beneath the parlor window. Next to the knapsack, casually, the woman set down her yankee camera. Sweat darkened her dress beneath the arms and a wet V pointed down to where her camera had hung on her chest. Despite her sweaty dress, she gave off a faint smell of gardens, of a newness that awed and rankled me. Her smile struck me as slightly greedy. Her teeth were too white.

Tere turned to me, her face wrinkled up into a question. I didn't smile back at the *yuma*, didn't ask her to sit. When strangers smiled for no reason, I thought it a bad sign. I was used to serious, embittered women like Ruth, or like the neighborhood women who sometimes passed by Ruth's porch and sighed tragically, looking into the void, saying things like, "It's so hot I've lost my senses," or "My nerves are standing on end," or "I've eaten so little my knees are buckling." I copied their expressions. At sixteen, I lived with old Ruth in her cavernous house out of necessity, not choice, and I honored my feelings by putting on dark, sullen looks.

The *yuma*, maybe thinking me simple like Tere, turned away from us and gripped the window bars. She peered rudely into Ruth's dark parlor. I didn't warn her. What was she trying to see? In the parlor sat only Ruth's ancient rattan couch and her rocking chairs, the stereopticon on the mahogany desk, and on the far wall the large portrait of the ugly baby—nothing, I thought, that could interest a fancy *yuma*.

And then, of course, it happened. The woman shrieked and jumped away from the window. She held her right hand in her left. Lucho, teeth bared, shoved his snout through the bars and growled, and old Tigre barked from inside.

The racket woke Ruth, and she clomped out to the dark parlor and shut away the yelping dogs in her room. Then she stepped out to the porch, her face puffy from her interrupted nap. When she saw the young woman gripping her own hand, Ruth looked hard at me. She took the stranger gently by the wrist, pressed the hem of her housedress to the woman's hand, and led her to the rocking chair. "Not to worry," Ruth said, "he's had his shots."

The woman winced at Ruth's pressure, and then, like Tarzan, pointed to her own chest with her good hand. "Mariela Ruth Vilar," she announced. *"Yo soy."*

Ruth held the stranger's hand. "You," she said to me. "Take Tere home."

3

That afternoon I ran from Tere's grandmother's apartment at the end of the block back to Ruth's house. In all my life no one had mentioned a pretty *yuma* who shared our last name, and Ruth had never spoken of family in *el norte* except for my deadbeat father, but, of course, he was no Vilar.

The blackout had started, and Ruth had lit a candle in the kitchen. She stood watching the pot of broth simmer on the gas burner. I rushed in, and she looked up at me, then back to the pot on the stove. She said only, "So she's my daughter."

Ruth's *daughter*.

I grasped the back of the chair and tried to catch my breath.

Ruth had always seemed nunnish, infertile; her long skirts and orthopedic shoes had always made her look old.

"She's upstairs now, resting." Ruth nodded toward the spare room above the garage. Music seeped into the kitchen from the Prietos' illuminated house next door. "I sent my daughter to *la yuma* years ago. She was a child. I sent her to an American family. She's had a wonderful life and that is all."

Ruth's *yuma* daughter.

If Ruth meant that this *yuma* daughter'd had a better life than mine, I thought the facts were against it: Ruth had apparently given her own daughter away. Mamá didn't do so willingly.

"You wrote your letters to *la yuma* to find *her*," I said. "You never tried to find my father."

This was a wild, foolish accusation. I'd seen Ruth write my father's name on many envelopes, address them to a place she called Eleya and spelled Hialeah; I'd seen her lick the stamps and give the letters to the mailwoman. But a sharp jealousy, stronger than Ruth's toward the Prietos, flared up in me at the arrival of Ruth's newfound daughter with her big, foreign camera. Until then I hadn't wanted an answer from my father. But now with the appearance of Ruth's *yuma* daughter, I burned for an answer from him or from anyone who'd care enough to write my name on a blue envelope. Ruth's past threat to send me to my father in the north now struck me as something worse—an invention of Ruth's, or maybe her last-ditch attempt to mold me to her ways and turn me into her grateful adoptee, sharing in her love of Jehovah, Ronald Reagan, and Jacqueline Gold-Digger Onassis, who'd made herself, in Ruth's eyes, "her own work of art." When I'd first moved into Ruth's house after Mamá's funeral, Ruth replaced my bedside picture of Yuri Gagarin with one of Onassis sprawled on a yacht, sunglasses lifted above her beautiful sunshiny face. "Something to aim for in this life, *niña*," she'd said at the time. It sickened me now that I'd let her.

"I tried to find your father, Jehovah knows," Ruth said. "But in His wisdom, He gives us what we need, not what we want."

"I want nothing."

I lied to Ruth. Sometimes I wanted to live alone in the thickets of the *manigüa* bush, dig up roots to eat, sleep, study, talk very little.

"Don't fool yourself, *niña*," Ruth said. "Even a cow wants, which is why she moos."

Ruth carried a bowl of the broth out to the small laundry courtyard, along the clotheslines, past the rusted washer, and around the gardenia pot to the room above the garage, where the visitor rested like Rapunzel in her tower. A candle flickered through the room's open window.

A hired girl had lived up in that room some years before the revolution, when Ruth and Mamá were children. The girl had cooked and ironed for the family, then loved a white boy from the neighborhood, fell into an "interesting state," and went off to have his baby. "We begged for her to stay, me and your mother," Ruth had said to me. "We liked her. Your mother especially. But your grandmother was a just woman." A green ceramic basin where the girl washed her face each morning still sat atop the nightstand up in the room.

I didn't think much of the story about the banished girl except as another of Ruth's racist tales—Ruth thought herself white as a Norwegian; the ends of her hair, she'd say with pride, had stayed blond till the age of ten. (My own hair, like Mamá's, was pitch-black, dry, and, according to Ruth, "hopeless.") But the night that Mariela Vilar, Ruth's *yuma* child, arrived, I wondered if it hadn't been the hired girl but Ruth who'd fallen into the "interesting state" and was made to ship the secret baby abroad by her "just" mother.

Ruth's new daughter, tucked away in the room above the garage, now seemed nearly a secret again. I could see why Mamá never told me about Ruth's secret baby, but why let Ruth pass herself off as the one who spoke to Jehovah and got Him to answer back?

Toward the end of that last winter in the Misión Street apartment, after Ruth had moved in with us to give Mamá her morphine shots, Mamá said to me, "Ruth means well. Listen to her." But Mamá never had. A Party member, she'd guarded the Old Havana streets with an ancient commissioned rifle while I slept. She looked out for counterrevolutionaries like her own older sister. Sundays Mamá and I woke early. Brooms in fists, she and I swept the streets with other volunteers; we carried homemade signs to the Plaza—*Socialismo o Muerte* and *Fidel estoy contigo*—and stood in the heat through the long day, roaring as the crowd roared. If I fell asleep on my feet, Mamá held me against her. "Revolution is like medicine, Yuri—bitter, but good for you," she said in my ear. Once I asked her why we needed medicine. "It takes a lot to heal a country," she'd said.

Now I opened Ruth's kitchen window. Soft music came in waves from the Prietos' illuminated terrace. I pictured Ruth's newfound *yuma* sleeping peacefully in her room above the garage, and I made my decision. Ruth could have the daughter she'd always wanted, but first thing in the morning I'd walk the four blocks to the Malanga-heads' cramped courtyard and ask my youth leader, Compañero Oscar Malanga-head Pita, for a spot in the Lenin boarding school for the coming year. That last winter in the Misión apartment I'd begged Mamá, a Party officer, to enroll me. "It's nothing to you," I argued, "and the Lenin's the best secondary in the country." But she'd looked at me, blank, and turned her face to the wall, and in the end, she let Ruth have me.

4

Who knows where we'd be now, Ruth and I, if that next morning I'd followed through on my intentions? But I was too young, too easily distracted, and in the end, I didn't walk the four blocks to the tiny Malanga-head courtyard. That day and that whole summer, nothing went as I planned. My two-person life with Ruth and the dogs in the Paladero house was nearly over, but I didn't know it.

I woke that morning to the kind of spread I'd seen only once, five years earlier, at Mamá's wake. At the sight of Ruth's heaped-up table, some of that old queasiness came back but also a big hunger. Ruth and I sat silent and waited for her *yuma* daughter to come down from her room above the garage. Fancy china from the cabinet—white plates painted with vines and tiny blue flowers—lay on the table, and blossoms from Ruth's gardenia bush floated in a clear bowl among dishes of fried eggs, the coffeepot with the small white pitcher of milk beside it, the breadbasket, and butter. Where had Ruth found butter? And at what cost? The country had started its "Special Period in a Time of Peace." Butter, cans of Russian meat, milk powder, and all Soviet products had disappeared from the stores; the corner bodega displayed mostly flies, buzzing or lying on the dusty shelves (*Look, niña, the German dust everywhere*) so that the ration book barely bought us a fistful of peas. Only a *yuma* visitor like Sonia Prieto next door, or like Ruth's new secret daughter, could get us past the militia at the entrance of the new Ultra dollars-only market stocked with the vanished eggs, chicken, steak, milk, rice, and coffee. I wondered if Mariela's dollars had already made this feast possible, and if it would be the first of many.

Finally, the clothes hanging over the patio moved, and Mariela Rapunzel Vilar, down from her tower, squinted in the light. She wore a wrinkled pale-orange shirt and dark loose pants, too sloppy for the grandness of Ruth's table. She was only a little pretty, and she stood as if a puff of wind could lift her off the ground. I saw nothing of Ruth in her, nothing of us sturdy, big-shouldered Vilars. "*Aquí soy*," she said, wrongly.

Ruth waved her in. "Good morning, *hija*." Ruth choked a little—on purpose, I thought—at the word *hija*. She looked giddy over Mariela's appearance, as if the young visitor proved something about Ruth herself—that maybe Ruth was a mother in her own right, and not the guardian of other people's reluctant and ungrateful children, or the caretaker of strays. Or that Ruth had been desired once—even if abandoned, so were many women, some beautiful with two good legs, abandonment so common as to mean no dishonor. Ruth would now join the ranks of the Prietos and shop for groceries at the Ultra dollars-only market, and there was no telling how many sparkling appliances Mariela Ruth Vilar could make appear.

Mariela sat back in her chair. She wrinkled her nose at the butter and eggs and the murdered flowers. "Excuse me," she said thinly, "I don't eat much breakfast."

Whenever I'd visited Ruth's house as a child, she'd made me sit at her table, hungry or not, until I swallowed what she'd dished on my plate. In Ruth's hierarchy of sins, wasting good food came second only to cursing the Holy Spirit (an offense that would get one's name struck from the Book of Life). To her *yuma* daughter she said only, "You must be tired, *hija*."

Lucho and Tigre circled beneath the table and brushed against our knees. I mopped up my yolk with a slice of bread, lathered another piece with Ruth's expensive butter, chewed loudly, clanked my fork on the plate, and took peeks at Ruth and at the *yuma* sitting quietly across from me. But my bad table manners got no notice. Ruth smiled expectantly at Mariela, who looked nowhere in particular.

A few minutes passed and finally the *yuma* spoke. "I would take a bath." Ruth rose at this—she would heat the water on the stove—but Mariela put out her good hand. "I have to learn to do things." She paused. "Yuri will maybe show me about the bath?"

I looked up, astonished to hear my name. Mariela's eyes were big and round and focused on me. I felt a little special for this. She smiled and slid her plate—her yolk still unpopped—in my direction. When I finished her egg, she rose from her chair, and I rose too, and the two of us walked past Ruth, who still smiled up at her daughter. The confused dogs stayed back, waiting for their scraps.

Out on the small courtyard inside a square of lichen-green

bricks lay the cistern's metal cover. Mariela watched me. I lifted the cistern's round metal lid, laid it to the side, then grabbed the rope attached to the pulley and hoisted the bucket, hand over hand. The bucket came up out of the dark iron-smelling water, swinging only a little, full to the rim. "Keep it straight so no water spills," I said. When the bucket reached the top of the well, Mariela leaned over the cistern and took the bucket from its hook. With surprising strength, she set it on the ground without a splash. I found it hard to resist her bright, attentive face; I'd never had a student before.

The brimming bucket sat on the ground between us. Mariela started then, "I can see the things Ruth says about you. You're smart." Her pronunciation was odd, flavorless—somewhere between yankee and native.

She'd said "Ruth." Not "Mother." And I doubted Ruth had said any good thing about me.

Mariela could see too, she added, that I was strong, like my name.

Having a boy's name was bad enough. I wouldn't admit to the *yuma* that after the first heady days of revolution, my mother and father had thought their baby would one day fly to the moon.

Mariela pressed her fingertips to the top of my hand. "Yuri," she said, "you and your classmates, the youth of Cuba, I want to tell you that not everyone who grows up in North America hates this revolution. Some love it. I love it. I have come to stay here for good and to work for the revolution."

I slid my hand out from under hers. This was quite a speech. But everyone knew that Cubans living abroad were still traitor worms despite their lavish green *fula* and would never be allowed to stay here "for good"—and besides, there was no such thing as a true yankee communist. Only Angela Davis, her hair a dark halo around her handsome face, could be called that. And she'd been in a yankee jail for her struggle. Where, I thought, had Mariela been with her cool, white photographer hands?

"I'm not going back to *el norte*," she said to me in a quiet voice. She sounded sure of this. I picked up the bucket. "For now," I said to her, coolly, "you know where things are."

◆

5

That evening, to my own bitter surprise, Ruth decided we'd attend the Prietos' nightly party for the first time. No more glowering or tsk-tsking from the porch. Ruth now meant to parade her own *yuma* like a beribboned pony past the Prietos and all the neighbors who flocked through the Prietos' front door. Her pride in motherhood—and the possible benefit that could come from it—seemed to tamp down any possible shame over Mariela's secret, out-of-wedlock birth. Or maybe Ruth wanted to strike first before the loose tongues in the neighborhood started flapping. Either way Ruth's bloated display of her *yuma* daughter made me sorry to be alive.

In the early afternoon Ruth introduced Mariela to Tere's grandmother Doña Barbara, and Doña Barbara's round face turned pink, then dark at the news of Ruth's yankee love child. Alarmed, Doña Barbara glanced at Tere on the floor beside Tigre. But Tere understood nothing of the fine points of Ruth's motherhood, and Doña Barbara and Ruth pooled their sugar rations and went in the kitchen to make a jar of dulce de leche.

They wrapped it still warm in a yellow towel, and like a group of gracious ambassadors, all of us took the dish next door in order, Ruth said, to make peace with the Prietos' good fortune. Ruth, of course, now beamed with her own good fortune, her *yuma*, bearer of gifts and giftee of Ruth's love.

In the Prietos' living room, the five of us made our way through a gauntlet of neighborhood old ladies sitting on folding chairs, balancing plates of fried foods on their laps. When Ruth introduced her brand-new daughter from *el norte*, the old women looked as startled as Doña Barbara had, but all were polite, smiled, shook Mariela's hand. One said to me, "Now you have a cousin. You must be so glad." I gave no answer. Mariela, looking slightly bored, shook the old ladies' hands, and Ruth, standing taller than I'd ever seen her, led Mariela from one woman to the next.

Past the old ladies I spotted a strange new contraption. A large white metal box, the size of a dogcatcher's cage, sat at the center of the Prietos' table. A group of neighbors stood around it, gawking. I forgot about Ruth and her beribboned daughter and went to stand with the other gawkers. Rosario Prieto, my classmate, opened and shut the door of the white metal box. A light went on and off inside. "Tiny wave," she said to me.

"*Micro*wave," corrected Sonia, the visiting cousin. She gave us the satisfied look of a teacher who's prismed a sunbeam into colors for a roomful of wide-eyed children. "It cooks everything," she said.

Ruth, introductions over, also came to look at the strange machine. Old Antonieta Prieto, Rosario's grandmother, took Ruth's elbow and leaned to her ear. "Glad to see you, neighbor. I tell dear Sonia we shouldn't let so many people in here. It gets so hot. But she wants to make everyone happy in the neighborhood." Antonieta gave her visiting niece a kindly smile. Then she whispered to Ruth, "We must be careful who we let in this house. But my daughters and granddaughter are young and the young will enjoy themselves. I have to let Dr. Cuevas in, or the CDR will shut down my sewing, you know how things are."

The room was stifling with the crowd gathered around the white metal box. A shirtless boy in front shouted, "Put a frog in it. The eyes will pop out."

Sonia lifted a long, yellow plantain from a basket, peeled it, and opened the door of the white box. She set it on a plate, placed the plate on the glass platter inside the box and closed the door. She pushed a button, and the light went on. The plate and plantain spun in slow circles, turning as if in a music box. No one said a word. When the gadget beeped, Sonia pulled the handle. "Who wants it?" she called out.

Tere and the children hollered and raised their arms. Ruth looked at the box with approval. "In a twinkling," she said to me and snapped her fingers.

"He owns a rabbit," the boy in front said, pointing to his friend. "Put his rabbit in."

The demonstration ended (someone in the group muttered that we didn't need to cook faster; we needed something *to* cook), and the small crowd wandered from the large white box. Antonieta then introduced the block's two *yuma* visitors, Mariela and Sonia, to each other. Both *yumas* had flown out of Miami only a few weeks apart.

"Enjoy your stay," Sonia said to Mariela. "It goes quickly." Sonia's thick fingers squeezed Antonieta's hand. Sonia looked a decade older than Mariela, although soon I'd find out that Mariela was thirty-four years old, not twentysomething as I'd first thought. Mariela, standing in the Prietos' dining room, hair loose across her shoulders, looked not much older than some girls who'd repeated grades and sat in the back of my tenth-grade classroom with their thick Cleopatra eyeliner and their bored faces, letting the clock on the wall run out so they could climb onto their boyfriends' motorcycles and live their lives full of sex and loud, forbidden songs on their stereos.

Mariela and Sonia stood beside the table and the large white box that had cooked the plantain in a twinkling. Mariela said in her odd, flat tone that she hadn't come to visit. She'd returned to her country. She'd come back for good.

Sonia looked at Mariela, then answered softly, "Not allowed, I'm sorry to say. The law forbids it. None of us can stay if we've ever received an exit permit to live abroad. We visit our families, then it's back to where we came from."

Mariela brushed back her dark bangs and said, "I didn't choose to leave. I was little more than a baby. That whole plane was full of children and babies."

Ruth opened her mouth but then said nothing. She shifted her weight to her thin leg, then back to the other.

Sonia asked if Mariela had grown up in Miami.

"Lincoln, Nebraska," Mariela said. She said she'd taken a train there when she was five. "I wore a big coat. They sat me backward." She smiled vaguely. "When the train started I felt—how do you say in Spanish?" Mariela put her hand over

The Tilting House

her belly and said a word to Sonia in English. I imagine now that she might have said *revolted*, or *woozy*.

"*Revuelta*," Sonia said.

"Yes. *Revuelta*." Loud Beatles music started on the terrace off the dining room. Julio Cuevas, the blond son of CDR President Cuevas, approached our circle and touched Rosario's shoulder. She smiled at him. Julio now attended the Lenin boarding school I had asked Mamá to send me to. On weekends he returned to the neighborhood and rarely left his house except to board the bus back to the Lenin, wearing his blue uniform and tie. His own mother had died early and horribly, dousing herself in kerosene and setting fire to her skirt the year before. Dr. Cuevas, wild with terror, had tried to wrap his wife in a blanket, but by the time the firemen and medics arrived, she had been "fully consumed." Soon after that, Julio was sent to the Lenin, but for the few weeks till his transfer there, he'd sat behind me in literature class and not said a word to anyone. I didn't dare to look back at him, but his slightest movement behind my chair made my heart jump and I could think of nothing else. He sighed sometimes, from boredom or disgust or pure sadness, I was never sure which. The day he finally left for the Lenin, I felt relieved and also lost, and for a while afterward I still felt him there behind my shoulders.

Rosario gave me a shrug of apology and she and Julio went to dance on the small terrace off the dining room. Julio pressed his hand against Rosario's back through "Yesterday."

Mariela continued her explanations to the rest of us. "The people here don't need gadgets. They don't need"—she pointed to the microwave on the table—"exhibitions," and in her crusading little speech, I saw a fleeting resemblance to her mother. Mariela said, as proof of her intention, "I've told Yuri, I'm here to work for the people, for the revolution."

Ruth, Doña Barbara, and Sonia turned to me as if I were to blame for the *yuma*'s delusions. I said to Mariela, "So you're staying for the cane harvest?" At that, Ruth, who'd stayed silent during Mariela's discourse, gave me one of her hard looks. I didn't care. Mariela's airplane full of babies didn't move me, nor did her big eyes on us now as if we owed her something. I'd had enough of her grand return. What did Ruth's yankee daughter know about us students chopping cane in the sun, bent to the stalks with machetes, or about the harvest goal itself set at ten million tons each year of my childhood? The goal had never been reached; still, that next January we secondary students would again head for the green fields outside Havana to bring in the sheaves at ten million tons, a number, Ruth said, far exceeding the Lord's requirement of seventy times seven.

Someone yelled into the dining room, "Greetings, Miss Astronaut." From the far side of the terrace, where tiny iridescent lights wrapped like a vine around the low brick wall, Hernando Malanga-head Pita, neighborhood thug and bicycle thief, called out to me and tipped an imaginary hat. His gang buddies laughed. Of the Malanga-head clan, only Hernando's older brother, Compañero Oscar, my youth leader, had made good on the gifts of education and equality promised by the revolution. Hernando, thin, wiry, attended a last-ditch vocational school and led a small group of scruffy boys eager to do what he said. I was surprised to see him and his buddies roaming the Prietos' house, bumping elbows with neighbors who would have shooed him and his rough friends from their own porches. Maybe the world really was tilting like Ruth said and all these unlikely people had tumbled in here together.

"Yes," Mariela went on. She would cut cane, yes. She turned to Ruth then. "I have no money for you. No gadgets."

Ruth's lips tightened. She took Doña Barbara's arm to steady herself. Doña Barbara turned pink again. She looked at Mariela, then at Sonia. "You two," she said, "are blessings to us all."

Mariela repeated, "No money." She lifted her chin.

I felt sorry for Ruth, holding on to her friend's arm. I also felt that this shock served Ruth right for having blown a month's supplies on one show-off breakfast and for having abandoned her child to the yankees in the first place and now inflicting her upon us. But Ruth looked stricken, her eyes shut as if a long-expected judgment had come down on her at last. I wondered if Mariela, like the dirty Soviets or the cruel yankees, would truly let us starve.

IT WASN'T UNTIL later that summer, after Ruth had lost most of her authority over me, that I learned more about Ruth's *yuma* daughter. In 1962, when Mariela was four, Ruth had boarded her onto one of those planes full of children and adolescents in an operation someone had named "Pedro Pan" in honor of that faraway Neverland populated by dispossessed boys.

Most of the children on those flights had been handed over by panicked parents following a wild rumor that Cuban minors would soon be taken from their mothers and fathers and "reeducated" in Soviet-style camps. Many parents had cajoled their confused and sobbing children onto airplanes bound for the land ninety miles north of us, where no child, it was said, could be forcibly separated from parents. The children were meant to stay with relatives in the United States or to be housed in church-run dormitories for a few weeks, until things "blew over" back on the island.

That was the parents' plan, but the Missile Crisis put an end to Cuba-U.S. relations, and months and sometimes years passed before the distraught mothers and fathers could make their way north and join their children. Some, like Mariela, grew up in Catholic institutions and orphanages. The nuns, she said, despite their gloomy rosaries, were kind.

For a little while, Mariela told me, she lived with a family, the Butlers, in the Nebraska countryside, cornfields in the back of the house, and chickens, and a donkey they called Boy. She showed me a picture taken from her bedroom—acres of corn, and above it, a stripe of pale-blue sky. It looked, through the rectangle of the window, like a strange flag. Mariela was returned to the nuns after a year. "I wasn't right for the Butlers," she told me. She seemed almost proud of the fact.

6

During the decades Mariela Vilar had spent with nuns in Nebraska, Ruth must have tried hard to join her daughter in *la yuma*. I had to believe this. Ruth could be fanatical and mean but not monstrous. What had stopped her from rescuing her daughter from an American orphanage? Visa trouble? Bad health? Lack of money? And what had gone through her daughter's heart in those years she'd spent with the nuns and in the few months she lived with the Butlers and their donkey named Boy? There was a hint of what, in Mariela's hard declaration of "no money" that evening at the Prietos', and in her taking off from the party without a word to anyone. Mariela's declaration scared me; it also made me like her a little. She seemed nothing like the puffed-up Sonia and her tiny-wave cooker for people who had no food.

Ruth, despite her shock, stayed at the Prietos' long enough to say her goodbyes. Before walking home in the late-evening light, she sent Tere and me to "bring back" her daughter. Mariela had apparently grabbed her camera from her room above the garage and walked over to the park. Tere and I followed her flashes of light past the Milo rotunda to the first bridge.

Music still reached the two of us from Rosario's terrace, and it was almost dark when we caught up with Mariela. She was bending backward, aiming her camera up at the mesh of branches crisscrossing the blue-gray of the sky. Lucho circled her, his pointy snout sniffing the ground. He sidled up to her, rubbed his ribs against her leg. He'd seemingly abandoned Ruth, wagged his tail, and switched loyalties to a stranger. Dogs, I thought, no matter how loony, couldn't shift allegiances as easily as humans did. But maybe neither dogs nor humans could be blamed for such betrayals. One's eyes could, like an infant's, follow brightness and movement and so go after Mariela's flashes lighting up the arc of leaves by the white cement bridge ahead of us.

When we reached Mariela on the green expanse by the foot of the bridge, she stopped clicking her camera. She bent down and scooped up some of the tiny orange-red flowers that grew all over the park in summer. Ruth called them *bolitas de coral*. Mariela broke one of the flowers at the stem and from the tip she caught a drop of dew with her tongue. She handed Tere and me each a flower. Tere opened hers and sucked on the stem. "Yuri, it's sweet," Tere said. I raised the stem to my mouth. It *was* sweet.

Hernando Malanga-head Pita appeared at the top of the bridge with two gang buddies, Reynaldo and Gelson. Lucho lifted his head and growled. Mariela bent down to Lucho and held him by the collar. Hernando scanned me, then Tere, and then settled on Mariela, who struggled with the dog in the grass.

The Tilting House

Fat Reynaldo Salderi whispered something in Hernando's ear, and Hernando walked down the decline a few steps, jumped over the bridge's wall, and stood before us in the grass, one leg facing out like a stage dancer. "We meet again, Miss Astronaut," he said to me. Then he extended his hand to Mariela, who held back the dog. Mariela seemed to take Hernando's courteous menace as a bit of a joke. She smiled, said her name, but didn't offer her hand.

"You a journalist?" Hernando asked her. "We know Miss Astronaut here and her idiot sidekick, but we don't know you." The gap between his front teeth showed. "You have a permit to take pictures? Of our flora and fauna?" He looked back at his boys standing at the bottom of the bridge. "If you don't have a permit, we may have to confiscate your equipment. Turn it in to the CDR."

Reynaldo said, "I'll confiscate her equipment." He and Gelson laughed, and Reynaldo came forward and stood behind Hernando.

Hernando held out his hand for Mariela's camera. His eyes were bright, but his face had changed. And still Mariela smiled up at him, ironic and friendly as if Hernando were a member of *her* gang with whom she could joke and tease.

Lucho quit snarling and sniffed something invisible in the grass. His ears flickered with excitement. I pulled on Mariela's arm. "We need to go." But she didn't move. Lucho dug his nose deeper into the dry grass.

I glanced back to Rosario Prieto's bright, noisy house—then to Ruth's. Ruth, still shaky from her secret baby's betrayal, might shuffle to her gate and try to call us in. I wanted to call out to her across the expanse of grass and the empty street, but Ruth's porch was dark.

Mariela stared at Hernando. I wonder now, looking back, why Mariela didn't leave the park that night when I asked her to. And I wonder why I didn't grab the dog from her and walk away—a simple action that would have prevented much of what followed.

Lucho stopped poking in the grass. He lifted his head, growled again, and then charged at Hernando. Hernando, like a dancer, turned gracefully to the side and in one swift pivot, he gave Lucho a vicious kick, lifting the dog off his four legs. Lucho came down hard on the sharp, glass-littered rocks by the bridge. He rolled on the ground once and whimpered, one leg kicking the air. Hernando yanked the camera from Mariela's hand, and he and the boys took off across the dry patch toward the Milo statue.

Mariela stared at the running boys, her camera swinging by its strap in Hernando's right hand. She didn't seem surprised, the way she'd been when Lucho bit her hand through Ruth's window bars. She knelt beside the dog and patted his head. "There now, there now," but her eyes followed the laughing boys, and in an instant, she took off after them and flew across the park's dry field. A dust cloud swirled in the air behind the runners, and then, as if it had all the time in the world, floated toward me and the whimpering dog and Tere crouching beside us with her soft, terrified weeping.

7

Sometimes, years after that night, I think this: Maybe the fine dust Mariela had raised running after the Malangahead gang boys drifted over to Ruth's house and wafted in through the windows and seeped under the doors, and Ruth and I, breathing it in and out for days on end, couldn't think right for a long time.

After Mariela took off across the park's field, Tere and I rushed to the Prietos' busy house for help. Doña Barbara bundled up Tere and took her home while Dr. Cuevas and a visiting nephew hurried back with me to the park. The nephew scooped up Lucho from his place by the bridge, and Dr. Cuevas and I led him to Ruth's house.

Ruth opened the door. She turned pale at the sight of Lucho bleeding in the arms of the young man. She limped to her room, where she laid out an old checkered towel across the bed. Dr. Cuevas's nephew Gabito, a veterinarian student at the Agricultural University of Havana, set the dog down. We stood around the bed and watched the dog's chest and stomach rise and fall unsteadily, the blood matted across the fur of Lucho's belly by his left hind leg. Ruth touched the dog's bloody fur gently, looked at her wet fingers, then at me. "Where is my daughter?" Mariela, I said, was out in the neighborhood, running after Hernando, who'd stolen her camera. Ruth took in these facts. "And you let her," she said, then turned again to Lucho.

Ruth's words sank into my chest. What I'd do with these words, or about them, I didn't know yet, but I was sure they wouldn't get dislodged except by a stronger, more punishing force.

Cuevas's nephew stretched the dog's legs gently and felt at the wound. "It's a deep one," he said to Cuevas.

"It's a stab wound," Ruth said. "Anyone can see that."

"Gabito studies agricultural animals, cows and chickens," Dr. Cuevas said.

"No chickens," the nephew said. "Bovine and equine medicine." He turned to me. "You saw a knife?"

"Hernando kicked the dog. Lucho fell hard on the rocks and broken glass by the bridge."

"An unfortunate accident," Dr. Cuevas said.

"No accident." Ruth's face turned dark. "An innocent animal is stabbed in the course of a robbery. That's a crime, not an accident." She looked at Cuevas, and before he could answer, she said, "My daughter, a guest in this country, is still out in the streets alone, in danger."

"The visitor couldn't have gone far," Cuevas said calmly. "This is a safe neighborhood." He turned to me. "The visitor"—he paused to clarify—"Ruth's daughter, she ran after Hernando?" There was something in this account Dr. Cuevas couldn't quite believe—Mariela's foolishness or his own bad luck at having to address it.

"Hernando took her camera," I said. "She ran after him to get it back."

Ruth said, softer now, "It's only logical that she'd run after the thief to regain her property." I knew this was Ruth's attempt to take back her poisonous *and you let her.* But I stood stiff; it wasn't enough.

Dr. Cuevas sighed and asked to make a call.

Ruth hesitated. She had always kept Paladero neighbors from wandering her house (not even Tere could go farther than the bathroom), and she applied this rule especially to the CDR president, who could note her possessions and their possible absence "should we have to sell some things quickly," she'd said to me, on the black market. But in the end Ruth looked at Lucho gasping on the splotchy red towel and pointed the CDR president in the direction of the phone down the hallway.

Mariela, of course, brought out all manner of exceptions from Ruth—and from all of us. First we'd had to make room in our minds for Mariela's secret birth and upbringing, then for her declarations of poverty, and now we had to allow that Lucho lay dying partly because of her stupidity (and also mine?), and that Mariela, a grown woman, was out pursuing small-time thugs through the neighborhood's dark streets to get back her camera.

"How much time?" Ruth asked Gabito. She walked to the side of the bed, where she could face Lucho's fearful, staring eye.

"He hasn't graduated," Dr. Cuevas said, lingering in the doorway. "He can't tell you for sure."

"Why'd you bring me here if you don't trust me?" the nephew asked.

"I trust you, Gabito, but life is unpredictable and hope is the last thing to lose."

The vet student looked at his watch and timed the pulse at Lucho's groin opposite the wounded leg. Ruth smoothed the fur on Lucho's head. The dog lay unmoving except for his labored breathing, as if he, too, had flown across the dusty expanse beyond the bridge with Hernando and his boys and Mariela, and was now simply trying to catch his breath. Ruth turned off the overhead light so Lucho wouldn't have to stare into the harsh brightness. She lit a candle on the dresser.

From down the hallway came Dr. Cuevas's loud "Uh-huh, uh-huh, *cómo no, gracias compañero*," and then, back in the room, he said with visible relief that Mariela was safe and her camera returned.

"Where is my daughter?" Ruth asked.

"Resting at Compañero Oscar's family home," Cuevas said.

"At the Malangones'?" Ruth raised her voice.

Lucho blinked and stared at Ruth. His leg shook.

"This little guy is not doing too well," Gabito said. "It's internal bleeding, something's punctured." Tears ran down Ruth's nose. I took her hand and held it the way she had held mine when Mamá died, and though it didn't help then, I thought it right to do the same for Ruth now. In a few seconds, Lucho stopped breathing. Ruth stared down at him for a moment, then gently closed the eye facing us, lifted Lucho's head, and closed the other eye. She thanked Dr. Cuevas and his nephew briefly and asked me to see them to the door.

Out on the porch, the two men lingered. They leaned against the iron rail and lit cigarettes. Dr. Cuevas glanced down the street, waiting, I imagined, for Mariela to appear. When she did, just before the tiny lights of their cigarettes had burned themselves out, she walked toward the house alongside Hernando's older brother, Compañero Oscar, each leaning toward the other as if engaged in a pleasant conversation. By Ruth's porch Mariela and Oscar paused on the sidewalk, and looking at our staring faces, Oscar apologized loudly for the "unfortunate accident" (Cuevas's exact words). At that, Ruth, who'd been watching from the window, opened the front door. She glared at Oscar and ordered Mariela and me into the house.

In the bedroom at the sight of the dog, Ruth sobbed a little, hanging on to Mariela's neck. She said she'd been "sick with worry"—the only reproach she'd make to her yankee daughter for taking her beloved dog along with a valuable camera to the park at dusk, and for running after the thieves. Ruth hung on to Mariela's arm and promised that the "culprits" would be charged.

Mariela slid the camera off her shoulder, then laid it on the bed next to Lucho as if she'd gone to get it for his sake. "We care too much about objects," she said. "It wasn't right that Lucho fell."

"Hernando kicked him," I said.

"That boy didn't mean to kick Lucho." Mariela paused. "He'll come tomorrow to say he's sorry. He promised."

"That's not a boy, *hija*," Ruth said. "That's a Malangón. A born criminal. And don't let Oscar's teacher glasses fool you." Her face reddened with fury at the thought of the two

Malanga-head brothers, but then she sniffled again and opened her arms to Mariela and me, and both of us leaned stiffly against each other and against Ruth's chest. Mariela's thin arms pressed against my back.

"We will bury our dear friend tomorrow," Ruth said, releasing us, "and everyone will see what was done to him."

Lucho, laid out across Ruth's towel, didn't look like himself at all (as most dead beings don't) but like a different dog we'd never known, stuffed and made up in Lucho's own image. I half expected the real dog to burst into the room and knock over Ruth's candle and set this dog impostor on fire. Instead, old Tigre, who'd gazed up once during the commotion in the room, woke now from his stupor in the corner and walked over to the bed. He sniffed at his dead friend and turned away. He seemed to accept nonbeing better than we did. Mariela took her camera from the bed and said to me, "Could you, maybe, come up?"

8

The worst part of that summer started for me then, worse than Mariela's sudden appearance and worse than Lucho's death.

I had never expected to be first in Ruth's heart. I figured I'd come in second after her dogs, or third, after the ugly baby in Ruth's beloved living room portrait. But the ugly baby in the painting seemed to have come to life now—no longer ugly—in Mariela, and my jealousy grew every day. Strangely, along with my jealousy, my desire for Mariela's approval, not Ruth's, also grew. It wasn't only Mariela's youth and foreign glamour, or even her stupid courage in crossing neighborhood lines drawn before Ruth's birth, that drew me to her. It was also that peculiar, approving smile of hers, which I'd hated in the first days of summer. Approval was something I rarely got from Ruth (or from Mamá in her last days). Mariela's encouraging voice sometimes drowned out the dry, low-pitched wind blowing inside me since Mama's death and telling me to head for the dark *manigüa* and disappear.

Ruth wiped her tears in the bedroom, straightened herself,

and nodded stoically as Mariela and I went through the dining room out the side door to the iron stairs, up to the room over the garage. Mariela dropped the camera on the banished servant girl's bed as if she no longer cared about her precious gadget, dumped it among several rolls of film, scattered photographs, pens, packets of chewing gum, a purple notebook, and a box of what I figured out were feminine pads. Of all the foreign things on display, her perfumy hygiene pads irked me the most. Every month my friends and I stuffed wads of cotton into homemade pouches that we pinned inside our panties. The pouches shifted and bulged and got stuck where they shouldn't.

Mariela and I sat on the edge of the bed. She slid an aluminum-wrapped stick of Doublemint gum toward me. It was the first time I'd chewed gum. The burst of flavor tingled in my nose and for a second my eyes watered. Mariela warned me not to swallow. Then she passed me some photos from beside her on the bed, one by one. She called them her "projects," and they were pictures mostly of herself, her face made up like a warrior's in bands of blue, red, and black, even the eyelids, and her head shaved bald like a mannequin's. I didn't know what to say, so I nodded, pretending to agree with whatever the crazy pictures meant. In some, Mariela seemed to scream at the camera, the veins in her neck bulging. In a final series, Mariela bent toward a patch of ground covered with a white canvas; she held a flaming twig and set off a snaking trail of fire that burned throughout the next few photos, in a long line zigging and zagging across the canvas surface, leaving dark meandering scars on the white background.

"What are they for?" I tried to sound breezy, but I felt

uncomfortable; I didn't understand what I was looking at. I'd never seen anything like it before.

"For nothing." Art, she explained, confronts time. All of us are thrown from the bowels of the Earth and all of us are returned to it. "What's the purpose in that?" she asked me. She didn't wait for an answer; she saw I had none. She gathered the photos and set them on the bed.

Mariela said that Lucho's burial would be her next "project." She opened her notebook. On several pages were colorful and black-and-white drawings of Lucho in various poses—jumping, sleeping on the couch, gazing up almost smiling, his tongue lolling from his mouth at what must have been Mariela seated before him. Mariela spoke of Lucho's "carnival spirit," his "creature joy," and then of the Day of the Dead and Mexican sugar skulls. In some of her sketches, Lucho's light-brown coat was purple and pink. His eyes were assorted colors too, even within the same sketch. I was flattered she'd shown me her Lucho pictures and wanted to say something smart. "Ruth keeps a notebook too. She calls it her Book of Days," I said.

Mariela frowned deeply. She shut the notebook. I blushed, ashamed. Obviously, Ruth's hurried lists, her scribbled sums, and her Palmer-looped Bible quotes couldn't compare to Mariela's sketches and diagrams by which she faced time and death.

Mariela slid the notebook under her bed. "I need some things to set off a few small rockets. Can you help me? We'll set them off at Lucho's burial."

Exploding homemade rockets at a dog's burial was far crazier than drawing a dog with a purple coat and wild pink eyes. A homemade rocket set off anywhere, especially by a dog's grave, was illegal and would, besides insulting Ruth, alarm everyone on our block. People still remembered Old Mario Prieto, who'd set off a pipe bomb at the Party Convention of 1975 and got thirty years for it. Mariela's rockets weren't pipe bombs, and they weren't exactly counterrevolutionary, but I doubted a *yuma* visitor was allowed to set off any kind of "carnival spirit" explosion for a dead pet in a public park.

Yet, in the half-dark of Mariela's cramped, disordered room, her eyes on me, she had, little by little, bizarre photo by bizarre photo, become less strange to me. Why that was, I couldn't tell, only that her voice was full of excitement, and suddenly I could see with her that exploding rockets might be, after all, the right salute for Lucho, who'd been a crank and a prankster in his short dog life.

I saw, too, that Lucho, the first to attach himself to Mariela for no good reason, was dead. I, the second to attach myself to Mariela for no good reason, felt the danger of my choice. But I told myself that Mariela would explode her rockets with or without me. *And I would let her.* When she smiled at me and showed me her list—cardboard, string, glue, some sticks, and the last item being gunpowder—I showed no surprise, as if she'd just asked for something as simple as a nail file or needle and thread. Mariela looked at me, patient. I read the list again. Then I got up (it felt more as if I watched myself get up) and led Mariela, an empty cup in her hand, down the metal stairs into the dark garage, where Mamá's old rifle hung by its strap from a nail on the back wall.

I'd held that rifle only a few times. Mamá had kept the bullets in the kitchen cabinet of the Misión apartment and the empty rifle next to her bed to load and take to her guard shifts in Old Havana. On what turned out to be Mamá's last night patrolling the streets of our neighborhood, she'd come back to our apartment in the early morning hours and leaned the loaded rifle against the bed and sat there as if thinking. The pain in her left hip over the previous weeks had grown sharp and sometimes made her cry out. After a long while, she rose and placed the loaded gun under the bed. It stayed there for the long months that followed.

That Mamá had never aimed the rifle at herself during those painful months seems less strange, looking back, than that I'd never emptied the weapon or put it away. And I didn't tell Ruth about it. I'd left the loaded gun under the bed. I had the absurd certainty that as long as the rifle remained within her reach, Mamá would find it a help in bearing what was to come. As she slept in short spurts and more and more refused the food Ruth and I brought to her, the loaded weapon turned into a strangely calming presence—a familiar monster under the bed that, in its way, was also there to protect us.

The rifle now hung by its strap in Ruth's garage. I pointed Ruth's flashlight and the gun barrel glinted. Mariela set the weapon on one of the boxes brought over from the Misión apartment. I pointed the flashlight where Mariela instructed. She removed the five cartridges one by one. She'd grown up in Nebraska, she said, "where the buffalo roamed and got shot to death" (she smiled) and knew her way around guns. She set the cartridges on top of the box. Later she'd stuff the gunpowder into small cardboard cylinders and finish the rockets up in her room. (She'd seen it done at an art exhibit in Chicago.)

"You'll light them at the grave." Mariela smiled and wiggled her hand toward the ceiling, imitating a rocket's path. She'd take pictures of the flying rockets, she said, her first project in her "native land." As Mariela pulled the bullet casings apart one by one with two pliers and shook the black powder into her cup, I pictured the rockets, launched by a flame in my hand, hurtling into the sky.

It was late. The Prietos' music had stopped hours before. I wanted to go to bed, but Mariela took the flashlight from me and aimed the beam at Ruth's fancy handwriting scrawled on the side of the next box. She set the flashlight on the sill; dust flew as she unfolded the top of the box. She tunneled through Mamá's skirts and blouses that Ruth and I had ironed and packed away with care. Mariela dipped her head inside the box and came up holding Mamá's blue linen dress against her body. The hem of the dress swept the dirty floor.

"Put my mother's things back," I said.

Mariela let Mamá's dress collapse over her left arm.

"It's okay," she said. "You and I are friends, yes?" She looked at me, her eyes big and round again. "I'd heard about your mom. This is why I came." She placed her right hand on my shoulder. "Yuri, I came here to meet you." Mariela's expression turned terribly sad then, as if she'd known Mamá for many years. I doubted her sudden sorrow over someone she'd never met, but the doleful squint of her eyes and the hard set of her jaw made me think that she knew grief, and in that moment I thought that I'd be able to stand her during the few weeks left on her visa, and even miss her a little after she was gone.

I took Mamá's dress from her, folded it, and put it back in

the box. I closed the top and breathed in the dust Mariela had raised.

She said in a softer voice, "I wanted to tell you from the first. That's the truth. But Ruth said to wait. She said to leave the past alone, that you have been through enough. But the truth is not harmful, it's the lies."

"I'm going to bed," I said. No more secrets, I thought, no more revelations.

"Look. She had me when she was very young."

"I know that already."

"Not Ruth," Mariela said. "Listen. Mamá had me. She was seventeen."

I closed my eyes for a moment, and then I heard Mariela's voice again. "No one knew about it but the two of them, Ruth and Mamá. Ruth hid me after I was born, left me with a family in the countryside, and when I was four, she put me on one of those flights full of children. Ruth paid money to some nuns and"—Mariela opened her hands to the air—"that was it." Mariela's voice was steady. "Mamá didn't know I'd been shipped off until after I was gone. Ruth kept it to herself. Understand?" I understood Mariela's words, which came faster and faster, but their overall meaning stayed just out of reach. She continued, "When Mamá found out, it was very hard. The two of them didn't speak for years. You know about that."

I knew of long, charged silences between Mamá and Ruth when they'd send messages to each other through me for months at a time, each of them asking me about the other. Sometimes Ruth would come by the Misión apartment with a flan while Mamá was at work and leave a note in a sealed envelope beneath the pan, along with a copy of *The Watchtower*. I thought of their on-and-off silences as normal sisterly fights or, as I got older, as ways in which two politically opposed sisters communicated. But Mariela was speaking of something different—an outlandish, secret rift between Ruth and Mamá about a shipped-off baby who was apparently Mariela herself. And what else was Mariela saying? Was she saying that Ruth, her newfound mother, wasn't enough for her? That she intended to take everything from me, not only Ruth's love and Lucho's life, but also my mother's bullets, her empty dress, and even the ghost of her?

Mariela continued, "All those years when I was little in *la yuma*, Ruth wrote to me and signed her letters 'Mamá,' as if *she* were my mother. At first, she wrote that she'd come to Lincoln and get me. Then she said she couldn't. She made excuses. The government wouldn't let her travel. Her health was poor. Later, when I was in school in Chicago, taking intensive Spanish, Ruth wrote that she'd come there. But she never did. After a while I gave up and stopped writing her. But the last time she wrote she finally told the truth." Mariela leaned forward and touched my shoulder. I moved away from her. Mariela said, "Ruth is not my mother. She's my kidnapper." She pointed to Mamá's box of clothes. "I came because of her. And because of you. Because we're sisters. Understand?"

I understood that I was stuck in a badly lit garage with someone who was batshit crazy or worse. I said, "My mother never told me about you. She would have told *me*."

"How do you know?"

"Because I *knew* her. You never saw her in your life."

Mariela winced at this, then said, "You and I go back to the start now. We're together. Mamá would have wanted it. She would have wanted us to know each other and be together."

She spoke as if this bond of sisterhood was something I owed her, something she couldn't imagine I'd refuse her. Mariela Ruth Vilar, the yankee who'd just gotten Lucho killed and had dropped gunpowder into a cup, now claimed that I had no first right to my loss and that I would have to share it with her, a stranger. I would not.

"Your story's shit," I said. "Go back to your buffalo town."

A dull light from the streetlamp shone through the garage window. The electricity had come back on; the hum of the refrigerator inside the house revved up. Mariela gave me a look of forbearance. When she saw it enraged me, she took the cup with the gunpowder from the windowsill as if picking up after a disagreeable child and turned toward me as if to say something. But Ruth's uneven steps approached outside the garage. Ruth opened the door and reproached us. "It's almost two in the morning."

Mariela hid the cup in the crook of her arm and headed out, mumbling good night.

"Get some sleep, my daughter," Ruth called out as Mariela climbed the metal stairs to her room. Then Ruth said to me, sharp, "Come inside. And for the love of Jehovah wash your hands and face."

IN THE KITCHEN Ruth threw linden leaves into a small pot of boiling water. She took *tilo* only in her most trying moments— sudden deaths, wakes, crucial mishaps, reversals of fortune, or other triumphs of the Confounder. Ruth watched the *tilo* simmer over the blue flame. I was afraid she'd blame me for whatever might have happened between Mariela and me in the garage. And at the same time, I thought that both Ruth and I were at the mercy of Mariela's tale; if Mamá had truly given birth to Mariela when Mamá was seventeen, I'd have to give up Mamá as I knew her, and Ruth would have to give up the fantasy of the *yuma* daughter she'd just found.

Ruth sat down with her steaming cup. "What were you two doing in the garage?"

I stood by the kitchen table. I was ready for her. "Your daughter's crazy. She says she's not your daughter."

Ruth looked up, exhausted. But she seemed ready for me too. She gestured for me to sit. I waited a moment before lowering myself into the chair across from her. Ruth started with a sigh, "Your mother broke dishes, tore dresses, muddied shoes. I cleaned up her messes. You know this. She had good legs and was born pretty and went off, and ran, and did, for both of us. It was that way." Ruth raised her cup and blew across the hot tea. "When we were little, she was a sweet child. Then I got sick, and it made her furious. She wouldn't look at my leg. After my sickness, she got quicker, maybe to make up for my slowness. She took more chances, helped herself to everything—she thought it was a kindness."

Ruth almost smiled, a sort of grimace with no joy in it. "One day I pointed to a red mango up in our tree in the farm in La Coloma. It was the end of the season and only a few mangoes, up in the high branches, were left. Your mother climbed the tree, grabbed the mango, peeled it with her teeth, and ate it sitting in the tree, watching me, her hands dripping with the juice. When she was done, she brought down a different mango, a small, yellowish one, for me. I asked her why she'd eaten my mango, and she said she hadn't; she'd brought me the one I wanted. See?" Ruth waited for my answer. I didn't see.

Ruth said, "I fell in love. A man in La Coloma. The cousin of someone in town, a farmworker, just passing through. Your mother and I were still girls. Your mother knew I loved this man. Sancho. His name was Sancho, can you believe it? But everyone called him San. Well, your mother went and had him one night in the fields while I slept innocently in our room. I hated her after that. She said she'd done it *for* me." Ruth paused. "Just like the mango, see? I loved your mother, but"—Ruth finished the sentence slowly—"that man's baby was mine." Ruth raised her cup and blew again into her tea. The calmer she tried to show herself, lowering her voice, sipping from her teacup, the more fury piled up in her words. "I wanted the baby and your mother didn't." Ruth kept her eyes on me. She put down her cup. "There was a woman who fixed such things for pregnant girls in La Coloma if you paid her. But your mother, she owed me. She stayed in La Coloma and gave birth, and *I* had the baby." Ruth closed her eyes, drew a breath. She looked at me and said, "But in the end what could I do with the child here in this . . . ?" Ruth swept her arm, pointing toward the kitchen window and to everything that lay beyond it. "I wanted my child to grow up happy and free. So I sent her to a good land."

In the days after Mamá died and I left the Misión neighborhood and moved into Ruth's house, I'd sometimes found comfort when reading at Ruth's kitchen table or doing homework while Ruth slapped meat on the counter and cut up onions. Now the kitchen seemed alien, as if I'd never sat in it before. The hard chair pressed up into my sitting bones; the light was from a different house or century or planet. I said, "Mamá knew that you sent Mariela to the north?"

"Listen. The baby was mine," Ruth said. "Your mother got mixed up shooting rifles here, calling for firing squads. You were born years later. You were hers to raise. But that baby was *mine*. Your mother and I had a deal."

"A deal."

"Between sisters," Ruth said. "I sent my child to *la yuma* and saved her life. And now I'm going to save yours. You don't know it yet, but you will. In the end your mother thought things over. She thought of how she wanted you to grow up. And it wasn't here, not anymore." I felt a stab of clarity: Ruth's letters to my father hadn't just been cries for a handout; all along she'd been plotting to send me away forever.

"You think you're going to ship me off with your kooky daughter after her visa runs out?" Ruth had gotten rid of one child before. No reason why she wouldn't do it again. Ruth shook her head; she looked wounded by my ingratitude. I leaned furiously across the table and said, "Your crazy baby doesn't love you. She's come to take revenge on you. She hates you for all the nice things you did for her—"

Throughout the years that Ruth and Mamá had argued silently, spitefully, I'd never seen Ruth's eyes narrow to such small points in her thin, unhappy face. I thought she'd lift her hand to me, but after a moment she fell back in her chair and said only, "What do you know about love? There are many ways."

9

Some transgressions were commonplace in those years. To break a window in the middle of the night, for example, and clean out a place; slip into your pocket some small, petty thing from a friend's house (a pen, an ashtray, a hairclip) and walk off waving and smiling; disappear sacks of cement and cans of paint from your workplace and sell them on the black market; creep in the predawn to rip tiles from an old, crumbling house. Or, in a column of numbers, switch digits, rearrange dates; sell shampoo bottles filled with watered-down detergent; bread a flimsy wet cloth with lard and crumbs, fry it, and sell it as a slice of cow steak (a woman in El Cerro was given three years for this stunt after someone half choked on it and nearly died). But to exchange a child out of pride, collusion—even love—was a peculiar transgression, then and now, and the child must sooner or later recoil from it.

Mariela did just that the following morning, when I told her what Ruth had said to me, that she and Mamá had made a "deal" and that Mariela belonged to Ruth instead of Mamá. My point wasn't innocent (I was intent on keeping Mamá to myself), but the more I defended it the more I saw that Mariela probably belonged to neither sister, which left her less than an orphan.

I couldn't blame Mariela for rejecting Ruth's version: conceived in pity or envy, birthed by committee, rejected by the rightful parent to be cherished by an impostor, who in turn gave her away to strangers in a foreign country. If I tallied it up, Mamá seemed no better than Ruth. All her life Mamá had mocked Ruth's weird religiosity, her stale dog-piss house and its turn-of-the-century doilies, porcelain figures, rocking chairs—a bourgeois cornucopia that Mamá had worked to smash in her own life, and in the country at large. Still Mamá gave her fanatical sibling a child to raise and dispose of, not once, but, counting me, twice.

In the hours that followed Ruth's story of Mariela's birth, I lay in bed with my eyes open in the dark. Finally, near dawn, without bothering with my shoes, I went up to Mariela's room above the garage. She was awake, cutting up cardboard for her rockets. I told her from the doorway that whatever had happened with her birth and childhood—whatever she'd made up or had been told—it couldn't be undone. "You were raised in *la yuma*. You're not from here. Go back and let us be."

Mariela shrugged at this. "I'm not here to undo anything."

All the same, her plans proceeded that summer as if she'd written them down in her notebook, step by step. And that morning as the sun came up and I sat on the floor amid her scissors and cardboard and sketches while she brushed away my versions of her orphanhood, I helped her put the finishing touches to her five rockets because, as Lucho lay dead and we would head out to bury him, Mariela seemed to me not good, but when compared to her two supposed mothers, the most innocent.

10

Sometime while I slept on Mariela's floor, Ruth and her *yuma* daughter must have agreed to bury Lucho in a spot in the park, on public land close to screaming children, gossiping neighbors, and teams of ragtag *beisbol* boys.

Ruth explained the plan as I drank my morning coffee. Digging a hole in the park without permission and lowering a dead dog into it was as reckless as Mariela's illegal little rockets. But after Ruth's admission the previous night (she wouldn't have called it an admission) about her despicable pact, I resolved to tell Ruth nothing about Mariela's rockets, or about anything else, from that point on.

On my way down the long hallway to the bathroom, I spotted Don Juanito Mustelier sitting on Ruth's sofa in the parlor. Don Juanito, Ruth's friend of forty years and Paladero's French tutor and black marketeer, was our first mourner, waiting, I assumed, for the dog's burial to begin. Ruth called for me from the bedroom, where she'd gone to dress and keep vigil. Lucho was sprawled across her bed and covered with a sheet. If Ruth had slept at all, it must have been in the armless chair in the corner beside the tall oak dresser. She had deep circles under her eyes and sat, exhausted, rubbing her bad leg. She asked me to take Juan his coffee.

When I came into the parlor with the tray, Don Juanito was watching Ruth's silent TV (audio defunct). He could, I thought, put in a word with Ruth and save us from harm if I told him of Mariela's rockets. He gestured excitedly toward the screen. Rows of uniformed men pantomimed gravely, and the doomed, famous General Jorge Luis Acha stood warily at attention, stripped of his uniform, during the fourth day of his televised trial. Charged with smuggling and high treason, the great general from the Angolan wars appeared drugged and half blind behind his thick glasses.

"That man was a titan," Don Juanito said. "Titan" Acha stood accused of stashing away a million dollars in African diamonds in a hidden cache. But for the bartering black marketeer Don Juanito—three cans of condensed milk for a bottle of shampoo, a bottle of shampoo for two pairs of sneakers, a pair of sneakers for ten cans of condensed milk—the huge sums of foreign currency Acha stood accused of embezzling must have seemed a towering feat.

Don Juanito's sudden enthusiasm for Acha's crimes made me doubt he'd bring reason to bear on Lucho's ceremony. He took his coffee from the tray and said to me, "*Niña*, I watch this parade every day on my brand-new Chinese TV. I have excellent sound. I hear every word they shout. But"—he tipped his head—"grand people can be the targets of envy." In Don Juanito's round, old, florid face was an appeal to consider him a grand object, too, of the envious tongues in the neighborhood.

"What if, *niña*," he said, "General Acha did nothing more than look distinguished in his uniform, like the bronze-skinned titan Antonio Maceo, straight-backed on his horse, machete raised against the Spanish barbarians?" Don Juanito lifted his right arm as if in battle. He disliked Spain and routinely exulted the French, including Robespierre, his Jacobins, and all their spectacular beheadings.

"Come sit." Reluctantly, I sat next to him on the edge of the couch. He sipped his coffee and smiled pleasantly. "I see your mother in you," he said.

His eyes were a beautiful, clear blue. Mamá, who'd been his best student, had thought him a fraud and a bore. "Some women, like your aunt," Mamá told me once, "go for Juan's refinement." Mamá, like many of her fellow Party members, denounced diversionist intellectuals, especially if they were gay. But Ruth had defended Juan and called Mamá's commentary "the kind of slander flung against every cultured man in this country. Quickest way to eliminate a foe is to assault his manhood. Our greatest man of letters"—Ruth meant the ever-present poet José Martí—"threw himself into battle and got minced because someone once called him a little sissy."

Don Juanito studied me. "You came to us a skinny stick last summer. And now here you are, a young lady chewing your sister's fancy *chicle* like Lana Turner."

I stopped chewing. "She's not my sister."

Juan's words alarmed me. He was known to trace gnarled family trees, neighborhood feuds, affairs, disputes, and simmering envies back generations—such information, Ruth had explained, was vital to his profession. He didn't usually make errors of genealogy. Juan's reference to Mariela as my sister could only mean that Mariela's claim to be Mamá's daughter was not only true but quite likely also known by everyone in the neighborhood except me.

Don Juanito corrected himself. "Your *cousin*. And both of you want to help Ruth."

The old schemer. He could be playing Ruth's messenger, appealing to me to ask Mariela for dollars or, more likely, angling for a *bisnis* of his own that Mariela could fund. He'd certainly heard Mariela's declaration of "no money" the previous night as he'd stood in the Prietos' kitchen whispering with Rosario's mother, the two of them in cahoots to sell a beet-juice-and-alcohol hair dye to foolish old women from the countryside.

"Mariela says she's poor like us."

He waved this away. "She has *chicles* to give you. You two, young and beautiful—you are friends." General Acha's face filled the TV screen in close-up. He was seated now—a shrimpy fool unable to look up at the shouting officials, his eyes unfocused and defeated.

"People tell me," Don Juanito continued, "that this is a Special Period. But what's so special about hunger? Maybe she's hungry too, this young *yuma* who gives you *chicles*. Don't say no." He wagged his finger as if I'd said anything at all. "Human hunger is of all kinds, *niña*, and always insatiable." He sounded glad of this, as if it guaranteed lifetime employment to him and to those of his profession.

"This hoopla about the dog," Don Juanito said, suddenly wary, "is it the *yuma*'s idea?"

"Ruth wants it too." I felt again the panic of saying nothing to Ruth, or now to Don Juanito, about Mariela's rockets. "You should talk Ruth out of it," I said. "It's stupid."

Mariela came into the parlor then, her hair wet and loose over her shoulders. She smelled of her foreign perfume. She extended her hand to Don Juanito with a faraway look of disregard, and Don Juanito stood and took Mariela's hand and made a slight bow. "I am pained by your loss," he said to Mariela. "Juan Mustelier, a lifetime friend of Miss Ruth. You and I met last night. I hope the poor animal didn't suffer."

"He did," Mariela said. "He died."

Ruth walked in wearing the black dress she reserved for human funerals. She turned off the TV. General Acha and his panel of accusers shrank to a small white dot, then disappeared. "My friend, thank you for waiting," Ruth said to Juan. "Let's head out before it rains."

"About this burial, Ruth, let's consider our position," Juan said, looking at me. I flushed with hope. But Ruth cut him off. "I have no position. I have only a duty to a friend who was murdered."

11

Ruth, Mariela, Don Juanito, and I filed off the porch, crossed the street, and walked along the edge of the park, looking for a spot to bury Lucho. Don Juanito, looking grim and breathless, carried across his right shoulder the dead dog wrapped in Ruth's checkered towel and fleece blanket as if to keep Lucho warm. Mariela carried in her hand Abuelo Alberto's shovel, and in a deep pocket of her dress the five small rockets she'd made from Mamá's bullets and toilet-paper-roll cardboard.

As we walked out in our peculiar procession, other households in Paladero and across the island probably sat entranced before their TVs, watching the foregone conclusion of Acha's proceedings the way one watches the known yet riveting outcome of a telenovela. Acha's defense attorney had looked like a bad telenovela actor himself during his closing statement, shown again and again over the next few days on one of the two official TV channels. Acha's young defense lawyer, appearing more pained than the accused, was said to declare something like the following: *The citizen, Jorge Luis Acha Calvo, hereby tried by the people's court, understands that he has betrayed the highest ideals of the revolution, the militia he swore to serve, and the citizens of his homeland, whom he had vowed to protect. He admits to committing Grand Treason and Fraud, as well as the violations enumerated by the people's court. The accused, knowing his crimes to be beyond rehabilitation, humbly thanks this Revolutionary Tribunal for bringing forth this proceeding and, respectfully, with admiration for the revolution's justice, begs for mercy, if any can be granted.* A few minutes later, after the maximum penalty was assigned—death by firing squad—the young defense attorney rose quickly, almost joyfully, and proclaimed that the accused stood ready to take his deserved punishment. The lawyer then thanked the revolution for its sure and measured justice.

Ruth, Mariela, Don Juanito, and I walked on, single file. The stench of the garbage pile from just beyond the park's edge reached us on a breeze whipped up by gathering rain clouds. Everyone called the small, seedy encampment beyond the park Llega y Pon: a patch of makeshift, tin-roofed houses whose dwellers had flocked to Havana from the provinces in hopes of jobs with the local militia or the army. Some of the residents were alcoholics; a few were mentally ill, but many others had fled collapsed homes in their small towns and the subsequent terrifying shelters assigned to them only to wind up in slapdash enclaves on the edges of neighborhoods like ours. Llega y Pon inhabitants at the park's far end had built their shacks from discarded planks and corrugated metal sheets, and they connected their electricity cables to street lines. As their numbers grew and Havana's garbage trucks dwindled from lack of fuel, a mound of refuse grew beside their outpost. Fuel shortages also kept water trucks from supplying the neighborhood. Official city water was piped into our houses for only a few minutes before dawn, and Ruth got up in the dark to collect it in the tub.

In our mourners' procession, we passed only a few neighbors out on their porches, sitting or standing, having their coffee, the men in undershirts and the women in housedresses. Ruth tipped her head solemnly to each, and some returned the gesture. "The Malangones killed my Lucho," Ruth said in a loud voice to Isabel Heredia, who lived next to the Cuevas's house. Isabel crossed herself. Ruth said, "I don't want my Lucho in the Llega y Pon heap." We passed the Milo rotunda, and a group of children standing around rocks placed on the ground to mark their bases stopped their *beisbol* game; the batter leaned on his bat and the players of both teams watched us go down the paved walkway toward the park's west end.

Finally, Mariela halted our small parade by the wide, gnarly ceiba tree. As if finding an X on a treasure map, she pointed to a swath of grass just beyond the tree's ripple of roots and overhanging branches. Around its thick trunk, the ceiba tree, sacred to African orishas, Taino spirits, and most supernatural powers who'd presided for centuries over the island, was littered with offerings of fruit rinds, withering flowers, and coconut husks. Ruth considered these offerings "pagan junk," yet she nodded to her *yuma* daughter-niece and let her pick this outrageous spot for Lucho's burial.

Don Juanito laid Lucho on the ground with a deep sigh and patted his forehead with his white handkerchief. The sky thundered just beyond the Llega y Pon. The old man looked up, tucked the handkerchief into his pocket, and took up the shovel with another sigh. Reluctantly, weakly, he started digging. No young men from neighboring porches ran out to help him as they would have for someone whose tire had gone flat or motorcycle stalled. I felt bad for the old man, red-faced and winded, digging up the earth where the tree's roots thinned just beyond the leaves bending in the threatening breeze.

Soon a small group gathered around, watching and whispering, some smiling a little, others standing idle, arms crossed. The boys who had silently stared at our procession abandoned their *beisbol* game and, holding their mitts, watched the old man pry dirt out of the ground next to the dead dog wrapped in a blanket. Doña Barbara arrived out of breath; Tere wasn't with her. "It's too much for her," Doña Barbara said to me, and I knew she was right. Tere had watched Lucho bleed on the ground; she'd watched his fearsome eyes stay open, fixed on some point in the distance. She shouldn't have to watch his stiff body lowered into a hole, and the thought of sparing her this sight gave me some peace.

The crowd rustled; Hernando Malanga-head and his boys were making their way through the semicircle. I should have foreseen their arrival. The Malanga-head gang never missed a neighborhood spectacle, making jokes on the side and mocking everyone by their presence, and in this way, I thought, they insisted on being counted as part of the common life of Paladero.

Hernando stepped forward and stood in his undershirt a few feet from Don Juanito. Ruth cried out, "Murderer! Get the authorities." She motioned to me to go fetch CDR President Cuevas from his house. "Now," she said. I put on a blank face and stayed put. After our talk in the kitchen the previous night,

I'd vowed to myself that I'd do nothing Ruth ever ordered me to do. Besides, if Cuevas showed up, he'd put an end to the burial and to Mariela's rockets, and a part of me (a wicked part, Ruth would say) wanted to see sparks sizzle over Lucho's grave and watch Lucho's anima ignite and release, as Mariela said it would, to the ether.

Ruth scowled at my betrayal. She turned to Mariela, but the *yuma* studied Hernando as if pleased to see him. Ruth said again, "Murderer." She urged the small crowd, "Someone get Cuevas."

But no one did. Neither did they shoo away the Malanga-head gang boys, Gelson and Reynaldo. No one would risk that sort of trouble. Hernando, magnanimous in his power, held his hand out to Don Juanito and the old man surrendered the shovel without a word, and with a neighbor's help, climbed from the shallow hole and went to stand in the deeper shade. Hernando started digging. Ruth stared uncomprehendingly at him, and at the small heap of soil growing beside the hole.

But someone must have gone to get Dr. Cuevas after all, or he might have appeared on his own. Either way, he made his way through the crowd with his usual authority, up to the edge of the hole. Ruth pointed to Hernando with the zeal of a TV prosecutor. "Arrest him," she said. "You know I'm burying my dearest friend and companion who was murdered. By him." I wondered if Cuevas, Don Juanito, or Doña Barbara, all of whom had known Ruth for decades, ever realized that Ruth's dearest friend was a dog.

"Ruth"—Dr. Cuevas was calm as he scanned the crowd— "this isn't right, you know that. Not on public grounds." He clapped at the neighbors. "Show's over, *caballeros*."

The Tilting House

Ruth stood defiant. "My Lucho was murdered in this park and will be buried here, in the place he loved."

"We got this, chief," Hernando said. Dr. Cuevas looked down at Hernando, the "murderer," holding the shovel, up to his calves in the hole. Hernando said in his mocking tone, "We'll plant a flower in the canine's name." He paused. "A white rose of friendship for the canine, beloved by all. He'll be missed." Gelson smirked behind Hernando.

Mariela stepped before Cuevas and explained, "Everyone is here now, *compañero*. This is important to all."

Cuevas frowned at the foreigner in the flowing orange dress; she was no *compañera* of his. But Mariela turned to the waiting crowd. "*Compañeros*," she said in her flat tone, "all of us are wrenched away from the place we call home, and then one day we are returned. Today I honor Lucho's return and my own." Mariela nodded to me. "We ignite this spot and see his spirit's light return to the earth and sky."

Cuevas said to Mariela, "You will not dig here without a permit."

"Yes," Mariela said enthusiastically in her odd Spanish. "You give permit."

Cuevas swept his arm. "*I* don't give permits. You're a visitor here and know nothing of our laws." His face reddened. "You need to go home now. All of you." He clapped at the neighbors again. "It's an illegal assembly and this"—he pointed to Lucho's body on the ground—"is a health hazard."

"That's why we're going to bury it, chief," Hernando said.

Ruth stood beside Mariela, arms crossed. The two of them side by side now seemed nearly mother and daughter again as they had in the Prietos' dining room in front of the microwave, and I felt a vague rush of hope that maybe Mariela's story of her birth was a fantasy, and maybe Mamá at seventeen (nearly the age I was) had never given away a baby or kept a dark family secret from me. I could go back to being her first and only child. But then Ruth's absurd tale of a sisterly exchange of a baby as if it were a mango came back to me, and I felt the same furious urge to move grimly forward—to Mariela's rockets and to Lucho covered forever by the dirt beneath our feet.

The neighborhood crowd, despite Cuevas's threats and the foul gusts from the Llega y Pon, and the dark banked clouds gathering over our heads, did not leave. The strange entertainment seemed to hold them there, by Lucho's hole, as if waiting for something extraordinary to happen.

Dr. Cuevas wagged a finger at Don Juanito, the black marketeer and safest target for Cuevas's indignation. "This will not fall on me, understand? If you want a permit, you bring Oscar here."

It must have occurred to Cuevas that local Party leader Compañero Oscar Malanga-head Pita, his young, watchful face softened by delicate, round spectacles, could kick Cuevas's balls and defend his brother Hernando in public. Oscar easily smelled disloyalty, mostly because he was a master and a product of it himself. He was a physics teacher at our school, and everyone knew that he was sleeping with shapely, soft-spoken Regina, our classmate and his student, while his own wife, Lissette, waited to give birth to their first baby, a boy. His "heir," Oscar would say self-mockingly in class. But nobody spoke up about it. To cross him was to risk one's academic file and university entrance—in short, one's future. Oscar's search for disloyalty had sharpened during the Special Period, as fewer youth seemed to believe in a future within the old-time revolutionary "process," and he scrutinized us for signs of disrespect or "diversionist" behavior such as growing dreadlocks or inking tattoos into our arms. Only within his own Malangón clan did Oscar seem to waver. He usually avoided his mother's apartment in a sketchy, dark alley that led to their small courtyard and front door. This was mostly his brother's territory, and on the rare occasions Oscar visited, he made it quick: indoors and then out, often after enduring his mother's insults (Hernando was her favorite and Oscar her useless, bookish turd of a son, too clumsy to fix her sink's faucet).

When leaving his mother's apartment, Oscar made his way stooped and silent around Hernando's boys and their sprockets and greasy chains spread out in the courtyard; then, down the street by the park, adjusting his teacher glasses, Oscar caught again his regal stride and looked as crisp and self-assured as when he stood before us in the classroom.

Hernando looked up from the dog's burial hole. "It's the hour of *jama*, chief. My brother partakes of breakfast. Family time. Doesn't like to be interrupted."

Cuevas's color deepened. "On your heads, then," he said. He surveyed all of us and made his judgment. "Defacing the people's property in illegal assembly." He turned to Don Juanito as if to predict that the old man's head would be first to roll. But Cuevas himself sounded unsure, his own head less than secure on his hunched-up shoulders. He stomped through the crowd toward his house across from the park.

Hernando finished digging. He and Gelson lowered Lucho, wrapped in his towel and blanket, into the ground. Ruth stepped forward, then looked at the dog bundle below and gathered herself. She opened her Bible; the pages snapped in the growing breeze. She found her passage and said, more reciting than reading, that dogs ate the crumbs that fell from the Lord's table. She cried a little. The neighbors, who'd inched their way forward to hear Ruth better, looked at one another, wondering if the peculiar ceremony was over, but Ruth flipped through the pages and read, louder, another verse, this one demanding one eye for another.

Hernando smiled at this last passage. He dug his shovel into the mound of dirt and little by little covered Lucho with fresh earth.

"Now we send him on his way," Mariela said.

"We what?" said someone in the crowd.

Mariela took the rocket tubes from her orange skirt and placed them randomly in the dirt of Lucho's grave. (Later she told me that she'd planted them in the pattern of the five brightest stars in Canis Major—her own private tribute to Lucho.) People pushed forward, tightening the circle around Mariela and her homemade rockets sticking out of the soil like flowerless stems. Rodolfo Heredia hooted. "This for a dog? More fuss than my father got, may he rest in peace." Several men chuckled and nodded, but all kept their eyes on Mariela, who bent down to the grave and lit four of the five long fuses with a wooden match until the match almost burned her fingers. Then she struck another match, cupped her hand around the flame, and as planned, gave it to me. She stepped back and lifted her camera to her face. I bent down, lit the last rocket, and shook out the match. The long fuse strings sizzled with white sparks that disappeared up into the small cardboard tubes until each rocket took off, pulling behind it a white, thin smoky trail into the gray sky. Mariela snapped her pictures. (They'd turn out well and, years later, would hang in a Brooklyn gallery, in what Mariela would call her "Dog in the Sky" series.) The crowd watched the four wobbling rockets ascend, then fall, ungainly and wriggly, back toward the Earth. The fifth rocket, the one I lit, stayed stuck in the dirt, sizzling on its stick, a few sparkles escaping from the glued-up tube. And then just as Lucho had managed, seemingly out of nowhere, to shove himself suddenly through the window bars and bite Mariela's hand on the quiet porch, the last rocket popped loudly on its launchpad grave and followed the four other rockets into the sky.

After a stunned moment, the last explosion faded and the neighbors around Lucho's grave beside the ceiba tree scattered without comment, heading in different directions toward their homes. Compañero Oscar, who must have arrived in the middle of the fireworks, grabbed me and Mariela by the arms and pulled us away from Lucho's grave. I looked back for Ruth. Oscar said, "Keep going." He shoved us along till we reached the sidewalk in front of Ruth's house, then said, "Stay here."

In the park beside Lucho's grave, two militiamen walked on either side of Ruth, escorting her to their patrol car.

PART TWO

Salons

12

The official announcement of General Acha's execution by firing squad was broadcast five days after Ruth's arrest. Rumor had it that he had refused a blindfold and had given his own command to fire. His firing-squad death and Ruth's arrest came together in my mind—both dark reminders, to me and to the neighborhood, of the price one might pay for extravagant gestures. Antonieta was the first to take heed, and she ended the Prietos' parties abruptly on the day after Ruth's arrest. The Beatles music stopped, the lights dimmed, and the Prietos' front door closed for the rest of the summer. Ruth might have smiled at the Prietos' sudden shutdown, but she was locked up in a five-by-seven-meter cell at the Ministry of Interior's Department of Internal Security (DSI) at 100 and Aldabó Street, a frightening place referred to in jittery street humor as 100 Y Se Acabó (100 and It's All Over). And what she felt or thought there, I couldn't begin to guess.

It was said that inside that placid blue building—it looked as pleasant and regular as the sky—no one told you your official charges and none of your loved ones were notified that you were there. We knew that Ruth was being held inside "for investigation" only because Oscar's unnamed contact in the DSI confirmed it. "For how long?" I asked Oscar, and at first, he made it sound like it was a matter of paperwork and Ruth would be home in a day or two.

But Ruth didn't come home in a day or two or for many days afterward, and I woke each morning in a sweat over what would or wouldn't happen to Ruth in that dark, cold cell, and by extension, over what would or wouldn't happen to me without her in the new chaos of the house.

In those first days without Ruth, I mostly lay around with Tigre on the cool floor tiles, suffering, thinking of schemes to get Ruth out of the DSI. And by the end of each day, with no progress to show for my scheming, I crawled back into bed, low and sick of myself. Each day that passed made it clearer that little could be done to get Ruth out. The most I could do was push Oscar to arrange a visit to Ruth in that terrifying place.

With Ruth gone Mariela took charge. As an adult *yuma*, she had the funds to feed the two of us—and she did, not just us, but other neighborhood guests including Oscar; his brother, dog-killer Hernando; and Hernando's gang, who in turn brought other boys from the Llega y Pon and girls who wore thick eyeliner and large hoop earrings and smoked and drank like grown-ups. Toward these strangers, Mariela displayed the generosity she'd denied Ruth at the Prietos' party, and in less than a week Ruth's parlor replaced the Prietos' as the noisy hub of Paladero.

At night young men on bikes delivered miraculous dinner boxes from Chinatown. While Ruth starved at the DSI, we scarfed down greasy noodles and pieces of pork fat with our chopsticks. I inhaled the food, almost forced it down my throat half chewed, as if to punish myself with every bite. Bottles of aguardiente and of homemade rum soon appeared, and the guest list expanded to young people from neighboring blocks and barrios outside Paladero. Dr. Cuevas attended these dinners, just as he had the Prietos' parties, and Don Juanito came too, now as Mariela's guest, not Ruth's.

On the fifth night without Ruth, Oscar brought over his mother's busted TV set (image blacked-out but audio working), and he placed it on top of Ruth's smaller, silent set. The two TVs looked like an inverted wedding cake, but together they had both picture and sound. We gathered in the parlor around the two stacked TVs, drinks and Chinatown boxes in hand, to watch the official summary report of General Acha's death. Nervous laughter spread across the room after the broadcast. The news seemed to make some guests giddy, especially those who broke the law daily in small or large ways to put food in their families' mouths, their petty crimes often overlooked by a few pesos under the table, or by an official's exhaustion or whim, or by sheer dumb luck.

This time only Acha had been "zapped," as Doña Barbara put it to me in our only conversation in those first days. She'd stopped briefly on the sidewalk on her way to the empty bodega with her canvas bag and commented on the Acha trial, and then, in a low, sad voice, asked me about Ruth. I could only tell her what Oscar reported each day. At my mention of Oscar's name Doña Barbara winced. She lamented, as if in passing, the sorry state of her "poor friend's" porch, littered with empty bottles "like a saloon."

"Shame," Doña Barbara said then and let the word hang in the air. She gave me an accusing look as if I were to blame for the desecration of Ruth's house. Doña Barbara herself didn't set foot in Ruth's parlor during our Chinese dinners, and she pulled Tere away from me. I knew what she thought of Mariela's "guests"—young men and women from poorer barrios, Llega y Pon squatters, small-time thugs, and worst of all in Doña Barbara's view, some *jinetera* girls known to "ride" mature foreigners in the city center for a few dollars and a decent dinner—a crime, in Doña Barbara's eyes, more disgraceful than Acha's.

In my brooding walks through the jumble of Ruth's house, Tigre behind me, I took to picturing Acha's last moments before the firing squad. I wondered if Acha's voice quavered when he'd ordered the row of uniformed men to shoot him. Ruth herself had stayed calm in the back seat of the patrol car, as if all her life she'd expected to be taken into custody. An officer, Don Juanito told us, had helped lift her skinny bad leg from the ground and place it inside the running car, and Ruth had said thank you to the policeman, and then, "Don't hurt my children." I'd watched the patrol car, shocked, without clear understanding, from across the street, where Oscar had planted me and Mariela. The car turned onto Dimas Street, and I caught only the dark silhouette of Ruth's head in the back seat.

After this Mariela rushed back into the house. Oscar followed her. Only Rosario and Julio stayed with me on the street, watching the police car disappear. Rosario put her hand on my shoulder. "They'll let her out in the morning," she said.

"It's my fault," I said.

Rosario shook her head in sympathy. "What made the smoke go so high in the air? It was pretty."

"Gunpowder," I said.

The Tilting House

At "gunpowder," Rosario's face turned serious, and I felt all the way into my bones that Ruth would not be getting out the next morning or the morning after that. My skin went cold. I realized that other than Mamá's death, this would be the worst disaster in my life. What would happen to Ruth in jail? And where would I end up? I had no other relative to live with while Ruth was gone, and Mariela couldn't stay here "for good" as she claimed. And because I'd helped set off Mariela's rockets, Oscar would now write "counterrevolutionary sabotage" in my school file, and the Lenin scholarship I half hoped for because of my good grades and excellent conduct and my new Communist Youth membership would vanish forever.

Rosario, Julio, and I went back to our homes. Night came, and I slept eventually and had vaguely scary dreams, and in the morning, without the clip-clop of Ruth's uneven steps on the tiles, I woke up to a cavernous new silence in the house. I made myself get up and walk to the kitchen through the empty rooms. As I passed the dining room window, Antonieta Prieto called out to me from her window across the way; she and Ruth often talked window to window over the narrow space between houses. "*Niña*, was it about the dog?" Antonieta asked. I shook my head. Antonieta saw that I was too choked up to speak and told me in a kind voice that I should come to her for anything I needed. "You hear me, *niña*? I'm praying for your aunt."

Mariela and Oscar, along with Don Juanito, sat at Ruth's kitchen table, discussing something in calm, reasonable-sounding voices. When I entered, they looked up from their coffee cups as if surprised to see me. But then the old man looked back down at his cup, and I knew the worst was true:

Ruth was still locked up in a terrible place, possibly for a long time. Mariela poured coffee from the pot and handed me a cup with casual authority, as if the pot and the cup now belonged to her along with all of Ruth's saucers and pans, the ancient gas stove, and the box of matches set by the stove.

"It was our fault, what happened," I told Mariela. "Let's go to the police now and explain. They'll let Ruth go."

The two men stayed quiet. Mariela, despite her previous veiled threats of vengeance against her "kidnapper," looked mostly sad and worn out. "Oscar understands. He knows it was my project," she said, low, "and that we meant no harm."

We. "So we go to the police now and tell them. They'll have to let Ruth out," I said.

Mariela didn't answer. Don Juanito sat rumpled in his kitchen chair and spoke softly. "One doesn't just show up at the DSI."

Oscar asked me to sit. "Let me explain," he said. "There are no charges yet. An evaluation for now. The ministry is analyzing the cause of the fire."

"There was no fire," I said, my voice high.

"We'll have to wait on the investigation," Oscar said.

"There was no fire," I repeated.

He cleared his throat. "I advise patience." He spoke impersonally, without bothering to look at me or at anyone, as he sometimes did at school to make us feel that we didn't matter and that our only choice was to follow his orders.

Oscar asked me suddenly about my plans for the next school year. I felt it coming then—his full-on condemnation. Now he'd break the news that my chance at a place at the Lenin school had vanished, and he might offer me something else if I was lucky, maybe enrollment at a vocational school to become a factory technician or a farming specialist in the countryside. But instead he said, "Our school's still allotted one spot this next year. We can still send one exemplary pupil to the Lenin." He looked at me closely. "You're an excellent student, Yuri, and your late mother was an exemplary Party officer." He smiled. "I don't see why not, if you really want it. Your future is still bright." He waited for me to nod. When I did, he said, "Well, in that case, we must behave as if we are *already* a Lenin student. We must display the correct attitude at all times."

Mariela thanked Oscar for his generous guidance; she shifted in her chair toward me as if it were now my turn to thank the *Compañero*. Oscar had made it clear, after all: Mariela and I would be spared. He'd issued his unofficial pardon of us and seemed willing to overlook our crimes. Why, I couldn't guess. Oscar had squashed others, ruined futures and lives for much less. I feared a price would have to be paid—something crucial and unbearable would be asked of me.

I took a sip of Mariela's muddy coffee and looked again around the table. Such a polite, violent tilt to my world: Mariela, the foreigner I'd met ten days before, and Oscar, the local Party boss speaking brightly in Ruth's kitchen one day after Ruth's arrest, both of them holding forth about my future like proud parents, urging patience and the turning of a new leaf. At that moment the tilting world became actual; the floor swayed and the walls spun for a few seconds or a few minutes—I couldn't tell because time didn't behave like itself. Then the room settled back little by little, and finally I saw Oscar, Mariela, and Don Juanito clearly again, sitting in their chairs with their coffee cups, oblivious.

I steadied myself. When the conversation paused, I asked Oscar if we were going to see Ruth now. He frowned, then used Don Juanito's words. "A person can't just show up at the DSI." I looked to Juan for a sign that he might be on my side, but the old man kept his eyes down as if reading the coffee grounds at the bottom of his cup. Oscar took a breath and said, "We work hard on your behalf, Yuri. But we recommend you don't lose sight of things. You have an excellent guardian now who looks after you."

There it was, the impossible thing I'd be asked to do: to forget Ruth and become Mariela's charge, her sister *and* her adoptee, and to be grateful for it. Oscar knew, of course, that no foreign visitor could become a minor's official guardian. But who other than Mariela could take up this role in Ruth's absence? My adult "sister"—if Mariela was to be believed, and why would Oscar doubt her—was my nearest of kin for now. And if she weren't here—I had to admit this—Oscar would have to send me to a shelter or an orphanage, and I'd become a ward of the State just as Mariela had been all her childhood in *la yuma*. Of course, if Mariela weren't here, Ruth wouldn't have been arrested in the first place, and I wouldn't need to live with a foreign guardian I barely knew.

Mariela said to me calmly, "Yuri, mix-ups happen. Some things take a little time and a strong shoulder." She put her hand for a moment on top of Oscar's hand, close enough to his strong shoulder. It was a bold gesture, I thought, toward someone she'd just met, but no one seemed to notice this. Don Juanito chimed in, "Compañero Oscar knows many people. Much can be done. Food's not the best there. The rooms can be cold. Ruth will need a sweater." The old man tried to smile at me, but he looked mostly afraid as he gave up whatever authority he might have had in securing Ruth's release.

He rose and excused himself; he had errands to run before lunchtime. He thanked Mariela for the coffee, and she shook his hand warmly. "We're grateful to you, Juan. Please let us know what's needed for Ruth and we'll provide it. We work together and soon this misunderstanding will be over."

I got up as if to see the old man politely to the door. When we came out to the porch, I took his arm and whispered, "I'll get you some money. Please." (I surprised myself with this proposal; I had no idea where I'd get any money.) "You know more people than Oscar does. Different people. Please help get Ruth out."

Don Juanito's mouth turned grim. "Ruth is my friend of forty years. You know that, *niña*. I will help, of course. Let's see what comes. Ruth is a Witness. A low-hanging fruit."

He shook his bald head, maybe thinking also of himself—low hanging enough for a neighborhood informant to grab hold of and give Juan's name to Oscar, or to the CDR, and maybe earn a privilege or erase a bad mark from a file. The old man looked at me. "Don't talk much, *niña*," he said. "And don't cry. I hate to see young people cry."

I wasn't crying. I was too scared.

"I'll look into a visit. Meanwhile we'll see if we can get a sweater to her." Ruth had only been wearing her black funeral dress when they took her away in the police car.

Don Juanito put on his hat and walked down the two steps to the sidewalk. I watched him turn the corner onto Dimas Street and disappear. Then I drew a breath and went inside the house toward the voices of Mariela and Oscar in the kitchen.

13

Ruth's imprisonment went on through the end of June. So did Mariela's nightly parties. During those crowded, noisy gatherings, I took to drinking aguardiente with the guests, and no one stopped me. Alcohol, I thought, might help me bear Ruth's absence and my guilt and make my new living arrangements tolerable. But it didn't. The aguardiente mostly burned my throat and made me stupid and slow. It didn't help me make out when or how Ruth would get out of detention, or why Mariela and Oscar had become such fast friends, joking and whispering in the hallway. Mariela's fun time with her new chums (her stash of dollars had clearly turned up somehow) and her playing grand hostess in her kidnapper's home made it hard to believe that she was working for Ruth's release. I brooded about this, and by brooding and drinking and doing nothing for Ruth, I felt I, too, was betraying her.

But on a late night, after the last guests had cleared out, Mariela gave me the first reason for hope. She was in Ruth's bedroom, now Mariela's, rifling through dresser drawers, and when I came in, she said, "There's progress in the case. Oscar needs Ruth's birth certificate."

I took her to the filing cabinet, stored in my bedroom beside shelves of Abuelo Alberto's rusted tools. The old pliers and wrenches and screwdrivers made the room smell of metal like an old factory. I liked the smell; it never reminded me of home.

Mariela, her head barely taller than the top drawer, held up the candle to the gray cabinet. I pulled out the first file, labeled "Births and Deaths." There was no birth certificate in it, only old envelopes and onionskin papers written in a child's hand. One yellowed sheet read:

> *Dear Mama,*
> *I hope you are good here we are fine. I don't cry with the injections. The doctor say I am good. Sister Dorothy gives cough syrup it is dark, I am sleepy. It snows and we dont go out for recess and I am good student. I have nothing to say more. 100 Kisses, Muriel.*

I handed the paper to Mariela. She looked at it without surprise and passed it back to me. "My American name. I must have been seven, maybe eight."

"You wrote this?"

"Justina, the cook, dictated it to me. She read Ruth's letters to me and to Sister Dorothy. Translated them to English. Then she'd help me write back to Ruth in Spanish. Justina talked to me in Spanish every day. The best thing the nuns did for me. Later I studied Spanish in school so I could read Ruth's letters and find out when she was coming."

I clutched the paper, stunned. All along, Mariela's orphanage story had been verifiable, stored in a cabinet next to my bed, ready for me to read. Here were the onionskin papers Mariela had written on when she was a child and still believed Ruth was her mother. There were fifteen or twenty letters in the file, the last few in English. I wondered if Ruth had understood those. She'd certainly kept them, dated the envelopes, and tucked them in a manila folder to preserve them. None of them proved that Mariela was my sister, but now I realized that the answer could be near, hiding in this gray cabinet just a few feet from my own bed.

Mariela sat on the edge of my bed. "Put those away. It's late," she said. "Look for Ruth's birth certificate."

Inside the same file, behind the yellowing letters, I found a picture of a dark-haired child holding the hand of a tall, pleasant-looking nun. The child looked into the camera, her hair pulled back from her forehead with a thick, light band. I held up the picture and Mariela raised her head and squinted in the candlelight.

"Me and Sister Dorothy."

"She took you from the plane full of babies?"

Mariela shrugged. "How would I know that?"

Another picture: Mariela, slightly older, wearing plaid pants and a light button-down shirt, a small tin pail in one hand. She was feeding chickens, their heads pecking at the ground around Mariela's feet.

I sat next to her on the bed. "You lived on a farm?"

"The Butlers' place. Sister Dorothy took me there when I was ten." Mariela yawned. She lay back and put a pillow under her head. "That was summer. Summers are short in Nebraska. All year you wait for them to come back. In winter your fingertips get numb, and you can't feel what's right there in your hand."

"But the snow must be beautiful."

"In pictures. But if you're in it, it's wet and gets into your boots and you can't think straight. Your thoughts come out of your mouth in a cloud." Mariela smiled. "Januarys are the worst. The Butlers had an outhouse right behind the barn and I'd have to walk through the frozen barn to get to it. Their donkey, Boy, watched me the whole time, his head sticking out of his stall. He was a sweet creature, but I hated him. I used to hold it in as long as I could."

"Did you like the Butlers?"

"The Butlers?" For the first time she sounded surprised. "I learned to hunt rabbits there. And I liked their horse. But Mr. Butler read a book about American presidents at the table after supper... Washington, Adams, Jefferson, Madison, Monroe, another Adams. I tried to keep my eyes open, but I guess I didn't. Mrs. Butler would wake me with a loud 'Muriel,' and Mr. Butler would say there was a paddle hanging by the basement stairs that he didn't like to use. Anyway, they took me back to the nuns."

"Why?"

Mariela yawned again. "There was this fruity gum I wanted, and chocolates from the little store on my way back from school. I needed a few coins. I meant to put Mrs. Butler's wallet back the same way it was, but I forgot." She laughed softly. "The nuns were better. They had indoor toilets."

She closed her eyes. I thought she'd fallen asleep, but then she said casually, "I wasn't right for the Butlers." She pulled the bedspread from close to the wall and wrapped it around herself.

"Ruth's birth certificate is probably in a different folder," I said. "Yours too."

"Mine wouldn't say anything true," Mariela said.

Soon she snored softly as she must have at the Butlers' dinner table. I got up and opened the second file drawer and took out envelopes and rummaged through old papers. There had to be a few rock-bottom truths in every person's life, such as where one was born and to whom. Mariela's birth, upbringing, and return still sounded outlandish, but it struck me for the first time that Mariela had, like me, refused to be adopted, and this refusal, defiant and apparently guiltless, impressed me. I rummaged through more papers, searching for facts that would fill in the blanks of her years away in the snowy north living with strangers.

I finally found Ruth's and Mamá's birth certificates. The two had been born three years apart in La Coloma, in Pinar del Rio, province of the world-famous mogote mountains and the green Viñales Valley. I set the certificates on top of the cabinet while Mariela slept quietly on my bed. I went back to the drawer and read the tabs on the old files. Toward the back of the drawer—there was no logical order to how the files were stored, neither alphabetical nor chronological—I found Mariela's birth certificate inside an old plastic bag. I held my candle close to it. Her last name was listed as Ríos, not Vilar; she was born in La Coloma, as Ruth had said. But the mother's recorded name was Ruth Vilar, the father's Luis Ríos. I'd never heard of him before. He certainly wasn't Ruth's beloved Sancho in La Coloma.

I roused Mariela. "I found your certificate."

Mariela opened her eyes, unrolled herself from the bedspread, and took the paper in one hand. I held the candle for her.

"Lies," she said softly and handed it back to me.

I blew out the candle and lay next to her in the dark.

Mariela breathed deeply. I said to her, "They say that if you change one thing from the past, everything else falls down like dominoes."

"What?"

"You'd be someone else now if Ruth hadn't—"

"Stolen me?" Mariela rolled up on an elbow and faced me. "Abandoned me?"

"Ruth didn't have to tell you what she'd done. She didn't have to admit you weren't hers. In her mind you were all she had."

"Listen, you think it's any different with you?" She paused for my answer, but I had none. "Ruth's been lying to you too. She told me herself that she'd tried over and over to send you off to that awful man in *el norte*. She wanted to get rid of you."

About this Mariela could have been right. My stomach pitched a little at her words. I said, "You can't keep Ruth in jail for what she's done."

"*I* keep her in jail?" Mariela raised her voice. "Last time I looked I'm the one trying to get her out." She took in a breath. "You think I'm stupid? I know both Mamá and Ruth didn't want me. Okay? Is that what you're getting at? But that old woman promised. I *waited* for her." She turned slightly toward the night table. "Like I said, it doesn't matter now. I choose

Mamá because she leads me to you. You and I stick together from now on."

Her decision that we stick together gave me a strange thrill. But it didn't last. Behind the thrill rose the old fury; maybe it didn't matter to Mariela whose daughter she ultimately was (though I doubted this), and maybe I admired her courage in saying so, but it wasn't that way for me. I knew who my mother was and where my loyalties lay. It never occurred to Mariela—not then and not ever—that her sisterly intentions couldn't touch this rock-bottom truth. She never understood that I wanted my own fate—not one latched on to hers out of desperation like an improvised bench nailed onto a bicitaxi.

Mariela took out a black-and-white picture from a plastic pouch—Mamá sitting with friends on the steps of the University of Havana. Mariela asked about the people in the picture, and I named the ones I knew. She asked for a pencil and wrote each name carefully on the back of the photo. She pulled more pictures of Mamá from the file cabinet. She wanted details—names, faces, dates—of each occasion. I tried to remember Mamá's stories, fill in blanks, re-create vanished people and events. Mariela sat on my bed, encouraging me, nodding as she studied the black-and-white pictures—Mamá at school, a smiling Mamá in front of a restaurant with other young men and women, Mamá wearing a sweater on the beach in winter, her hair pushed back by the wind. Mariela kept nodding and scribbling on the back of each photo. At some point I felt I couldn't go on—I wouldn't turn Mamá's youth into Mariela's notes, or my childhood with Mamá into one of Mariela's projects. Little by little, I started to lie—small lies at first, then bigger. This cheered me up. I gave wrong names and dates on purpose, put Mamá in places she'd never been, with people she'd never met. Mariela ate up my stories, especially those of revolutionary struggle, machetes in the countryside, Party congresses, military parades—she loved Mamá in her militia uniform, ready to stamp out all counterrevolutionary worms.

By lying to Mariela, I thought I'd keep something of my life with Mamá to myself. But as I spoke, the fake memories started to edge out the real ones and I worried I wouldn't be able to tell from then on which details I'd invented and which ones had happened, or to tell the real Mamá from the one I was making up, and so I would lose her again, this time forever. Mariela took out her camera, which recorded my face as I spoke, and as she aimed her bright light at me, whatever she asked, I gave the bright light whichever answer came first.

14

Despite Mariela's high-handed speeches about working for the revolution, she never did a thing, never picked up a broom to sweep the streets on Sundays and never signed up to chop cane in the countryside. Instead, she lay around the house brewing pots of coffee, sketching furiously in her notebook, and dressing up in the evenings to meet her guests. But what she did on those evenings, in the manner of grand hostess, changed the neighborhood in unexpected ways.

Under her reign few things were forbidden, and young people (Hernando especially) could make politically dangerous jokes that had only been told in secret before, in a shut room among trusted friends. For example, Hernando now openly greeted Mariela's guests with a sardonic "Welcome to Perestroika House." Oscar hated this greeting, but Mariela found sarcasm clever, dissent amusing, and taking offense dull—so Oscar, freshly showered and combed, his face placid in the dim light of Ruth's parlor, grinned at his younger brother and pretended to approve of the impertinent name, Perestroika House.

In turn, Oscar called Mariela's gatherings *salons*, an old-fashioned word not heard since the poet-patriot José Martí had held court abroad among his nineteenth-century poet friends and fellow anti-colonial agitators. Sitting in Ruth's plushy chair, Oscar raised his glass in honor of those Parisian salons, where "our Latin American rabble-rousers hatched revolutions and poems in those frigid countries of exile." Of course, to neighbors like Doña Barbara and Antonieta Prieto, Ruth's reconfigured household—its unholy alliance of the Malangones and the crazy Nebraskan yankee—was no belles-lettres gathering place but a perverse carnival scene and the ultimate mockery of Ruth's old-style dignity. But to Mariela's guests, high school girls and boys from rough barrios or from the Llega y Pon, Mariela's salons became, during that Special Period of terrible scarcity, a respite of free thought, alcohol, and, most importantly, a decent dinner.

Ever since Soviet goods had disappeared from store shelves, Paladero neighbors had found themselves scraping together strange dishes of ground soy protein mixed with cow organs—intestines, liver (if you were lucky and could make a deal for it), stomach, and whatever leftover slop could be thrown into the mix. The smell of this fried offal wafted through the neighborhood each night at dinnertime. The Prietos ate this too now that rich cousin Sonia had gone back to *la yuma* when her visa ended and the Prietos' resources had dried up overnight—not because of long-distance stinginess on Sonia's part, but because Sonia, back in her Miami office after her Havana visit, had found a security guard at her office door on the day she returned. According to Rosario, the guard told Sonia to pack the framed pictures from her desk into a box—he'd handed her the box—and to follow him down the escalator and into the sunny Miami morning. It turned out that the bank Sonia worked for had gone, she'd said during a weepy phone call to the stunned Prietos, "a bit too far" in selling what she called "dicey mortgages." Things took a "bad turn," and she and a number of her coworkers were "let go." It probably didn't help, she added, that because of her visit to Havana, some coworkers denounced her as communist to her Miami branch manager.

Ruth, dispenser of harsh judgments, might have said something like, "Antonieta's golden goose got cooked in the microwave." But that was the old Ruth. As to the actual thoughts coming to the new Ruth in the DSI, I could only guess, and such guesses didn't keep me sober or help me sleep at night. Often I lay awake for hours wondering if Ruth was awake too, her terrors more harrowing than any I could think up. With each day that passed, I felt us moving away from Ruth, abandoning her (Oscar repeated over and over that no one could show up to the DSI without approval). So Ruth, though she herself was an old hand at abandoning her nearest and dearest and even plotting to send me away to *la yuma*, now sat alone in that frightful DSI cell, and the thought of her there continued to keep me awake, some nights until dawn.

At breakfast, after a few hours' sleep, I repeated my questioning of Mariela: Did Ruth's birth certificate bring any results? Was the investigation moving forward? Mariela answered yes to both questions, but when I'd press her for details, she'd only echo Oscar's bland insistence on patience. I didn't believe her or Oscar, and her calm manner as if she was humoring me filled me with gloom. She'd smile and pour me the muddy coffee she brewed in Ruth's pot. "You'll see. Things will turn around soon." Her words reminded me of Ruth's hopeful prediction—"our turn will come"—which in the end had brought us only disaster.

From day to day, I couldn't tell whose turn was coming or what would happen next. At Mariela's salons I often milled about hazy eyed and half drunk through the smoky rooms while, in the parlor, Oscar held forth to a group of friends on global markets, yankee exploitation of resources, or the Soviet question. He clicked chopsticks with his buddies, ate noodles straight out of his white carton, and swatted away the predicted End of Socialism. In those days everyone talked, as Ruth had, of Endings and Unravelings. But Oscar swayed with drunken optimism and instead spoke of True Beginnings while Mariela, half pupil and half hostess, smiled at him. Mariela's smile seemed to hint to the chief Malangón, and to all of us, that his life—maybe all our lives—could be grander and more significant than we'd ever thought possible.

One night, during one of Oscar's speeches on globalism, Mariela declared herself committed to the "Third World" and "her people." I'd never heard of three worlds before or who'd decided on this ranking. Oscar looked stumped as well and maybe a little indignant at coming in third. He protested in a low voice that we were "second world," but Mariela, who often threw down shots of the clear aguardiente but never seemed drunk, restated her pride in casting her fate with us in third place. If there were indeed three worlds and not one, I thought then that Mariela was not from ours, and that in any case, her siding with us didn't exactly call for gratitude.

Oscar took advantage of Mariela's little speech to go stand near her by Ruth's desk and raise his glass to her. "You were snatched from us and from your birthplace," he said in his orator's voice. "The revolution now corrects this wrong." Mariela, solemn, walked over to him, and the two of them clinked glasses as in a wedding, the high pleasing note rising above everyone's heads. Oscar's mother, Amadora, smiled at her older son—a rarity—and seemed to overlook Oscar's treachery toward his wife. Was it the power of *jama*, our love of eating and drinking and talking freely, that made us put aside all judgments? The other guests also raised their glasses and cheered. Oscar and Mariela looked around the room, then at each other, and they kissed on the mouth, becoming a couple even as Oscar's young wife rocked his newborn son to sleep at home. I stood on the other side of Ruth's desk, watching their public celebration of commitment to global struggles and to each other. The two of them huddled close; they bent their heads together toward Mariela's sketchbook opened on Ruth's desk. Mariela spoke to Oscar about her new project—large figures she planned to paint out in nature, by a mountain or a boulder, she said, to "celebrate the enduring Taino and Yoruba spirit of this land."

Surely Oscar, who taught ninth grade physics and called himself a Marxist-Leninist materialist, would never go in for Mariela's wacky projects, her warrior faces and screaming poses. But now, his arm around her waist, he nodded wisely at her kooky sketches. This gesture hit me hard. I leaned back against the wall and closed my eyes; the aguardiente was making me weepy. It suddenly seemed clear that Oscar, despite his Party airs, was only a neighborhood swindler and could never deliver on any of his promises—our visit to the DSI, Ruth's release, or what he touted now to Mariela as his many "contacts" in the art world who'd grant the necessary permissions for her projects and exhibits in Havana's most important galleries.

I turned away from the two of them in disgust, only to find beyond the open front door Hernando at work on his own swindles. He and a young man, a bicycle propped between the two of them, shook hands on Ruth's porch, and then the young man wheeled the bike down the steps to the sidewalk. The exchange looked simple, crisp, even natural, nothing like Oscar's grandiose declarations. In that moment, I envied Hernando's smooth dealmaking. Compared to Hernando's "business" and Mariela's lofty projects, my own desires to get Ruth out of jail and escape to the Lenin boarding school struck me as puny and desperate—not much more than wishful thinking.

Hernando saw me staring. I walked off, but not before he shouted from the porch his usual "Miss Astronaut."

From that point on I remembered nothing until around midnight, when I woke up in a corner on the parlor floor. The room was quiet, the electricity back on, and one of Ruth's old scarves, draped over a lamp, had turned the parlor a reddish gold. Oscar had left and only a few guests lounged on the floor and on the couch. I felt sick to my stomach and very low. I was furious at myself. Mariela and the Malanga-heads never cared for Ruth, it wasn't their job to help her; it was mine, and I'd done little more than fret and drink myself into a stupor.

Mariela leaned down to me. "You look terrible. Come on, let's fix you up." She led me to Ruth's bedroom and sat me on Ruth's former bed. Mariela had moved her things into Ruth's room on the day of the arrest. She'd changed the bedspread that lay under Lucho's body to one embroidered by Ruth many years before, bright with birds from exotic jungly places like Costa Rica or Guatemala. She'd put away all of Ruth's pictures, keeping only the framed photo of Mamá and me at the beach, Mamá's hand cupped over her eyes against the sun, her teeth visible beneath the shadow of her hand, and me, a toddler, sitting within her folded legs. Mariela had decorated the picture with a few pink construction-paper flowers.

She had me change into one of her three loose, bright dresses, a little tight around my shoulders, but the dress was a pretty blue. She combed and braided my hair, her cool hands resting sometimes on my shoulders, and her touch made me feel less lonely. When she was done, she turned me around and rubbed blue eye shadow on my sleepy lids, clasped a pair of her golden hoops on my ears, and took me by the wrist to Ruth's bedroom mirror.

"Dreamy," Mariela said to the costumed drunk girl in the mirror. She pulled my shoulders back, and my breasts pointed themselves at the mirror. "Show yourself off," she said, and turned my face toward hers. "Talk to people, Yuri. Show off your mind. You and that funny boy, Hernando, you're both clever. You should be friends."

"Hernando's a clever killer of dogs. His bikes are stolen. He's out of juvenile detention only because of Oscar."

"I was in juvenile detention once," Mariela said with no emotion. "Doesn't mean what Ruth says it means." She spoke again to the "me" in the mirror. "Smile a little at the boy and he'll stop needling you. He wants your attention."

"I don't care what he wants."

I followed Mariela out of the bedroom. The hall bathroom door was open, and inside two "pre-university" girls played with Ruth's silvery set of rouge and face powder, laughing and rubbing it into their cheeks.

I said to them, "That's not yours."

The shorter girl looked at me, at my bright eyelids and large earrings. She set Ruth's face powder down beside the sink and said, "This? This dried-up shit is for Methuselah. For mummies." She stared me down, then said, "It must be for you." Both girls laughed. They stepped out of the bathroom and walked past me and Mariela toward the parlor. Mariela said, low, "Try to make friends, Yuri."

The girls were right; Ruth's ancient face powder *was* dried-up shit. Ruth's preciousness about her possessions had always struck me as ridiculous, and yet, since her arrest, I found myself leaping Lucho-like to guard her old things including, apparently, her 1950s cosmetics. It unnerved me how easily one's presence could be erased, even from one's own withered objects, and I felt part of the erasure machinery myself. Ruth could soon be ground down to old powder, to dust; a casual wind would blow away what remained of her. But I couldn't say this to Mariela. I said instead, "People are stealing Ruth's things."

"Everything belongs to everyone," Mariela answered.

I didn't think so. "We need order."

Mariela glanced at the soiled towel hanging from the rack and at the dirty tiles where Tigre lounged and shed his long brown hair. She picked up Ruth's abandoned compact from the powdery sink. Surprisingly she admitted that things were getting "a little sloppy."

Back in the dim parlor, Mariela approached Amadora Malanga-head, who sat rocking contentedly in one of Ruth's chairs. The two girls who'd thrown down Ruth's makeup with a sneer were gone, as was everyone else except Hernando and one of his gang friends half sitting, half sprawled on the couch. Amadora, her hair pinned back from her heavy face, looked tired, possibly relieved to rock herself by the reddish glow of the scarf-covered lamp. Mariela asked Amadora politely if she could please come to the house in the mornings, to help "straighten up things a bit." I hoped Mariela meant strip the beds, wash the clothes, collect dishes, make decent coffee, cook something other than scrambled eggs, empty wastebaskets and ashtrays. Amadora nodded. Whatever Mariela would pay her in dollars would be more than what she made cleaning the high school, and so Mariela, who'd thrown her fate in with third world peoples, had just hired the first Vilar servant in thirty years. And shamefully, I was glad. As for the dollars that made this extravagant transaction possible (the stash Don Juanito had sensed was somewhere, despite Mariela's declarations of poverty), I wouldn't come across Mariela's actual money until months later, when it would prove a slight reprieve for Ruth and end up condemning Hernando.

Amadora didn't wait till morning. She rose from the rocking chair, set the parlor vase upright, straightened the pictures on the walls, collected trash into a burlap sack that someone had used to bring bottles of aguardiente and supplies, and dragged the sack noisily past her youngest Malangón son and his gang buddy Reynaldo. "You ill-born bums, go home and sleep it off," she yelled at the drowsy, confused boys, who stood quickly, looked about the room, and made their way to the front door. I was grateful to her and also embarrassed by my own laziness. In my worry and stupor, it hadn't occurred to me to clean up the mess myself. Now I went through each bedroom, picked up dirty clothes and towels, then threw them into the ancient washing machine in the courtyard, turned it on, and listened for several minutes to the whoosh it made. The late-night air cleared my head, and I felt useful for the first time since Ruth had been jailed. I went to my bedroom. I thought I'd hide some of my valuables, keep them out of the hands of any wandering guest or "pre" girl looking for something to mock or steal. I tucked some things in a small box—pictures from the Misión apartment, Mamá's silver pin, her water-stained copy of *Le Père Goriot*, then walked down the hall and into the kitchen. I climbed on a chair to hide the box in the highest cabinet. Amadora came up behind me. "Good," she said when I explained what was in the box. "Let's keep it away from traffic." I nodded, shut the cabinet door, and climbed down. Amadora rinsed a rag and wiped the sticky counters. She said, "Don't worry, we'll tighten the screws around here." For a while she was the only person in Perestroika House who made me feel at ease.

THE NEXT MORNING something strange happened. The night before, I'd looked clownish to myself caked in Mariela's makeup, but now, after waking with black smudges under my eyes, I stared at myself and thought that I'd actually changed. I washed my face and looked again in the mirror; it was as if Mariela had magically redrawn my features the previous night with her eyebrow pencil and lipstick. My lips appeared fuller; my nose seemed longer and thinner. It was impossible to have transformed overnight, and still, some new version of me stared back from the mirror. Stranger still, I saw for the first time, in this new girl's eyes, the possibility of a life beyond Ruth's house, beyond Mariela's and Oscar's salons, maybe even beyond the potholed neighborhood. I wondered what else might have changed in me as I slept.

I found out at that night's salon. Things started as usual—the Chinese dinner and chopsticks, and my intention to stay sober, which didn't last long. But instead of the fog that filled my head each time I had aguardiente, my mind turned sharp. I felt bold, ready to cause a stir, tilt something, break it. I leaned over to Don Juanito, sitting beside me on the parlor's wicker couch, eating his noodles. I raised my voice over the room's chatter and asked him to take me to see Ruth right then. Some guests turned to look at us. "No more excuses," I said to the old man. "We go now."

Juan half nodded—yes, of course—his eyes blue and clear, his lips shining with noodle grease. "I would take you, *niña*," he said. "But just now I have a situation." (Don Juanito often had "a situation.") "Besides"—he nodded toward Mariela—"your sister is your guardian. She should take you."

"She's not my guardian. And she's not my sister. You know that."

Don Juanito looked up at me. He sighed dramatically. "Ruth

was my friend of forty years, *niña*," he said, then whispered that Ruth was charged with serious violations that barred visitors, such as "dangerousness" (a legal term that covered a broad swath of unnamed past, present, and future offenses) and an "elevated lifestyle."

"Ruth *had* no lifestyle," I said, "much less elevated."

The old man shook his head. "I wish she hadn't served that butter..."

"Ruth," I spoke louder, "is in jail because she served butter?" More guests turned toward our voices.

Juan continued whispering: "Look, *niña*, where do you find butter in times like these?" He paused as if what followed were obvious. "It would have been better if Ruth had purchased her butter from a friend of forty years... hmm?" He tapped a wise finger to his forehead.

There it was. Ruth's butter. So rare it had to come from a different, better-connected black marketeer, and Don Juanito had found this out. Ruth's crime then, according to the old man, wasn't gunpowder or rockets or even black-market purchases but black-market purchases from someone other than himself. Was the old man implying that this other untrustworthy merchant had told on Ruth? Juan saw my fury and said, "Stay calm, *niña*. Alcohol is dangerous for a young lady."

I walked across the room toward Oscar and Mariela. The two stood watching a young man play guitar beside the two stacked TVs. I stood behind Oscar and said, loud, "Is Ruth in jail because of rockets or because of butter?" Oscar and Mariela turned to me. Oscar tilted his head as if amused; he raised one hand and lowered the other, palms up, drunkenly weighing the difference—rockets or butter? Butter or rockets? Then he put a hand on my shoulder. "Stop worrying. Ruth is cooperating. The investigation will clear her soon."

"Clear her of what?"

"Of the charges," Oscar answered, and he smiled wide, terribly pleased with himself.

Only one thing seemed clear; there were serious charges against Ruth, and those, I knew, could only lead to harsh convictions. Oscar turned back to the young man playing the guitar and swayed with the beat. The young man's wavy hair went past his collar, and at one time Oscar would have denounced him, maybe charged him with "dangerousness." Long hair in men, at first an homage to the shaggy revolutionaries of 1959 shooting their guns in the mountains to overthrow Batista, had morphed into a sign of ideologically diversionist thinking, especially after the Beatles and the Rolling Stones and the hippies in the mountains of California took up such haircuts and the decadent, drug-taking attitudes that went with them. But now Oscar didn't seem to mind the young musician's hairstyle; he wanted to appear tolerant and bohemian before Mariela, and his hypocrisy enraged me.

I put my hand on Oscar's shoulder and tried to turn him back to face me. Oscar shook off my hand and turned, his eyes dark and cold. I asked him, loud enough that Mariela and other nearby guests could hear, how his wife was feeling today. I'd seen the *Compañero*'s wife, I said even louder, at the market that morning, and she looked exhausted. Circles under her eyes. Pale. Oscar faced me, more astonished than angry. The young man with long hair looked up at us from his guitar but kept playing. I continued: Was Oscar's wife planning to visit us with the baby this evening?

At the end of each night Mariela strangely made a point of asking Oscar to bring his wife and baby to the next day's festivities, and Oscar, holding the plate of food he was taking home to them, promised he would. Then the next night Mariela would nod sympathetically at his reports of the baby's colic or cough, and the ritual would continue, unchanged, for another night. I understood now that just as Oscar and Mariela lied to each other each night about Oscar's wife and baby to keep up appearances that no one believed, so had they been lying to me about Ruth's charges and her future release. And I'd let them make me their fool.

Oscar drew a furious breath, but Mariela quickly took me by the shoulders before Oscar lashed out. "Yuri, my love," Mariela said, "say hello to your friend." Mariela rushed me toward Julio Cuevas, who stood beside the desk, arms crossed, watching the guitar player with admiration. Then she returned to Oscar, who gave me a vicious stare from across the room. Mariela gently turned him back to the guitarist.

Julio gave me a quick nod, friendly but distracted. He was waiting for Rosario Prieto to show up, but as the salons had grown rowdier and Mariela's guest list expanded to tough barrios like Alamar and El Fanguito, Rosario's family forbid her from attending. Julio and I had to call her from Ruth's dining room window, across the gap between our houses, and beg her to sneak past her grandmother Antonieta and join us.

I stood beside Julio, proud of my boldness in insulting Oscar, but also, as my buzz wore off, shaky; I'd never confronted anyone that way before—and certainly never someone like Oscar, who could do me so much harm. Don Juanito had reminded me that Mariela was, for now, my "guardian," which meant I could go on living safely in Ruth's house, eating and drinking and waking up to Tigre asleep in the bathroom. And I knew I owed Mariela's designation of "guardian" to Oscar's approval. What if he reversed his decision now? My current life, as much as I hated it, could turn much darker if Party leader Oscar decided to make it so.

Julio said to me, "Watch that son of a bitch." I thought he meant Oscar, but Julio was pointing to the young man's fingers racing up and down the neck of the guitar. I looked at Julio's handsome face for what I feared was too long and, partly to cover this up, I asked him about Ruth's case: Was it ever mentioned at home? Did Dr. Cuevas talk about Ruth's charges—her dangerousness and black-market butter and her elevated lifestyle?

Julio frowned. "Are you drunk already?" He looked surprised at my stupidity. "What charges? Don't you know anything?" He turned back to the guitarist. "They've probably looked at everything in this house. They've probably done their inventory."

His ferocity scared me. "Who's *they*?"

Julio said more softly, "They're probably in business." Julio tapped his foot lightly to the music. He nodded toward Hernando and added, "Who knows what the Malanga-heads are up to? But I bet when their little business is over, your aunt comes home."

Hernando lay curled up on Ruth's sofa, an arm thrown over

his head. The sight of him on the couch half asleep while possibly full of malicious intent filled me with dread. Don Juanito, after finishing his food, also rested peacefully, eyes closed, in the rocking chair. Could Juan close his eyes and sleep peacefully in Ruth's house if the Malanga-heads were plotting some "business" against Ruth—and wouldn't he, of all people, know if they were?

"I have to leave this place," I said to Julio. "I don't trust anyone here. I need to go to the Lenin like you. Get away from all this."

Julio frowned again. He watched the guitarist's spider fingers running up and down the neck of the guitar and without looking at me said, "Forget the Lenin. No *jama*. Watery beans, rotten spaghetti. Every night you fall on your bed stiff like a board after working in the fields. We're farmhands. Serfs. Get it? We clean the toilets on our knees with our toothbrushes." I had a hard time picturing Julio as a serf; his tanned arms and handsome face seemed no worse for all the farm labor.

"But you study," I said.

He looked at me at last. "Pay attention, *chiquita*. Learn what's what. It's not in any of their books."

When I said nothing, he looked at me and shrugged with mild pity. "Come on," he said, and nudged me down the hall to the dining room window as we did most nights, to shout Rosario's name across the few feet that divided her house from Ruth's.

I followed Julio, stunned and confused by his accusations. He'd just implied that Oscar and Hernando—and, if Julio were telling the truth, others too, the same people walking in and out of Ruth's door, eating and drinking from her plates and cups—were plotting to steal from her and, worse, possibly working to keep Ruth locked up for as long as their schemes required. I glanced at Hernando sleeping off the aguardiente on the couch and tried to imagine him carrying out a secret plot to keep Ruth in jail and take her things. Hernando was a small-time gang leader and thief, taking a bike or a camera, maybe even a radio or a TV. If he wanted anything of Ruth's, he would've already taken it. But nothing much, as far as I could tell, was missing except for a few plates and spoons, which could have been swiped by anyone. As for Oscar, I didn't think he'd risk his standing in the Party in order to steal Ruth's old Methuselah junk. Yet Oscar was already risking his Party status by granting easy pardons to Mariela and me for the gunpowder rockets, and by attending these decadent parties and carrying on an open affair with the guilty *yuma*.

My head throbbed. Julio leaned out of Ruth's dining room window and called Rosario's name, and soon Rosario came to her window and made her usual excuses. We went back to the parlor and the music, but in a few minutes, Rosario appeared at Ruth's front door wearing her tight *yuma* blue jeans. After her arrival I gulped down more aguardiente. I'd promised myself to go easy, cut down on the drinking for a few days. But I didn't. I wanted to feel sharp again, and bold, the way I had at the start of the evening. I wanted to question Julio, figure out what to do with his hints and accusations, and confirm or disprove his suspicions about Ruth's house and her imprisonment.

But the more I drank, the less I thought about Ruth's stay in the DSI and the supposed Malanga-heads' plot to steal from her.

The Tilting House

I acted silly around Julio and Rosario, and then sulky whenever the two of them touched or nodded or smiled at each other. I tried to tell myself that because this was Perestroika House, the two of them had come to visit *me*, and I was somehow part of their courtship and their secret Romeo and Juliet love—Julio, the CDR president's son, and Rosario, granddaughter of a bomb-throwing traitor. I saw myself as their cover and witness, a job I assigned to myself in my drunkenness. But when Julio called me *chiquita*, *niñita*, or something else equally demeaning, I realized that I was only their dumb, excitable little Nurse. I flushed with shame. Even Hernando noticed my humiliation and called out from the couch, "Miss Astronaut, third wheel of the spaceship."

The rest of the night I sat in a corner, low and desperate. I drank until all feeling left me and watched the door open and shut behind the guests going back to their own neighborhoods. Only later, when the music ended and no one noticed me or cared, did I finally do something to prove that I wasn't a dumb Nurse.

Julio and Rosario were standing before the ancient record player in the corner of the dining room. Julio was going through Mamá's old, prerevolution record albums. They hadn't been played in years. Julio flipped through each one and studied their covers. He removed one record from its sleeve, set it on the spindle, placed the needle at the edge of the record, and turned the stereo on. (Usually, late enough in the night when almost no one needed it, the electricity came back on.) It wasn't dance music, but Rosario and Julio started dancing, or mostly hugging and rubbing their bodies together, Julio pressing himself against her jeans, and Rosario pressing back. She, too, had downed a number of shots of aguardiente. Julio smiled at her, and then at me. He took his arm from Rosario's waist and reached out and grabbed my wrist, and I stood from the floor and the three of us turned in a circle in Ruth's dining room. The strange, sad melody on the record player made the game thrilling.

Dancing, swaying to the strange music, our arms around each other, Julio kissed Rosario full on the mouth. He held me tight while the two of them kissed, his hips and mine mashing hard together, our arms around each other, and after he raised his mouth from Rosario's, he kissed me too. He pressed his mouth to mine hard and batted his tongue against my lips. I opened my mouth to him but also kept my eyes open, and when he pulled back, I saw he beamed with daring. "Kiss," he said to Rosario. And then to me, "Kiss." Rosario looked at me and didn't say no, and I kissed her, a flavorless, soft kiss. I batted my tongue in her mouth without aim and bumped her teeth against my teeth.

Julio held on to the two of us. I looked at each of their faces and loved them both in that moment, and didn't want to let go. Julio was smiling, first at me and then at Rosario. But Rosario looked away then and the thrill of my naughtiness left me. Suddenly I wasn't sure why I'd kissed Rosario. She slipped from Julio's arm. It was late, she said, and she left through the carport. Julio smiled at me, sly and drunk, released his hand from my waist, and followed her out. I feared she'd never speak to either of us again.

All the aguardiente I'd had that night filled my head and I had to lean against Ruth's table. Someone behind me said,

"Nice job," and then, "Easy." Hernando was then holding me up, his hand in my armpit. He took me to the bathroom, where I bent over the toilet and threw up long strings of Chinese noodles and bile; my nostrils and throat burned. Hernando held my hair back, and when I finished heaving into the bowl, he cupped the cool, saved water from the tub into his hands and told me to rinse and then spit. He didn't seem to mind the awful smell or the disgusting sight of the toilet. He dipped a towel into the tub and put it to my mouth and forehead; then he flushed the toilet with a bucket of water.

"Not used to earthly beverages?" he said quietly. "I don't drink myself. My sisters drink. I've seen them puke many times." I'd never heard him speak in this low voice before. He patted my forehead with the cool, wet towel. "Your face is red, and you don't look pretty." He set me on the edge of the tub, and when he could see that I wouldn't fall off, he stepped into the hall and called out to his mother.

He and Amadora helped me walk to my bed. Hernando pulled the top sheet to one side, and after I lay down, he stepped back to the lit doorway as if to give me privacy. Amadora pulled the sheet up to my waist. The wall behind Hernando, spotless under Ruth's watch, was stained with candle soot, and the house, my sheets, my hands smelled of aguardiente, smoke, sweat, and bad living.

I closed my eyes; the invisible room still spun a little. When it slowed down to a manageable speed my thoughts drifted, not to Hernando's kindness or to the three-way kiss with Rosario and Julio, but to Julio's word, *inventory*. I saw toothbrushes, toothpaste, shampoo, soap bars swirling and making their way out of Ruth's house, for use or resale, in the pockets of the Malanga-heads and of Mariela's guests. I wondered about Don Juanito and his bulky bags earlier in the night when he'd chatted with Oscar, the two of them standing before the sheets on the line, their hands waving in the air as they talked. As I drifted toward sleep, I felt Hernando watching me from the open doorway. I was startled that he now knew me like this. Not many people in Perestroika House, Ruth's house, knew me at all.

THE NEXT MORNING I woke to Mariela's shouts on the phone. "I work in public. Yes! Yes. No. Not permanent. Please explain. Of course. I record the process. No one else. Of course. No, my camera. My camera only."

I put on clean clothes—couldn't find any panties—and rinsed my parched mouth in the bathroom. My head felt huge. In the kitchen, Amadora looked me over, and without a word she dropped a spoonful of bicarbonate in water and mixed it in a clear glass. She handed it to me along with two aspirins.

I thanked her and tried to swallow the gritty mix. "I wonder if people are taking my things," I said to her. "I have no underwear."

Mariela looked in from the doorway. "People are taking your underwear?" She pointed to her fancy panties hanging from the courtyard's clothesline. "Have one of mine," she said, cheerful. "But what you'll need soon are good hiking boots. We're going to Viñales. Steep hills. The permit for my project comes any day." She glowed with this news. She'd apparently secured, with Oscar's help, a permit to wander about painting and sculpting in the countryside. As for securing Ruth's permit to leave the DSI, she'd clearly not made the same effort.

"We can't go anywhere until Ruth gets out," I said.

Mariela put an arm around Amadora's shoulder and scrunched her close. "Amadora will take care of Ruth if we're gone when she's released. Anyway, we'll be back in a few days." She went on, "It's beautiful out in Viñales." She got her map and spread it on the kitchen table while I tried to eat a few bites of the toast Amadora set on the table. Mariela had circled sites on the map with her colored pencils. "These," she said pointing, excited, "are the mountainsides where I'll make my paintings."

I didn't understand why we had to travel hundreds of miles to paint pictures of mountains when Mariela could paint anything she wanted to in the city—a bowl of bananas, the ceiba tree in the park over Lucho's grave. Only later did I understand that Mariela wanted to paint *on* the mountains, on the sides of large, stony caves. I said, "There are no mountains in Viñales. They're mogotes. Flat as tables."

"Are they?" Mariela beamed again.

I knew of the famous Viñales mogotes only from pictures. People from Havana rarely traveled beyond the city, having no transportation, little money, and few country places that offered good food or extra beds. For sanitary reasons too, Mamá had never taken me to the countryside. She thought I could catch dengue from mosquitoes or parasites from unclean water.

"I'll stay here till Ruth comes out," I said to Mariela.

She looked up at me, angry. "Your hard head won't bring her home any faster." She turned to Amadora. "I've been patient, don't you think, Amadora? I've explained. Now I'm finished explaining." She folded the map and said to me a bit softer, "I thought you wanted to live out in the *manigüa*."

I'd made the mistake of telling Mariela, in one of our late-night drunken talks, that after Mamá died I'd wanted to live alone in the bush among wild plants, speaking to no one, reading in the day, and watching the sky at night. Now I was sorry I'd said it. Still, a part of me also felt important, being begged like Julio begged Rosario. Mariela smiled. "Of course you want to come to Viñales," she said. "I see it all over you. We'll only be three days."

After saying this she looked absent, as if she were done with us and had already left for the countryside to complete her important projects. Turning her face toward the grand future that she'd set in place by her will, she seemed as if she could be, after all, Mamá's daughter. And if she was Mamá's daughter, whose daughter was I, who longed for my limping, fanatical aunt to come home and set our lives in strict order? But maybe Mariela had it right: Ruth wouldn't come home any faster if I refused Mariela's bright excursion to the "real Cuba," as she called it now—its "rivers and lakes and green hills" known the world over, the reason why cruel Columbus had called the island the "most beautiful land human eyes had ever seen." (Quite a stretch, I learned later—an urban myth repeated by Cubans on every corner of the Earth, despite the more dazzling beauty of Italy, New Zealand, or Hawaii.) What sort of fool, I thought, gave up Mariela's adventures for Ruth's austere, wrath-ruled world? Yet I longed for Ruth to return and put everything in its proper place; I was also ashamed of this longing and burned to betray it.

"Where can we get some boots for Yuri?" Mariela asked Amadora. Amadora shrugged and rubbed her thumb against her fingertips.

"I know it costs," Mariela said. "That's why we're going on this trip. So I can feed everyone around here." She didn't say this to boast, only as a matter of fact. She never seemed to require gratitude. She touched my arm lightly. "Come with me to the post office. I'm sending a cable. The fresh air will sweeten your mood."

Hernando's bike parts and tools were gone from Ruth's porch, and the two rocking chairs leaned against the railing, stacked one on the other in a corner as if Ruth had just mopped. My head throbbed again in the sunlight, and a strange thought came to me: Hernando—dog killer and bicycle thief—might help me get Ruth out of the DSI.

Across from us in the park, Lucho's grave, sunk in green shadows, was probably indistinguishable now from the rest of the bushes, vines, and weeds grown around it. I pointed in the direction of the dog's burial spot, but Mariela didn't bother to look. After taking the pictures for her project, nothing more about Lucho's death or resting place seemed to interest her.

At the post office she sent a cable in English to a Robert Sands, a "friend who helps me," and she seemed happy afterward. On the sidewalk, sweating in the July sun, she shook the neck of her dress to cool herself and claimed the Earth was warming up; soon all would burn and disappear. This thought seemed to cheer her. Strangely, it cheered me too—I, and everyone else, could stop worrying about how things would turn out. "We're probably in the final times," Mariela said.

"That's what Ruth says."

"Not because of Jehovah. That's superstition. Because of us." We were animals, Mariela said, and like all species, we showed up for a while, and then, sooner or later, vanished like the dinosaurs. The old Ruth, before Mariela arrived, would have railed against such paganism, but what would Ruth say now in a hell her scriptures hadn't described?

"I'll go with you to the countryside," I said to Mariela. "But we see her today. We go to the DSI today. We go see Ruth."

Mariela stopped on the sidewalk. "Listen, Yuri. I see you changing, okay? It's okay to try new things." Her eyes lit up then and her face was suddenly beautiful. "Fun things, young things. It's okay to be young and be alive, understand?"

Ruth had described to me the "road to perdition" as a garden of birds chirping, music, reveling, and beautiful people milling about until, unaware, self-satisfied, they carelessly slipped over the edge and plunged down the sudden drop-off to everlasting flames. In the half-light of the salon nights as I'd make my way dizzy and happy from Mariela's aguardiente and from the joy of speaking and of being spoken to by Julio and Rosario and by young people I barely knew, who glowed and hugged each other in the dark, I felt I might have edged close to Ruth's drop-off point. I thought that because Ruth's own way had been hard, she'd convinced herself that only a harsh, lonely path could save any of us. I told Mariela about this once, late at night, when people I'd never seen before lay huddled in corners groping or kissing or sleeping. But Mariela had sent me to bed. It was normal at 3:00 a.m., she'd said, "to feel a little gloomy."

Now, in the bright sunlight of the sidewalk by the post office, her cable on its way to her friend in *la yuma*, Mariela went on, cheerfully, "I saw you with your two friends last night." She lifted her face. "Boys are like an arrow, no? But girls are a whole world." She smiled, pleased. "Was it fun?"

Heat rose to my neck and ears. I said nothing.

At the corner down the block from Ruth's house, I asked again about seeing Ruth.

"We can go see Ruth if you want," Mariela said. "But it doesn't change things. Your fate is not with Ruth. I've told you, Mamá wanted us together." She stopped and grabbed my arm. "You pretend that what we do in Perestroika House doesn't mean anything to you. But can you say you don't want a life beyond this neighborhood?" She pointed in the direction of Ruth's house and the old, faded houses around it, and it was clear that she meant the entire island, even if, up until then, she'd praised our poverty as a badge of honor she'd been deprived of. Now I saw what she really thought of it, and of us. Mariela said, "We do everything for Ruth, but Ruth's away and Mamá is gone, and I am here. In the end, you belong with me."

It was almost as if she'd said I belonged *to* her. Maybe Mariela intended to swallow me whole like Jonah's whale. I saw her mouth open, ready to suck me into her insatiable belly and never let me out into the sunlight.

"I know you've thought about this," she said. "Ruth is old and if anything happens, like now, you'd be alone."

"Anything" hadn't happened, of course. Mariela and I together had *made* things happen. Bad things. It could be that, because of my badness, I did belong *with* Mariela. Maybe we'd already plunged together over the ledge of damnation. Or maybe I was still falling, not yet reaching bottom. "Ruth got arrested because of us," I said. "You and I lit the rockets at Lucho's burial."

"No one meant for Ruth to get arrested. You didn't, I didn't."

"But it's our fault. And you're not sorry about her arrest," I said. "You take her plates, her desk, her bed, and now you want to take me. You take everything. You think you're owed everything because your fingers got cold in the winter and you had to pee in front of a donkey."

Mariela looked at me, surprised. "I care about you, Yuri. I don't *take* you. You decide your own fate."

I saw that out of some last-ditch effort to remain myself, unmovable, untouched by influences, I'd resisted, first Ruth, then Mariela. But by Mariela's logic, Mamá had left me to Ruth, Ruth had left me to Mariela, and now Mariela's and my own orphaned DNA had gotten twisted up and we could end up as sisters after all, banding together in a harsh world and all that, as Mariela claimed that Mamá had wanted.

But in the end, it wasn't true. We got to the corner of Dimas and Velasco, just a few doors down from Ruth's house. I said to Mariela that I'd go out to the wilds of Viñales and watch her make her paintings on the mogote walls. "But now we go see Ruth." And that time, to my surprise, Mariela said okay, and we went back to the house to get Abuelo Alberto's Chevy.

IN THE KITCHEN, Oscar rose from Ruth's table, his arms stretched out toward Mariela. "Armando Hart's office is involved," he said, a little breathless. "He's the top guy, the minister. His assistant just called my house."

15

The green, sloping lawn leading to the DSI building in the quiet suburb of Boyeros gave the place the clean, stately air of an embassy. A row of yellow and white flowering shrubs ran along the front wall, and except for the two armed guards out front and the barbed wire fence toward the back of the compound, one could imagine grabbing a discreet briefcase and leaving from here to an important diplomatic mission abroad.

Oscar pulled into the compound's driveway and stopped the car by a white narrow booth. He passed his Party ID to the guard inside. "*Las compañeras* have a relative inside," he said.

The guard took Oscar's ID but didn't look at it. Instead, he examined Mariela and me with an invasive little smile. "How do they know their relative is here?" he asked.

"They've been notified," Oscar said quietly.

"Is that so?" The guard was stocky and short and could have stretched out his arms and touched the walls of his one-man house. I was sure he'd turn us away, even lock us up for daring to appear without permission before his tiny white guardhouse;

Don Juanito and Oscar had been right—one didn't just show up to the DSI.

I realized then that I didn't know for a fact that Ruth was actually inside, or that she was even alive. I calmed myself by remembering that Oscar had driven us here; he wouldn't have bothered if Ruth were dead. He'd made it clear back at the house that this visit disgusted him, that he had no intention of entering the DSI compound himself, that he had no great love for Ruth, a counterrevolutionary Jehovah-worshipping worm, and that we, especially me, should consider ourselves lucky that he was willing to use his influence to get us through the DSI's terrible gate. And now here he was, at the wheel of Abuelo Alberto's Chevy, nervous but firm, and I thought, yes, Ruth was alive behind those pale, placid-looking walls, and nothing mattered now except seeing her face, watching her breathe, touching her hand.

The guard lowered his head and studied Oscar, his starched linen shirt and his professor glasses. Oscar stared straight ahead, enduring the inspection, one hand on the steering wheel. The guard cocked his head and looked again at Mariela sitting beside Oscar, and at me in the back seat. "The *compañeras* should know it's not visiting time," the guard said. He grinned.

"*Compañero*," Oscar said, "I spoke to Dr. Grener on the phone today."

The guard squinted at Oscar.

"Dr. Enrique Grener," Oscar said casually. "We studied together." Oscar took from his shirt pocket a paper that named Grener and himself as officers of the University of Havana's Student Federation in 1979. Underneath the paper was a twenty-dollar bill.

The guard took the paper and the money. I waited, sure that the guard would now have to arrest us for attempting to bribe a DSI officer. But he nodded slightly, still full of mockery, and told us to wait. He stepped out of the booth and walked to the building's tall beige door and opened it. Then he signaled for us to get out of the car. Mariela looked at me, her usual confidence drained from her face, and we got out. Oscar said that he'd wait for us by the curb. From this point forward we were on our own.

When we reached the beige door, the guard spoke briefly to another guard. We followed the new guard through a heavy metal door down an icy windowless hallway. After several corners, that guard opened another door with a key chained to his belt and let us out onto a bright cement patio. After the darkness inside, the light was blinding. All around was a tall mesh wire fence. The sky was cloudless.

Mariela and I sat across from each other on two of the benches around a square cement table. The noon sun burned the tops of our heads. A trickle of water wet the ground in the corner where a thin pipe wrapped in moss ran along a wall. A quick whistle of wind passed through the mesh wires.

Neither of us spoke. The savage heat drew the long hallway's cold from my hands.

A different door opened, and Ruth came out, holding on to the elbow of a big militiawoman. Ruth wore a flimsy tentlike gown and lifted and set down her bad leg with effort. Her hair was brushed flat against her scalp, and her face was pink like a baby's. She shaded her eyes with her right hand.

The militia woman walked Ruth toward us and sat her at the

table on a bench between Mariela's and mine. "I'm cold" were Ruth's first words to us.

The militia woman explained that neither the case nor conditions of detention could be discussed or the visit would end. "Five minutes," she said. She stood behind Ruth.

Mariela took Ruth's hand. Ruth looked at Mariela's fingers. I took Ruth's other hand. Her fingers were icy, crinkly as if wrapped in onion paper.

"How good to see you," Mariela said.

Ruth looked up with a bland expression devoid of all the fiery Jehovah judgments with which she had made her predictions and interpreted the world.

Mariela said, "At home we're all fine. Yuri is fine, see? I'm taking care of her."

"Tigre is doing fine too," I said.

Ruth turned to me. "You have enough to eat?" Her voice was scratchy.

I nodded. I didn't ask if she had enough to eat. I could see she didn't.

The militia woman touched Ruth's shoulder and Ruth gave a start. "I am well," Ruth said to us.

"We see that you are well," Mariela said. "We see that you are doing fine." We talked loud and slow, as if Ruth were hard of hearing.

"We're going to Viñales next week." I didn't know why I said this. Maybe to fill the silence. Or to confess our badness and have Ruth forbid our useless, selfish trip. "It's only a couple of days," I said.

"Always pay attention to instructions," Ruth said.

"Everything is being done to help you," Mariela said to Ruth.

"Everything." Ruth nodded. "It's my turn, *hija*," she said to Mariela. "Don't worry about me." Mariela let go of Ruth's hand. It sat on the table, palm up.

"Are you less cold now?" I asked. The sun was fierce above our heads.

"I'm not going to die, *niña*." Ruth looked at me then as if she were herself again, and I remembered her kindness—how she'd washed Mamá on the bed, with patience and without fuss, and tried not to hurt her, an impossible task toward the end.

"Time," the militia woman said, though it didn't seem that five minutes had passed yet. She took Ruth's arm to help her stand.

"We'll come back soon," I said. "We'll come see you."

Ruth scrunched up her lips and blew a kiss. "My children," she said to the militia woman as if to introduce us to a friend.

OUT BY THE curb, Oscar sat in Abuelo Alberto's car with the windows down and the radio on. We approached and he leaned to his right and opened the passenger door without a word. Mariela looked pale and shaken, as if for the first time she'd grasped the workings of the machinery she'd set in motion with her pyrotechnic tribute to a dead dog, which more and more struck me as a tribute mostly to herself. Maybe this was why she'd put off a visit to Ruth in the DSI; she hadn't wanted to see where extravagant whims could lead to on this island she'd come back to "for good."

Ruth and I had always known where such whims led. And still I'd helped Mariela build her rockets with secret gunpowder, and I'd lit one in a public park without a permit. Ruth herself had approved of Mariela's plans to bury Lucho under the ceiba tree. I wondered then at the unseen forces that move us toward harm, and at our arrogance in thinking we can escape them—decide, plan, command, and direct our lives instead toward clarity, or peace, or grace.

I shook in the heat of the car's back seat just as Ruth had shaken when the militia woman sat her on the burning cement bench, and I thought of the day when Ruth, sitting on her porch chair, had said with stubborn confidence that our turn would come—back when she'd still hoped for a golden visitor from *la yuma*. What had Ruth, at the DSI's cement table, meant by *her* turn? Did she think her punishment fit her crimes? Even Ruth's Jesus shuddered at the outsized torture he'd agreed to and tried to wriggle out of it, and in the end, he had cried out the unanswerable question: why. I wished Ruth had cried out in the DSI's courtyard, or that I'd cried out for her. Instead, I was crying now, silently, hiding from Oscar's sightline in the rearview mirror.

At some point on our way back to Paladero, Mariela switched off the car radio. She said to Oscar, who'd asked nothing about the visit, "Ruth is fine. A little thin. I'd like to provide some extra food for her. Let's take care of it." Mariela must have felt rattled to issue orders to Oscar; it wasn't her habit to speak to him as if he were the butler.

What followed marked the first breach in their alliance. All summer Oscar, using Mariela's cash, had happily managed

Mariela's salons; he'd arranged for Mariela's Chinese food, drinks, and music, and he had installed his brother as handyman and swallowed his pride when his old mother washed our dishes and mopped our floors and scrubbed our bathroom on her hands and knees. He'd secured a permit for Mariela's Viñales project and had driven us here to visit Ruth at the infamous DSI. But despite the cash and lust and mutual admiration, Oscar wouldn't be ordered around like an errand boy. He drove on in chilling silence through the shade of the overhanging trees of Havana's backstreets toward Paladero and Ruth's occupied house. Between him and Mariela the power wasn't all one-sided, and he wanted Mariela to know it.

In the silence of the car, I sensed an opportunity. Ruth's raw, pink face, her tent dress, her slow, painful walk, filled me with desperation. Yet her steadiness too, her kindness under the punishing sun gave me courage. I tapped Oscar's shoulder. "When can Ruth get out of that awful place?"

It was as if I'd touched him with a live wire. Oscar jerked away and shouted, "What the hell am I now? Do I pull rabbits out of a hat? Am I a fortune-teller?" He lost his salon cool and slapped the dashboard with his free hand in his full street-tough persona. He shouted at Mariela. "I've put myself at *risk* for you and this stupid girl." His voice filled the car. "I drove you to that shithole. I got Hart's office *on the phone* for you."

"Thank you," Mariela said softly as we turned onto Dimas Street. "We're grateful for all you've done." She didn't look at Oscar as she said this.

Oscar shouted more insults: we had him confused with a lapdog for yankee imperialists like the old bat at the DSI, who *belongs* there, he yelled. I thought he might go on and say we belonged there too and that he'd build a file on me and would get Mariela kicked out of the country, or worse. But he held back. He stopped the car by Ruth's curb and yanked up the brake lever, then got out and slammed the car door. He headed down the street without a word. Mariela went into the house and shut herself in the bathroom; she used up the day's water in a long bath. Then she spent the rest of the afternoon locked up in Ruth's room.

    I lay on my bed, sniffling beside Tigre, and eventually in the quiet of the house I fell asleep. In my dream, Ruth appeared healthy, young; she clumped her bad leg into the middle of my classroom between the rows of desks as my classmates and I bent to our work. This was the only time I dreamed of Ruth, then or in the many years afterward. None of the other students in the dream classroom noticed her. They wrote across their dream papers. Ruth came to my desk and asked me, "Are you in the Truth?" This was how Ruth's Witness friends had greeted me, not in dreams but in real life when Ruth was still part of the Kingdom Hall, before they kicked her out over the question of skirt length. (Ruth had argued that Kingdom women should cover their shins, not just their knees, and this was finally too much for the women in the Brotherhood, especially when fabric was scarce, which Jehovah surely understood and made allowances for. "Ruth is too severe even for the Witnesses," Mamá joked at the time. "She wants to cover her bad leg, but it has nothing to do with modesty, and the other women know it.") In the dream, I said yes to Ruth. I said, "Yes, I am in the Truth." Ruth scoffed at my answer. She opened a pamphlet on my desk to a picture of fishermen scooping up whole schools of silvery mackerel in a net and said, "Eat the fish of his flesh."

THAT EVENING OSCAR came to Mariela's salon late and looking unusually disheveled (as a rule, he presented himself groomed and cologned), and he and Mariela shut themselves in Ruth's room. They emerged a while later, both of them disheveled now but also looking transformed as if lit from within. They stood close together and held hands throughout the night.

Part of me wanted to tell Rosario and Julio about my visit to Ruth, but they weren't there that night. Hernando sat on the porch, joking with his gang and his ragged Llega y Pon audience. I heard the rise and fall of his voice from my place by Ruth's desk. I thought he might listen to my news about Ruth, but despite his having held my head as I puked into the toilet and then helped me to bed the previous night, when he came into the parlor now, he avoided my gaze. His indifference stung. I took another shot of aguardiente and a surge of rage replaced my shame. I followed him back out to the porch, where he was showing off a brilliant new bike he'd "found" and restored, praising the silver handlebars and yellow grips and leather seat, saying to his boys, "I'm keeping this one for myself." Everyone knew this was a lie; he only meant to drive up the price for anyone who might approach him for a secret transaction.

"You stole that bike," I said.

Hernando ran his hands down the handlebars, tipped his head toward me, and threw back an imaginary slug. His audience laughed.

I said, "You belong in prison, not Ruth."

He set the bike gently against the railing and came toward me, at last looking me in the eye. "What's wrong, Miss Astronaut? Your blond boyfriend left you crying tonight?" He gripped my arm and brushed his mouth across my cheek to my ear. "Quit slobbering," he whispered. "Clean yourself up, eh? Let's have a little chat."

I yanked my arm from his hand. The small crowd on the porch hooted.

And still I did what he said. Out in the courtyard I knelt beside the washing machine, lifted the cistern's cover, and leaned over the iron-smelling well. I let my head hang down; the cool air from deep within washed over my face. I closed my eyes and listened to my breath, hollow in my ears. I stood and pulled up the heavy bucket, spilling much of the water. I set the bucket on the ground and scooped cold water over my head with my hands.

I took my time. I hurt in places I couldn't account for, my chest, my arms, the back of my knees. I waited, but Hernando didn't come to look for me, so I went back out to the porch, my hair and shoulders soaked. Hernando stood now by the curb, leaning against Abuelo Alberto's car as if it were his. He opened the passenger door with a grand, mocking gesture as if he were my footman. Of course, everyone standing by the car understood it was the opposite: if I walked to the car and got in with Hernando, I'd become his girl, or, in Ruth's and Doña Barbara's words, his "little slut"—I'd belong to him as did his gang boys and his bikes.

Hernando's friends opened a path for me. I slid into the

passenger seat. The boys hooted and made obscene gestures and pounded the trunk as we drove off.

On the ride, Hernando turned silent and shy again, the way he'd been while standing in the hall outside my bedroom as I lay drunk under the sheets. He drove for some minutes, glancing at me sometimes but saying nothing. I felt strong in this new silence, sure in my apparent weakness. He'd have to use his voice, his command. And what was all his strength without my weakness? He needed me; I was sure I'd win.

We reached the outskirts of the giant Ciudad Deportiva Stadium off Via Blanca, where decades later the Rolling Stones would play to five hundred thousand people. Hernando stopped the car behind a long mesh fence. Across the grassless field, the craggy round walls of the weather-beaten stadium were a blur of shadows and peeling paint beneath a few tall shining lights. We got out of the car, still silent. Hernando climbed up onto the hood, gave me his hand. I didn't take it. I climbed up beside him, keeping a good distance between us. We lay against the windshield. Finally, Hernando lifted his chin to the evening sky and pointed. "Alpha Centauri. Your home turf."

"Quit the astronaut bit," I said. "I'm tired of it."

He pretended to think on this while looking at the stars. Then he silently rose onto an elbow, stretched over to me, and lowered his mouth against mine. I pushed him back easily.

He lay back against the windshield again. His silence now had a sting. Finally, he said, "Look at you. If you gave someone shit on a plate in exchange for your blond Lenin boy, you'd lose a good plate. But there you are, night after night slobbering over him and his girlfriend." He paused. "Truth is, Miss Astronaut, you're a lush and you're not my type."

I didn't know, any more than I knew Alpha Centauri, whose type I could be. But something was in me now, something different from what I'd felt around Julio. I let it grow and wasn't afraid.

The lights around the stadium switched off with a fizzing hum, and the surrounding houses went dark too. The power grid had gone down. More stars appeared. Hernando said, "Just in case, let me save us some time. I'm not here to make a deal to help you get your crazy old aunt out of jail, understand? I make deals in my business but that is to *resolver*. I'm not here to solve your problems, and you're not here to solve mine."

I hadn't mentioned Ruth, wasn't thinking about her. I said, "You're useless."

"Exactly," he said, looking up at the sky. "A teacher once told me: never turn yourself into a commodity. The only thing I learned in school." He paused. "You're some kind of studious girl, right?" He pointed to where the blacked-out billboard stood beside the stadium, made a megaphone of his hands as if we were at an official rally, and shouted the slogans we'd learned since childhood, *If I move forward, follow me. If I go back, push me. If I stand still, kill me. It's better to cease to be than to cease to be a revolutionary.* No one was around, but I told him to lower his voice. He gave me an ironic grin. "You believe all that shit from Comandante Tutankhamen?" He turned his back to the darkened billboard and said, "Back at the house, you said I was a thief. But *they* have stolen everything. *They* have turned everybody into Llega y Pon beggars. I steal to live. *They* steal to boss me around."

"Who's *they*?" Same question I'd asked Julio, but now I hoped for a different answer.

"They. The whole lot of them—all the way down to my shithead brother."

His mention of Oscar surprised me. I felt a sense of relief, even joy, and I said, "I hate Mariela."

"Who wouldn't?" Hernando's voice was quieter. "The two of them think they know a lot. But they know nothing."

The stadium lights tried to reignite, flashing bright a few times, and I shut my eyes and followed the orange squares and flimsy ghosts floating behind my eyelids. The stadium lights went dark again, but when I opened my eyes the squares and ghosts continued flashing and swaying.

I asked Hernando if he saw them. "The ghosts," I said, "the swirl of the lights behind your eyelids."

He said he didn't. But he liked ghosts, real ghosts. They showed up sometimes, he said. He'd seen a couple of them, an old uncle and a cousin who'd died in childhood—no one he knew very well. "They're fine, they're real," he said.

"Ghosts, spirits, God, they're all the same to me. I want something solid," I said. "Something I can pound my fist against."

"I hope it's not me," Hernando laughed. "You're an eye-for-an-eye type of girl? Like your crazy aunt?"

Ruth's Jehovah talked big of retribution, I said, but I didn't see *his* hand in anything. "Or maybe his hand is in *all* of it, and one can never tell who gets zapped and who doesn't. A person barely knows when to duck."

Hernando surprised me again. "You gotta trust something, though. Can't duck all the time."

The stars were everywhere now, and he rested against the windshield. "No faking with Ma," he said. "I trust *her*. She's smarter than me and my brother put together. And she likes you."

The mosquitoes had found us, so we went inside the dark Chevy. We closed the windows against them. I slid my hand toward Hernando's. He closed his fingers quickly around mine.

He leaned toward me, and this time I kissed him. His lips were thicker than Julio's and warmer, and his tongue went into my mouth, delicate, light.

I pulled back from him. I needed to make something clear. "I'm not a *girl*," I said. Hernando opened his eyes. I said, "I'm not some *girl*. Not your *girl*. Not like that. I'm not *anybody's*."

He nodded, serious. "All right."

He kissed me again. I opened my eyes afterward but couldn't look at him long. He kept his eyes on me, and I pressed up against him and finally didn't look away. I decided. We kissed again, and I took his hand and set it down on my leg, and he slid it under my skirt. I moved slightly against his hand. We lay down on the back seat, and he said my name. After some time, I heard from myself low sounds like those that came sometimes through Mariela's and Oscar's closed door.

Later, back in the house, I saw a little blood on my panties and touched some of Hernando's sticky goo, but in the car with him I didn't worry; I held on to him and didn't let him go, even after I couldn't feel him inside me.

16

We drove back from the stadium, and as we pulled into Ruth's driveway, I braced myself for more hoots and obscene gestures from Hernando's gang. But the porch was deserted. In the parlor, Mariela looked up from the couch as we came in, and Oscar sat rocking slightly, nervously, in the rocking chair. They had sent everyone else home.

Mariela made room for Hernando and me on the couch. "How was your ride in Abuelo Alberto's car?" She smiled, teasing us both. "I guess the old Chevy is ready for our trip, Oscar. The shocks obviously hold up." Hernando looked down at his knees, grim. Oscar smiled now too, and he said to Hernando, "Have a drink, *socio*. You look like you've been to a funeral."

Hernando leaned toward me, and I felt his breath on my neck as I had in the car. I was relieved not to have to sit alone in this room of parents by proxy. I took his hand. A few minutes earlier, in the car with Hernando, I'd felt safe, his body on mine like a kind of shield. But now there was a slight, hollow place in my gut, a tiny warning I was trying to ignore. I knew

Hernando was a small-time thug, only a year older than me, and as much as I wanted to, I couldn't exactly see us together beyond one desperate summer in a Special Period of disaster. Still, as my "parents" made their jokes and Hernando's hand lay in mine, I knew I wouldn't undo any of what we'd done.

"Hernando, you'll come with us to Viñales, no?" Mariela ran her hand through my hair. She said to me, "Now that you have a boyfriend, it'll be an adventure."

"But someone should be here when Ruth comes home," I said.

"Not you," she said softly. "I need you with me."

I tried another tack. "Why don't we go to Varadero Beach? It's a one-day trip. None of my friends go to Viñales. Everybody goes to Varadero."

Mariela stopped playing with my hair. "You wear me out," she said. Her cold look scared me. Only Mariela had the dollars to send Ruth extra food in jail; only she could arrange for Ruth's release. "I'm sorry," I said, but she didn't hear me. Someone was at the door, and she and Oscar jumped to their feet.

Oscar let into the parlor three carefully shabby men. He embraced them, laughing and slapping their backs. Two were about Oscar's age, and the third, a Victor Flores who wore nice jeans and a starched white shirt, was a little older, possibly forty. His haircut was sharp and his temples dark gray; he seemed to be the boss of the other two.

The three visitors were artists and professors at the Escuela de Artes Internacional. Spiffy Victor Flores said to Mariela, "That was you. In *Art of the Americas* magazine." Mariela beamed. I watched her, amazed; Flores had finally confirmed that someone, somewhere, thought Mariela's wacky projects were things worth doing and not just pranks to ruin other people's lives.

Mariela seemed prepared for the visit. She asked everyone to sit. Hernando and I took a spot on the floor tiles, and the others sat on the couch and rocking chairs. From Ruth's desk, Mariela retrieved a folded map and a stack of photographs. She passed them around as she narrated each. Oscar, smiling knowingly to the rest of us, pulled out a joint from his shirt pocket (where he got his weed, I couldn't imagine). He lit it, inhaled. The joint followed the photographs, moving first to Luis Valdes on Oscar's right. Valdes then took a puff and passed it to Roberto Bursini.

In Mariela's first photograph, taken in some field outside Chicago, she'd marked a wide circle of black gunpowder on a swath of grass. Inside that circle lay a pile of *yuma* paraphernalia I'd only learn about years later—a Barbie doll, a box of Joy detergent, a plastic Oscar Mayer Wienermobile, a Doris Day movie poster, a cap gun, and a few other colorful items from popular U.S. television. In the next photograph, Mariela was lighting the gunpowder trail with a bristling sparkler and then, photo by photo, the pile ignited, and the yellow flames ate up the gathered objects. The last photo was a bird's-eye view (Mariela must have climbed a tree to take it) of the charred junk and ashes. She called this piece *(L)arsony*.

The men studied each photo in turn. When the joint came my way, I took it and pretended to know what to do. No one stopped me or helped me with it. I took a shallow puff, tried to inhale, coughed it out, and passed the joint. I set my head down, half hiding, in Hernando's lap.

Mariela said, "From the time I was Yuri's age—my little sister." She paused and the men glanced my way. I blushed, wondering what they thought of me, a pot-smoking minor sprawled on the floor in a wrinkled-up dress, her head in a young thug's lap. "I knew that crime and art were siblings. Art's a crime if it's good art."

"Friends," Oscar said in a plume of smoke, "barriers are falling. Right now, the world is fusing. Look at us here."

The door to the carport was open, and outside, Don Juanito, again loaded with bags, chatted with Cuevas. I was surprised that they were still in the house. Wisps of their conversation made their way to us in the parlor. As I strained to listen, Oscar signaled to Hernando to shut the door. After he did, Hernando lingered over one of Mariela's pictures and asked, "How did you feel when the pile burned up?"

"Empty," Mariela said.

Oscar said to the men, "Mariela is an Earth artist."

Flores, who'd looked charmed to meet Mariela when he first arrived, now swatted at Oscar's pronouncement. "Everyone thinks they do Earth art." He turned to Mariela. "Some of your work reminds me of others—Abramovic, for example. I hope you'll pardon me, but you bring a North American, even European, perspective. It's very Christian, really. Ashes, resurrection, rebirth."

Mariela let him finish, then said, "The Chinese used gunpowder for medicine. And in our country"—she meant Cuba—"gunpowder was used against our ancestors, Africans and Tainos. I use European weapons to reenact our ancestors' extermination and bring back their power."

Flores considered this with his grave, ironic face, then said, "For us the thing is not to be narrow or voyeuristic. We must move away from the merely personal. Or emotional." The word *emotional* had the sound of a slap. The two other visitors, Valdes and Bursini, watched the exchange with neutral expressions. "Your work," Flores continued, cool and professorial, "doesn't speak to our current historical process."

I'd never heard anyone put down another so casually; I'd never met an intellectual before.

Flores explained to the rest of us, now half stoned, "In *el norte* her colleagues love us brown people. Not that you're especially brown," he said to Mariela. But Flores wasn't either. Of all of us, only Hernando's skin was a golden brown, his brother's slightly lighter. Hernando rested his chin on his raised knee and turned his head left and right, following the voices and the outwardly calm, reasonable-looking faces.

"They cook us in their soup for spice," continued Flores, "then chew us up and spit out our bones."

Roberto Bursini, stocky and unshaved, spoke for the first time. "Victor went to Princeton one summer, so he thinks he knows what everyone in *la yuma* thinks."

Flores ignored this. "The left of North America," he said, "they think our revolution has restored the dream of socialism that Stalin killed long ago. So they bring you to their parties, put you on display, give you a nice, puzzled look, and then talk about you as if you weren't there."

"Isn't that what you're doing now?" Valdes asked. "Talking as if she's not here?" He spoke without looking at Mariela.

Mariela didn't move. Her voice softened to what I thought

was a calculated sweetness. "I know this country is not mine the way it is yours. But this is not my fault. I'm also one of those the Americans chewed up and spat out."

"You're not looking too bad for it," Valdes said. He and Flores laughed, and even Oscar seemed to like the remark. He stretched his arm confidently across the seat of the couch behind Mariela.

"I am hoping to work in my homeland." Mariela placed her folded map on the floor. "I ask you, *compañeros*, if it's possible for me. I'm between cultures, between worlds."

"Wait a minute," Valdes said. "That wasn't you in *Art of the Americas*. It was Tanya Valenski, I remember now."

"We were in the magazine at different times," Mariela said in a sour tone.

"On the cover?" Valdes asked. "You were on the cover?"

All of us looked at Mariela. I hoped that she'd clarify this important detail and put Valdes in his place. But Mariela turned to Flores, who smiled benignly, apparently pleased at her acknowledgment of his authority. He leaned forward and settled the matter. "Let's not be provincial, gentlemen. Of course it's possible for you to work here," he said to Mariela.

Mariela nodded at Flores and opened her map. She laid it in the middle of the circle and pointed to the Viñales countryside. "I plan to paint on the sides of mogotes."

Bursini said, "Some of those are UNESCO World Heritage Sites. They won't let you paint there, unless . . ."

Oscar, his eyes hazy from the last of the joint, interrupted him and said, solemnly, "*Compañero*, the *comandante* has said it is better to sin through excess than through timidity, which can only lead to failure." He leaned across and tapped Bursini's knee for emphasis. "In our youth we got complacent. We thought the world wouldn't change, that our friends wouldn't leave our cause. We were young, the revolution was young. But now we've matured." He sat back against the seat of the couch.

"Complacency is a crime. Art is not."

I lifted myself from Hernando's leg. Suddenly the weed, like the aguardiente, went to my head and made me fearless. This art talk was mostly above my head, but one thing seemed clear to me. "The rockets we set off weren't a crime," I said. "They were art. So why is my aunt locked up?"

Oscar looked at me. His eyes lost some of their glaze. "Yuri, I've explained a hundred times."

Bursini said to me, "You set off a rocket?"

"Mariela and I set off little firework rockets for her project. It wasn't a crime." I turned to Oscar. "Why did they put Ruth in a police car and lock her up at the DSI?" The men looked alarmed at this. I pressed on. "Ruth hasn't come back. This is *her* house we're in." The visitors turned to Oscar and Mariela for an answer.

"There was an incident," Mariela explained calmly. "Things are getting cleared up." Then she addressed me in her cool, faraway voice. "Yuri, we're all concerned about Ruth. You know this. We're all upset. But soon she'll be released. In the meantime, we must help ourselves to what's given to us now. Please, Yuri, don't think yourself a beggar all your life. Whose house this is, whose tiles"—she tapped the floor—"whose radio or TV or plates or silverware—possession of property, possession of nature, that's what ends up killing people and species and the Earth itself."

The men seemed to consider the wisdom of her babbling. I started to say that many things kill people, like jail and hard-heartedness and lies and shouldn't she know this by now, but I was too enraged, or too high, and couldn't get the words out right, and finally Hernando stood and pulled me to my feet.

"I'm hungry. Time for some *jama*," he said.

"Yes, thank you, please bring snacks for our guests," Mariela said.

In the kitchen, Hernando whispered in my hair, "Wrong pitch, Yuri. Don't go at the two of them like that in front of big shots."

Amadora skewered several slices of old bread onto two forks and held them above the blue flame of the stove. Hernando kissed my neck lightly. "Let them talk their stupid talk, they're all stoned. And anyway your aunt's release isn't up to my brother. Nothing's ever up to him."

"Who's it up to?"

He pointed to the ceiling. "Higher." This was not Ruth's "higher" but someone somewhere above Oscar's rank. Hernando said, "Your sister, maybe. Her *fula*. Try not to piss her off. She doesn't want the old lady in jail, does she?"

"She's not my sister. And I don't know what she wants."

Amadora took the slices of bread from the flame. She cut pieces of yellow cheese.

"Help me," I said to Hernando.

He set the toast and cheese on a serving plate. "What do you think I'm doing?"

In the parlor, after finishing the food, the three guests exchanged promises and dates with Mariela and Oscar. Then they walked to the front door and out to the porch, Oscar's arm around Flores. Mariela stood in the dim light of the doorway, watching the men hug and shake hands. With a wave, Oscar came in and shut the door. Mariela kissed him, and they stood there, his hand cupping her small breast.

17

Over the next week, with the backing of art critic Victor Flores and with official approval from Hart's office, all maneuvered by Party leader Oscar (and by means of Mariela's stash, courtesy of her American friend), Mariela finished her preparations for our trip to Viñales.

Mariela's *fula* could have easily paid for a full week at the Varadero Beach and Resort, where Party families (and, during the Special Period, much-needed foreign tourists) stretched out on the white sand and watched the famous turquoise waves break on the shore. But instead, she insisted on dragging us inland through the July heat toward tangled brush and looming palm trees, past spooky Jurassic caves bubbling with underground streams and subterranean plants, and—Mariela grew excited at this—bats thriving on darkness and mysterious echoes. Centuries before, the caves housed Guanahatabey and Ciboney tribes, and according to Mariela, some of their paintings survived on the inner walls. I pictured ancient drawings of hunters and long-antlered deer, hidden for centuries in the dark; I also pictured my classmates' vacant, mocking stares at the beginning of the school year when I explained that I spent my summer vacation with blind bats and subterranean fish.

Mariela and Amadora gathered a collection of tools—chisels, hammers, rasps, gloves, masks, handkerchiefs, plastic sheets for tents, Abuelo Alberto's shovel (still caked with some of the dried soil of Lucho's burial), a folding ladder, many colored paints, and bags of white powder Mariela would make plaster with. These either came from Ruth's garage or were "acquired" by Don Juanito through third parties who lifted them from construction sites. (Was this the purpose of the mysterious bags the old man sometimes hauled in and out of Ruth's house in the pitch of night?) Don Juanito also brought over a pair of boots for me, secondhand but in good shape, all bought with Mariela's secret money.

Mariela planned to paint her figures—Nadies ("Nobodies," "The Forgottens")—onto the sides of the valley's flat-topped mogotes. "Impermanent," she repeated to me about the Nadies and showed me her sketches of fat, small-headed, large-torsoed figures. Between their legs she'd drawn giant grotesque vulvas in bright orange and yellow and blue. Despite their loud colors and ridiculous, ballooned bodies, the Nadies struck me as strangely gorgeous, dignified even, especially when compared to the silly Viñales mural the government commissioned a decade earlier to cover the side of one of the famous mogotes: a giant snail, a dinosaur, and a family of Neanderthals smiling dumbly from a looming rock-side. The childish mural, meant to promote a cartoonlike version of Darwinian evolution to the mostly still-Catholic population, attracted very few Catholics (or atheists for that matter) since few among us could afford to haul ourselves out to the wilds of Viñales to see it.

Mariela's project promoted nothing, and still it required Abuelo Alberto's Chevy, gas, food, a driver and amateur mechanic (Hernando) in case the old Chevy broke down on the road, plus a bureaucrat (Oscar) to smooth out legal or political wrangles Mariela could run into. But there was no reason the project needed me.

My protests went unanswered. Mariela hadn't spoken to me directly since I challenged her and Oscar in front of the visiting artists. What I said in front of those important men while stoned on the parlor floor had clearly stung her. She felt I'd betrayed her, and she kept her distance in the house after that night, leaving a room if I came in, or getting up from the table if I sat down. I tried to shrug off her silent comings and goings, but as usual her iciness frightened me. I felt the truth of Hernando's remark: enraging Mariela would not help bring Ruth out of the DSI.

Yet despite my fear for Ruth, something kept me from making peace with Mariela. It wasn't honesty or ethics but a kind of obstinacy, some hard kernel of refusal in me that I loathed at times but wasn't able to change. Seeing Mariela's mountain of supplies on the dining room table, I couldn't summon up friendliness or tact. Instead I said, "If Ruth stays in the DSI much longer, she's going to die."

Mariela wordlessly examined the thermoses on the table, the crackers, condensed milk cooked to a sweet brown paste inside the can, the can opener, a few green mangoes, and green bananas that would ripen along the way. Finally, after taking in a breath, she said, "Do you always bite the hand that feeds you?"

I'd never heard this phrase before and didn't understand it. I wasn't Lucho snapping at her through the window bars. Without looking at me she said, "We're going to the *manigüa*. Like it or not, you're coming." And then she added, half amused, half contemptuous, "You told me this was what you always wanted. Live under the stars with nature or some such." She paused. "I guess you never meant it. But I mean what I say. This is what *I've* always wanted." And she ordered me again to go on the trip with her, not because she wanted me there (how could she at that point?), but simply out of spite.

Hernando also didn't think much of Mariela's excursion. "What's with the gloves and masks?" he'd asked, sprawled in my bed one night. "For sissies." He smiled at his own hateful swagger as if he didn't exactly mean it. He routinely called his gang buddies "faggots," "retards," "turd eaters," as if his barrage of insults would keep Reynaldo, Gelson, and the others obedient enough to ride a stolen bicycle to Hernando's house and help paint it fresh or salvage enough parts from a dozen stolen bike carcasses to build a new one. It was a kind of performance.

Hernando stroked my face and sat up. "You and your sister don't look alike. Like me and my shithead brother." Hernando was lanky, Oscar fuller, slightly taller, his good looks hidden a little by his glasses and his humorless, bloated ways. Hernando's nose was sharper than his brother's, his hair curlier, his face ironic and charming.

"She's not my sister."

I pulled him down to me. Hernando's face then seemed to me as chiseled as those of the Taino chiefs Mariela liked to sketch from her book, *The Ancient Civilizations of Mesoamerica*.

One of those old-time chiefs, Hatuey, was said to have refused redemption from the Spaniard priest who'd offered it to him if, while captured and tied to a tree, Hatuey repented of his savage ways. Hatuey answered that he'd rather not share heaven with his Spanish captors, even with the good ones—and the Spaniards burned him alive, unredeemed. His feathered head, gold loop in his ear, now decorated the labels of Cuban beer bottles. In those days I knew as much about Hatuey as I did about Hernando, but for most of that summer I felt that Hernando was on my side, and I on his.

THE MORNING BEFORE leaving for Viñales, Mariela spoke to me again, this time more softly, almost seductively, the way she'd spoken to me when she first arrived at Ruth's house with her bulging blue knapsack. She took my hands and said, "Let's stop fighting. I need you with me. I want you to see this." She meant not only the lush green Viñales Valley and its monstrous flat-topped blue mogotes, but also the giant figures she'd paint there. "You're the one I care about, Yuri. You understand what I do." She had to know this was a whopping lie; I understood nothing of what she did. I was also sure that she didn't need my understanding. And she certainly didn't understand me at all. Still, I was relieved that she'd ended her cold treatment. Her voice came the closest it had in the time she'd been here to showing shyness or shame, both of which, I'd imagined, her hard childhood had wrung out of her. She sensed my surrender and squeezed my hands. Then she went back into herself and her preparations.

The Tilting House

After a lunch of beans and rice, Mariela, Oscar, Hernando, and I piled into the Chevy with supplies in the trunk and a few packed bags at our feet. The seats were terribly hot, and we rolled down the windows to let in some air. Amadora had come to see us off. She waved as Hernando turned the engine over. The car rattled and hummed to life, but then Hernando leaned forward as though listening for a distant station on the radio. His eyes widened. He flicked his wrist and turned off the car, but a strange shaking continued. It wasn't the engine's familiar rumbling; it seemed to come out of the ground up into all four wheels of the car, shivering into our feet and legs and into the car's seats. Hernando said without raising his voice, "Everybody out." He opened his door and ran toward a thick cloud of dust curling from the side of Ruth's garage.

The growing tremor hadn't come from the Chevy at all. It was rippling out *toward* us from Ruth's house. "Out!" said Oscar, and he, Mariela, and I threw our doors open and clambered from the car as the walls of Ruth's garage crumbled under the weight of the upstairs room. The kitchen wall followed. I called out Hernando's name.

I held my breath as the creak and rumble and roar of the collapsing house subsided. A few seconds later, Hernando appeared in the driveway pulling Amadora by her housecoat, both of them covered in a white gritty silt. Amadora plodded forward, staring unfocused to where the three of us stood next to the car. Blood was on her forehead and cheeks. Oscar cried out, "Ma," and Hernando let go of his mother's housecoat and leapt toward his brother, pinning Oscar to the side of the Chevy, his hands at Oscar's throat. "Fucker." Hernando's teeth were set. "You could have killed Ma." Oscar grabbed at Hernando's wrists as Hernando knocked him back against the car.

Mariela and I each took Amadora by an arm and pulled her away from the wreckage and dust. Rubble covered the driveway and part of the sidewalk. I tried to take in the extent of the disaster. Ruth's garage, Mariela's upstairs room, and part of the kitchen had crumbled. Roused by the thunder of the tumbling house, Dr. Cuevas and a few neighbors came out to the street and stared in amazement at the sheered wall of Ruth's kitchen and at the white dust drifting left and right down the block.

A few men separated Hernando and Oscar, and Hernando said to me, breathless, "Get in the car, Yuri. We'll take Ma to the polyclinic." Then he said to Oscar and Mariela, "You two go fuck yourselves."

"Look." I pointed to Amadora—I didn't know why I said this. "She has a spoon." And all of us turned to Amadora, a white-looking ghost holding a large stirring spoon in her right hand. I remembered my box of Mamá's things, tucked away in the high cupboard, all of it flattened by now, buried. I walked toward the house to find the box. But Dr. Cuevas pulled me back. "No one's going in there, it's not safe," he said.

And then came the strangest thing Mariela ever said, stranger than her false pledges to the revolution and her tales of holding in her pee because of a donkey. Mariela told Dr. Cuevas, "Please take care of this until we get back from Viñales." Astonishingly, she thought we were still going off to the countryside to paint her Nadies on the mogote walls. And more astonishingly, Dr. Cuevas nodded at her request, even as the smoky dust floated through the air. I thought he hadn't understood.

I grabbed Mariela by the shoulder. "We can't leave. We have to fix this. What will Ruth come home to?"

She took my face in her hands as when she'd first told me that Mamá had given birth to her at the age of seventeen and that she and I were sisters. "Yuri, listen. I was going to tell you in Viñales. Our efforts have paid off. Ruth is coming home on July thirtieth. We wanted it to be a surprise." She paused. "We were fixing the garage and the upstairs a bit for Ruth's return. Taking out boxes and scraping the mold from the back bathroom." She looked back at the collapsed walls. "There must have been a crack. But it'll get fixed. It's not as bad as it looks."

I stared at the pile of rubble and broken beams. I didn't see how any of it could be fixed. But suddenly that didn't matter. "Ruth's getting out?" I asked.

"July thirtieth. We were fixing things up for her. There must have been a crack somewhere," Mariela repeated. "Ruth is coming home."

Beside the porch were layers of debris, scattered along the driveway and sidewalk. Only the front of the house stood. In the mirror of the car window, I saw that I, too, was white with dust. "What home?" I asked.

The neighbors huddled on the street and talked in low voices as if at a funeral. Mariela squinted at the ruined house, as if to pinpoint the exact calculation that had failed or the tiny detail that had escaped her.

"We'll end up in a Llega y Pon shelter," I said.

"We," Mariela said calmly, "are not Llega y Pon people. This is an unfortunate accident. That's all. But trust me, after Viñales, you and I will be fine."

"And Ruth?"

"Ruth too."

More neighbors gathered, talking louder now, pointing to the house's exposed innards. Some of Ruth's scattered objects were old and useless, but others were well-preserved, even fancy, certainly better than what some neighbors had in their own decaying homes. I pictured Ruth coming out on July 30, standing among the broken shards and timber in her prison gown, as exposed as the house itself.

Hernando called to me. He stood with one foot inside the open driver's door. "I'm taking Ma to the polyclinic now."

He got into the car. Mariela guided Amadora into the back seat and slid in beside her. She said, "Yuri, look at me. Dr. Cuevas and Don Juanito will secure the place. We'll get cleaned up at the polyclinic and then head to Viñales. We can't let a little accident decide things. Our fate's not here." Oscar took the passenger seat beside Hernando.

"People will grab everything of Ruth's," I said, though it wasn't clear to me that Ruth owned anything anymore.

Dr. Cuevas held the car door open and waved me toward the Chevy as if half of Ruth's house had not buckled and we, our car full of bananas, mangoes, and crackers, were off to a picnic. "It's not safe here," he said. "You can't stay."

If I left, whatever was scattered in the rubble would vanish—Ruth's mahogany desk, my bed in the room of metal shelves, the shelves themselves, the tools, even the clotheslines in the courtyard. My life with Ruth in the house would disappear, and Mamá's and Ruth's stories, and my hours as a child in the garage thumbing dusty books and pretending to drive Abuelo Alberto's stranded car.

Tigre came out from the rubble then. He limped, miraculously, toward the car. I'd forgotten Tigre! My forgetting felt like the house's hidden crack, invisible and catastrophic.

Dr. Cuevas bent down and picked up the dog. I put my hands behind Tigre's ears and touched my forehead to his dusty warm head.

"He'll be fine. I'll get my nephew to check him," Dr. Cuevas said to me as if Lucho hadn't died in Gabito's care.

But Tigre's eyes were open. He saw me and knew me. And astonishingly, I let go of him and slid into the back seat next to Mariela. Hernando restarted the car. I left Tigre and what remained of Ruth's house. I never saw Tigre again.

18

Manigüa

So it was that my old wish to live in the woods far from everyone, digging up roots and studying and speaking little, came true in this frightening way—not by heading toward peaceful silence and a time for grieving but by running away from disaster inside a crowded car, in the heavy silence that follows shock. We drove on and the landscape outside the window struck me as too lush and wild and blurry, and I realized immediately that I'd never wanted to live in the woods; it was only a lifelong foolishness that had made me think so. Looking back years later, I see that the price for my young foolishness was steep, the lesson harsh. But who was I then, in that speeding car, to set the terms of my own schooling? On that silent drive to the woods, I vowed that whichever way the lessons came from then on, and whatever pain they caused, I'd keep my head down and learn what I needed to know to stop being a fool.

We arrived at Las Brisas Hotel in the village of Viñales in early afternoon. We showered in our rooms, washing off the last of the dust from Ruth's crumbled house, and ate on the hotel's terrace overlooking the green and orange and blue valley below. No one spoke of the ruined house. We were the only diners, taking in the majestic view, maybe pretending that we had escaped not only the house's wreck but also the old city's decaying streets, the Llega y Pon garbage heaps, the cold cells of the DSI, the lies and destitution and the schemes of the black market. A cloud nearly the length of the valley floated at a surprising speed across the sky and pulled beneath it a gray blanket of shadow, exposing the bright, dull, shining, flashing, striped, rolling greens behind it. When the cloud passed, we clapped like children at a magic show. None of us had seen such a display before.

After lunch we went to meet our guide. Oscar had arranged for a young man to show us to the stable a few blocks from the hotel. Mariela had never mentioned horses, but there we were, at the entrance of a horse hotel. Pedro, the guide, held the white gate open for us. He was short, thick, with a deeply tanned, coppery face under his straw hat. His eyes were keen, dark, and amused. He wasn't much older than me and Hernando, but I couldn't imagine joking around with him. He had a tough, solid physical presence, which I imagined he used to command animals and, from what I could see, also humans.

We fell in line and followed him into the stable. Eight horses, four on each side, stood in individual stalls among shit and hay. Pedro guided Hernando and me to a black, looming horse. I looked into the creature's brown, disdainful eye, and shuddered. He was larger than I'd pictured Mariela's Boy, the Nebraska donkey. These horses seemed massive and, I thought, even if they stood there in their stalls doing nothing, terribly fierce.

Mariela considered each horse, then stroked the splotchy

black-and-white muzzle of one. Pedro gave permission with a slight shrug, and she climbed the stall's gate and used the wall to climb gracefully onto the horse's back, as if she'd been born riding in the Nebraska hills. Hernando copied her gesture and threw himself onto the back of our own fire-breathing horse, who took no mind of his presence. He settled himself and urged me to climb the planks of the stall. I grasped a plank and pulled myself up, then threw threw myself forward in a leap of fear and faith. I didn't quite make it over the hump of the horse's back, but after some struggling and a hand from Hernando, I pulled myself up behind him. The ground seemed a dozen feet below us.

When each of us had managed to get ourselves and our supplies up onto the back of a horse, Pedro opened our stall gates and walked us single file out the stable door. He shut the door behind us, then mounted his own horse. We followed him down a dirt path that descended into the valley. There, the famous blue mogotes rose out of the undergrowth, their giant limestone tops flattened by wind and rain over the last hundred and sixty million years. I saw the *manigüa* I once thought I'd longed for—green and red hills, the strong breeze against my face—and for a moment my wish to live in the woods didn't seem foolish to me; I felt a new clarity absent in the city and available only in this country air.

Our horse followed Mariela's and Pedro's horses up and down stony trails, then rougher nontrails for about an hour toward Mariela's chosen mogote wall. I pressed my chest against Hernando's back. We went in and out of the shade through wild brush, sometimes dismounting and stumbling on foot, scraping ourselves. Hernando took it all with humor, joking with Pedro about hunting wild pigs and slaughtering cows in the countryside. "We don't do that here," Pedro said, with a serious look. Everyone knew that the *comandante* loved cows and killing one outside the state-run co-ops was a punishable offense.

"But if a train hits some dumb cow, what can you do?" Hernando said to Pedro smiling, repeating the tale of how cattle were secretly slaughtered for consumption and profit in the countryside: tie the animal to the tracks, wait for a midnight train, then carve up the carcass, eat some of the meat, and sell the rest on the black market in the city.

After riding along narrowing trails for another hour, under mosquitoes and flies and leafy, long branches and the strange cries of birds, we arrived at a small clearing. A rocky outcropping rose some fifteen feet above us. Mariela got down from her horse and approached the wall of stone; she felt along the smooth surface the same way she'd stroked the long neck of her piebald in the stable before sliding onto its back. She said this was "the spot," the same words she'd used when choosing Lucho's doomed burial plot.

The huge sun wobbled over the silhouette of trees at the western end of the valley. It was twilight, too dark to go back to the hotel. Hernando and Pedro ran some twine between trees, threw our plastic sheets over the taut lines, and made three tents, securing the bottom of each with rocks. Pedro started a fire in the clearing. A gray hawk screeched in a tree above our heads. I watched it give what seemed a significant look to a smaller bird nearby and then fly after it; the small bird was her meal and she wanted him to know it.

Sparks rose from the fire. Hernando leaned against me and

stroked my arm. He had told me, talking over his shoulder as we rode on our frightening horse, that he'd called home before we left the hotel. Amadora was fine. Tigre too. But where, I'd asked him, would Ruth, Tigre, and I end up now? I saw us huddled, me, an old woman, and a dog, if we were lucky, between two ramshackle lean-tos in the Llega y Pon. I asked Hernando again as we sat by the fire. He said, "Your sister'll get you a good place." His answer surprised me. He didn't trust Mariela any more than he trusted Oscar. After the debacle of the house, his contempt for his brother had exploded. Oscar had opted to remain at the hotel in Las Brisas, supposedly to keep "communication with Flores" in Havana. Hernando had called him a liar and shouted, "You're staying 'cause you're shit-scared of horses. And of me."

But now Hernando said to me, "Who knows, maybe your sister can get everything you need." He might have been trying to calm me. Or maybe, in this clearing surrounded by blue mountains and stars rising over our heads, he was feeling, as I did, that improbable things might happen, things like Ruth coming out of the DSI on the thirtieth and all of us leaving behind the dust of her crumpled house just as we'd left behind the old, tired city, maybe becoming better than we'd been before.

We ate the sandwiches the hotel waiter had packed for us and drank coffee from thermoses. Night noises rose. I closed my eyes, and the sound became a steady, pulsing thrum. I was feeling full, almost calm; the fire kept the night coolness from creeping in. Hernando finished his coffee, set himself on the ground in front of me, and leaned back against my legs, then as if conjuring a campfire scene he'd seen in a movie, he asked Pedro to "tell a spooky story. From this place."

Pedro's fire-lit face looked a bit ghoulish. He gave Hernando a scornful look, but Mariela said, "Yes, Pedro, if you don't mind. It'll be fun." Mariela used the word *fun* too often; so many things struck her—and so few struck us—as "fun," and if anything ever seemed "fun" to us in those years of scarcity, we wouldn't have had the bad taste of saying so. In the Special Period and possibly long before that, many of us came to believe that we'd jinx any enjoyment by calling attention to it. If we ever took pleasure in the sky, a flower, a good record, or the juicy details of a neighbor's family fight, we often covered up our "fun" with casual mockery, aimed at all things and people, including ourselves.

Pedro closed his eyes as he considered Mariela's request; then he looked at each of us around the fire. "*Bueno*," he said, "here's one for you. From these parts." We leaned forward to hear him over the crackle of the flames and he started: "They say some evil spirit stays in these caves. A funny one. This spirit comes back once in a while from Coabey to tell lies to the living. One day he says to the people, 'I saw a guy with a moustache who has many women in Coabey.' The people nod. 'Yes, we know that guy. It's Martí, the patriot.' 'Sure,' the spirit says. 'Martí sits in the land of the dead with Chief Hatuey and they smoke cigars together.'" I could picture the sophisticated, martyred, bookish Martí sitting back, lighting up with wild, martyred warrior Hatuey, two anti-colonialists chatting in the afterlife. "Martí says to Hatuey that the yankees are even worse than the Spaniards, and Hatuey says back to Martí, 'How can that be? Spaniards swell up and drool at the sight of gold.' Martí says, 'So do yankee women at the sight of diamonds. I've known those pretty little monsters in *el norte* and their pretty little insides.'" Pedro smiled at Mariela. "'And, boy, how I miss them.'"

He laughed softly. He'd apparently told the story to annoy Mariela or come on to her, trash her, mock her, belittle her—maybe all these at once. Some of us thought of Mariela as a yankee, others as a long-lost Cuban revolutionary artist returning to her true homeland. Either way, looking back years later, she appears to me in Pedro's story as an object of both derision and desire, both colonizer and colonized.

Mariela wasn't bothered by Pedro's little tale. She ignored (or didn't get) Pedro's lewd twist to Martí's famous quote—that Martí had known the "monster north" from having lived in New York, a phrase brandished on billboards across the island to warn us about the imperialist enemy ninety miles from our shores. Mariela also brushed aside Pedro's oblique reference to herself as a diamond-drooling yankee woman. Instead, she rose and aimed her camera at him, its lens flashing gold across the fire. "Okay," she said. "Say the joke again."

THE NEXT MORNING the two reversed roles and Mariela asked Pedro to film her. Camera in hand, he followed her around for much of the morning while Mariela felt along the rock walls, climbed up and down the ladder, sketched with her rainbow chalks, moved the ladder left and right, stepped back and forth and high and low until her first colorful Nadie, short legged and round bodied, emerged out of the wall's gray surface.

She mixed water and powder inside a small bucket, took gobs of the stuff in her hands, molded a blob, and smacked it onto the

The Tilting House

Nadie's chest. She took my wrist in her muddy hands. "Here, do it with me." Hernando encouraged me with a nod, and I climbed up beside her on the ladder. She guided my hand around the cool plaster of the Nadie's multicolored heart. When she declared that we were done with the Nadie's bright chest, we climbed down.

I thought Mariela would rest, but then Mariela replenished the plaster in her hands, climbed halfway up, and shaped a giant vulva between the Nadie's legs.

As the plaster dried, she spent hours painting and climbing up and down the ladder. Her project of rainbow-colored, plaster-hearted, and bulging-vulvaed Nadies, bright and ridiculous in the sunlight, soon turned even stranger. Pedro kept filming as multicolored Mariela crawled into her plastic tent. I thought she'd gone in for more tools, or maybe to take a short break at last. But she came out carrying Mamá's rifle. I stared at it, unbelieving. I thought she'd only brought tools for her work—certainly not a weapon. Mariela gripped the rifle purposely around the stock and walked directly to me. "You go first." She thrust the old rifle toward my chest. "Shoot her in the heart."

The sun was high, and I stared at the Nadie, round and somehow glorious, electrified with wild colors on her rock wall. I wasn't going to shoot it or shoot anything else. But Hernando sat himself on a fallen log. With him watching me, waiting for me to pull the trigger, somehow the Nadie's carnival balloon heart, blue and orange and green, not a drop of red on it, became a bull's-eye.

Mariela as usual assumed I'd do what she said. She turned to Pedro and spoke to the camera lens: "I always felt I must have done wrong to be sent away from the land of my birth. Tainos and Africans must have felt they did wrong too, for their goddesses to abandon them. Now we enact the violence against those goddesses, unknown to us—Nadies, 'Nobodies,' 'Forgottens'—and in this way we reaffirm their power." Mariela turned to me and Pedro shifted the camera in my direction. "Go ahead," she said.

I'd never shot Mamá's (or anyone's) rifle. As Mariela positioned the rifle in my arms, it occurred to me that Mariela and I would finally get arrested, go to trial, get the punishment we deserved, and I felt a strange relief, as I imagined Ruth might have felt in the police car, finally caught, brought down, judged, and punished. But Mariela, Pedro, Hernando, and I were deep in the *manigüa*. Only birds and valley creatures would hear my gunshot. No one would take us away in handcuffs to the DSI.

At the end of the rifle's sights, tall and bright, loomed Mariela's Nadie, its splotchy rainbow heart swelling out against the purple and green and yellow chalked-in background of her body, the sky blue and cloudless above. We'd waited for hours in the heat and clouds of gnats for Mariela to shape and paint her ridiculous balloon woman. And now we'd blow her up, much like Mariela had blown up Ruth's house.

Mariela pressed herself against my back, her hands on my outstretched arms. "Take a breath and pull the trigger on the release."

Mamá had carried this weapon in her nights of vigil, maybe even pointed it against a counterrevolutionary out on the streets during curfew. The big, rainbow heart of the Nadie now bulged against her colorful chest. I closed my eyes. Mariela's arms held mine and when she said, "Do it," I opened my eyes and pulled the trigger. The gun's pop echoed across the valley. Mariela caught me as I bounced backward from the recoil.

There was no bullet hole, no wound. I'd missed the wet heart, the head, the colorful vulva, and the entire Nadie. Mariela took the rifle herself, aimed, and shot at the Nadie's big heart, opening a dark hole in the lower left that bled the bright-blue paint that Mariela had sealed inside it. She watched, then went to see behind the camera lens. "Good," she said to Pedro. "Shut it off." She handed him the rifle and went back to her work on the rock wall. Mariela didn't look at me, walked past me as if I weren't there. The towering Nadie kept bleeding blue rivulets down the rest of her body. Mariela shifted back and forth and up and down on the ladder. From the shade, Pedro said, "The sun's going to get her." Then he turned to me. "It's going to get you too."

NO ONE HEARD our rifle shots and no one was arrested. Actually, this one ceremony, far from parks, CDRs, and other human ears had been legal; Oscar, through Flores, had arranged for permits for Mariela's shootings in the bush of Viñales.

By the end of the next day, after sculpting more Nadies and their creepy vulvas and shooting the rifle at their paint-filled hearts, Mariela began to slow down. She started to move a little like Ruth, hunched over and stepping with effort, her arms and legs red, blotchy, her skin creased and purplish beneath the eyes from squinting for hours in the sun.

We went back to Las Brisas for more supplies. In our hotel

room that night, Hernando asleep beside me, I admitted to myself that I burned to shoot Mamá's rifle again. The gun's loud pop had gone through my breastbone, and I'd felt like laughing, then I'd felt sadder than at Mamá's funeral. But after asking me to shoot her first Nadie, Mariela had nothing more to do with me. She didn't beg me to return to the rock wall the following morning. She didn't order me. She walked away from my locked door, saying nothing I understood; I wondered if it was English. I went back to sleep and woke past noon. Hernando woke then too, and after ordering lunch in bed like royals, he and I had long, slow sex and then lay with our legs tangled, picking at restaurant leftovers until late afternoon. It was dusk outside when I came around to asking him the question I'd been forgetting on and off, half on purpose, since we'd left Paladero. "Why did you say that Oscar could have killed Amadora, back at Ruth's house?"

"My brother fucks around with things he knows nothing about. One time he screwed up our bathroom wires and almost blew up Ma. He wanted to show her how he'd fixed the light, but he'd crossed the wires and when Ma threw on the switch, it popped and flashed, and she burned her hand. You've seen the scar."

"How did Oscar fuck around with Ruth's house?"

Hernando rolled his head on his pillow to face me. "I guess he set out to fix the garage and the top room like your sister wanted. He probably cut the wrong beam or who knows. Everything he touches turns to shit. I don't get mixed up in my brother's business."

Maybe *business* meant nothing more than "tasks," or "stuff," but I remembered that back in Ruth's parlor, Julio had used the same word. He'd meant "inventory," someone counting the things in Ruth's house and doing "business" with them. "What business?" I asked Hernando.

Hernando shrugged but I pressed on. "What business does Oscar have with Ruth's house?" Hernando sighed, then finally said, "Look, your sister's behind the wheel with all that, not my shit-eating brother." He turned away.

I took him by the shoulder and rolled him back toward me. "I thought *you* were behind the wheel."

Hernando sat up. I continued, surprised at my own venom. "Aren't you her driver? Don't you bring the car around whenever she orders you?"

My insults astonished Hernando and he got up from bed. "I may be the driver, but you're like those three little monkeys." He shook his head in disdain. "You act like you don't see and you don't hear, but you talk plenty of nonsense. If you care so much about your crazy aunt, what are you doing in this room with me? You play the lost orphan, but you put my guilty dick in the same mouth that chews your sister's fancy food." He grabbed his shorts, furious and, I thought, a little afraid of his fury, and left the room.

HE DIDN'T COME back all night. Close to dawn I fell asleep for a few hours. The sun's hard light woke me. I dressed in a panic, packed my bag, and went to the lobby, intending to hop on a truck or a bus or take an early train back to the city—though where to in the city, I couldn't picture. I told myself I'd beg Don

Juanito or Dr. Cuevas to put me up for the night, or maybe I could pitch my stuff in a still-standing room of Ruth's house. On July 30 Ruth would be out, and we'd go somewhere, anywhere. But what if Ruth didn't want to live with me in a corner of the Llega y Pon? What if, even after the DSI, she still preferred her *yuma* child?

Outside the hotel's front door, Hernando leaned against the Chevy by the curb. I walked past him pretending not to see him, my bag of clothes under my arm. He followed me and took me by the arm gently. "I got carried away last night," he said softly. He didn't look at me directly. His face, serious and thoughtful, showed that he'd met some limit in himself, some part of him that his wise-ass bullying couldn't brush away. "Those two," he said, finally looking in my face, "my brother and your sister have nothing to do with us. Fuck 'em. Let's start the car and go back to the city. Just us."

"She's not my sister," I said.

I let him put my bag on the back seat and the two of us rode through Viñales's quiet streets, under the old power lines and by the city water tank, past the few men and women sweeping the sidewalks or walking to work. The morning light seemed to scrub the tired buildings. The store windows flashed as we drove by them.

I felt calm, sleepy. We rode on for a while, mostly in circles. In the end we were hungry and had no money and the car was low on gas, so we headed back to Las Brisas. Hernando turned the corner to the main square and the hotel, peeking at me as he drove. I knew he'd decided about us. And my heart sank because as I looked back at him, I knew I'd decided nothing.

The Tilting House

ON OUR FOURTH day in Viñales, blankets of rain swept across the mogote mesas, and Mariela and the rest of us stayed in Las Brisas. The following morning, the five Nadies' purples, oranges, blues, and yellows had turned muddy brown. Only the blurred hands and the head of one Nadie, a shoulder and an arm of another, and part of the grotesque protruding vulva of a third Nadie remained. I'd hated the Nadies, had enjoyed shooting at one of their hearts even if I'd missed, but now I felt rattled by their ugly beauty in ruins, and by their almost washing away from the rock walls.

Stranger than anything that had gone on in that green Viñales Valley—the cries of birds, Pedro's lewd story, the towering rainbow Nadies, the slam of energy through my chest and arms after shooting Mamá's rifle and it echoing back to me from far away—was Mariela's reaction to her ruined project. She ran her hands over the muddied, faded figures, then turned to us, thrilled. This was much better, she said. "On top of Troy, Troy." She pressed a piece of red chalk against the rock and retraced a Nadie's outline, exhilarated. Oscar, Pedro, Hernando, and I looked at one another, then went to the shade, and Mariela alone rebuilt two of the five Nadies, changing them as she went: one ended up big-bellied, small-headed, and green, and the other mostly purple, with color-swirled breasts. Neither had eyes or noses or ears. It took her most of the day, stopping, rebuilding, resketching, shooting the gun, recording it all with her camera. (She never asked me to shoot the rifle again.) The other three Nadies exist only on video. I don't remember them.

PART THREE

El Focsa

19

Mariela turned out to be right. In the end, we were not Llega y Pon people. While we'd been riding our horses up and down the Viñales hills and shooting at Mariela's grotesque, gorgeous Nadies, Oscar made many phone calls from his room in Las Brisas Hotel and, through Flores and other contacts, arranged for Mariela and me to move temporarily to the towering El Focsa highrise, one of the best residencies in Havana. Our new place was on the eleventh floor overlooking the bay. Even Hernando was impressed. Exactly five days after we stood before Ruth's crumbled house, he and I now stood on the Focsa apartment's balcony, my hands sweaty at first from the height. We took in the city skyline, bright and glorious, and the seawall and the blue-green ocean beyond.

The apartment was small and bare, covered in white walls and beige tiles, and it contained no living plant or animal. Every day my hot shower brought me a guilty joy, as I thought of how Ruth spent her days and what sort of view she had from her cell. I still didn't know Ruth's official charges, and Oscar's and Don Juanito's reasons—Mariela's rockets, Ruth's religion, her black-market butter—never added up. Her detention still felt like a curse, a punishment that didn't square with any actual crime. But I knew I was lucky—we all were—to be able to await Ruth's release in El Focsa.

Flores had arranged for a feature article on Mariela titled "The Archaeology of Revolution," and it appeared in the important *Juventud Rebelde* magazine. Mariela was photographed standing beside her colorful Nadies on one page (before shooting them up and before the rains had washed them away), and on the facing page she held up Mamá's rifle like an actual *guerrillera*. Photographs and videos of the Nadies, and the sketches Mariela produced in Viñales, would make up a solo exhibit at the Galeria de Arte Internacional in September. Thus Mariela's triumphal return came to pass as she'd envisioned in all her grievance and arrogance and grabbiness.

Success made her more beautiful. Her sunbaked skin eased itself into a smooth, glowing tan. Her hair, the ends made golden by the hours spent in the hard light of Viñales, was down to the middle of her back. She wore it loose and wavy. She swanned around the apartment, kissing me on both cheeks like a Spaniard, or coming up suddenly behind me and hugging me for no reason. She laughed at herself, and I laughed with her. She was terribly annoying and sweet and charming, like an actual sister, and I had to admit that as uneasy as I often felt around her, I also liked her a great deal. She'd say to me, beaming, "Think Ruth would like this place?" I didn't know. It was not her house, the one she'd loved all her life. "But do *you* like it," Mariela

The Tilting House

insisted. I did, unfortunately, and said so, and she kissed me then and danced with me on the beige Focsa floors. In those moments I felt grateful to live with her in that youthful joy and exuberance she claimed I deserved. I breathed in the ocean's salt air in a modern apartment, waking up as I pleased, eating sausage and bread for breakfast, having sex with Hernando at all hours, drinking beer and soda from wineglasses—in short, what Mariela called "fun." She bankrolled our lifestyle without grudge. Maybe because of her life with the nuns, she'd never known the fear of hunger or felt the full-on corrupting power of *things*, how they bind you and how their lack pains you, and maybe this made her generous and clueless. Or maybe she'd felt this lack brutally during her years with the nuns and the Butlers and had chosen to always float above the raw need for *things*— after all, she'd refused to be owned, so why wouldn't she refuse to own objects and people?

Except when it came to me. I felt her hang on to me with cheerful greed. And I almost forgave her for it during our time in El Focsa. I put aside as much as I could, tried to forget how recklessly (or criminally?) she'd ruined Ruth's house. The high bay breeze and salt air and city lights helped me do this. When the thirtieth came, I told myself, Mariela and I would redeem ourselves by taking care of Ruth in whatever state she arrived.

The first day after our move to El Focsa, I called Dr. Cuevas from the white phone in the living room. I said we were ready to pick up Tigre. Dr. Cuevas cleared his throat and said that Tigre had found a new home too. Gabito had taken him to the countryside to stay with a family. Tigre had recovered, Cuevas said, and he roamed the hills with the couple's three children and came inside only to eat and sleep. He wouldn't like it in a high-rise, Cuevas said. I protested that Tigre was Ruth's dog. He couldn't just give him away. Ruth would want to see him when she got out. Mariela listened to my end of the conversation, then took the phone from me. Instead of asking Cuevas to bring Tigre home to us immediately, she *yes, of coursed*, and said, "Exactly . . . just what he needs." She hung up the receiver and said, a little sheepishly, that Tigre was happy and that this was a small apartment in a high-rise, with no yard or nearby park. She promised that we'd go see Tigre after Ruth came out of the DSI, drive the Chevy out to the dog's country home and spend an afternoon. I sobbed and argued, but the decision had been made. I moped for days. The last part of Ruth's life we'd been entrusted with, we'd lost. But I finally came to admit that Dr. Cuevas and Mariela were probably right—it'd be sad to shut Tigre in El Focsa now that he had the scent of country air, his own lazy *manigüa*, in his nostrils.

    Mariela tried to distract me with crafts and projects. She decided to "personalize" the apartment, and we sat at the table with lengths of wire and a wire cutter and made five interwoven concentric circles she hung on the wall above the gray couch. Late afternoons, light from the balcony crept along the wall and the five wire plates gleamed one by one. They looked stylish in the bare apartment. The two small bedrooms down the hall had only the essentials, white bed and dresser and nightstand, and were both for Mariela; one served as her room and the other as her art studio, bed upended and pushed to the wall. Hernando and I slept in the tiny room in the back (ex–servant's quarters seemed to follow us).

The Tilting House

Not everything lived up to El Focsa's grand reputation. The water pressure was temperamental. Hernando sometimes had to make our toilet flush with a wire hanger. In the kitchen only one burner worked, and the fridge, a 1950s Westinghouse, rumbled noisily and kept the food barely cool whenever the electricity was on. When it wasn't, we and nearly everyone in the building lit candles and walked up the pitch-black stairwell to La Torre, the restaurant on the thirty-third floor, to drink lukewarm beer and eat sandwiches of pimento paste and stare at the magnificent darkness out the tall windows. Past the outline of the seawall, the yellow torchlights of the old Morro fort wiggled in the black water.

In the restaurant's entrance hung a black-and-white photo from the old days—a man in a pinstriped suit, a neat part dividing his shiny hair, sipped a drink with a cabaret girl. Maybe no one had taken down this prerevolution relic because it lent a sly, festive air to the melancholic bar. The national TV studio was a few blocks away, and on our first night at La Torre—when the lights came back on suddenly—I spotted a famous actress sipping beer at an animated table of actors I didn't recognize. The actress, who played a detective on a popular program, was more beautiful in person; her green eyes, gray on TV, were set off by her golden-brown skin.

It was no coincidence that TV actors chose to gather at El Focsa. The building had a dilapidated sort of glamour. The apartments were often reserved for members of the Central Committee and for foreign professionals—surly Russians and Romanians, a few Venezuelans (loud and sometimes funny), and a handful of other South Americans who'd sought asylum years before, having fled the strong-armed regimes in their native Chile or Argentina for our own friendlier but also strong-armed regime. On that same night at La Torre, we met Laura, a Chilean girl about my age who lived two doors down from us. She carried around a mysterious notebook, smaller than Mariela's sketchbook, and she jotted notes and "impressions" in an impossibly neat hand. I didn't mind this affectation in Laura, whereas the same preciousness from Mariela often filled me with disdain.

MARIELA SOON PLAYED hostess again, this time to a better crowd. Painters and sculptors from Havana's Art Institute; actors, directors, and scriptwriters from the Institute of Cuban Cinematographic Arts and Industry and journalists from the National Union of Cuban Writers and Artists regularly gathered in our apartment. They seemed to know each other or of each other, and whether they liked one another or not, they made their way up to the eleventh floor of El Focsa. Mariela served trays of snacks from the supermarket on the ground floor (not even Oscar was allowed to cross the market's threshold; his hungry face, Hernando said, gave Oscar away as a dollarless native). Laura and her parents, Ernesto and his lonely-looking wife, Cintia, came over sometimes. Laura's parents were foreigners like Mariela but looked as poor and hungry as any of our old friends back in the neighborhood. Their living room was empty except for a colorful Andean rug they'd tacked to the wall and a card table with three folding chairs. Laura's mother kept the blinds shut at all times against the "tropical glare" that made her apartment "noisy with light." She suffered from migraines and took many pills.

I drank less at El Focsa and entertained myself mostly by listening to the conversations rising and falling around me. I felt myself changing, not like the overnight transformation I went through after Mariela decked me out in large hoops and blue eyelids in front of Ruth's mirror, but something quieter and farther-reaching. It was then that the idea came to me, over those long, slow days; I thought I wanted to be a writer. Not a poet like Laura with her "impressions" and rhymes but a recorder of reality, something like a journalist, or a human version of Mariela's camera. I had no clue how to make this happen, or whether this wish was as foolish as wishing to live alone in the bush, but I fantasized about it as I moved around Mariela's guests. I thought of myself as a kind of ghostly observer, taking mental notes of kaleidoscoping interactions and the one-upmanship often on display in the casual chatter. I never wrote down a thing, but I tried to record in my mind words and the sound of words and the highs and lows of the talk in the apartment. One evening, a short, wavy-haired man with a jutting chin, who'd go on to make famous movies in Italy, spoke to Mariela about producing a documentary of her art and early life. Mariela smiled and passed him the tray of cold meats and sandwiches from Rey Supermarket, and the wavy-haired director said, "That supermarket is our cathedral." He took a sandwich in his hand and wrapped another carefully in a napkin and put it in his blazer's inside pocket. "And you," he said to Mariela, "are our high priestess." Mariela laughed at this, but it seemed again that *jama*, the precious and rare animal protein and not just Mariela's celebrity, brought out her new and illustrious friends.

Besides Mariela's charm and protection, the tasty *jama*, my terror of Llega y Pon shelters, and the official proof of Ruth's release (I'd seen the ministry's letter) kept me bound to her. But in the middle of my "fun" and relief I also worried. Could these three mostly bare rooms in the celebrated El Focsa, "the seventh wonder of Cuban engineering" according to an ancient plaque in the lobby, help Ruth bear the loss of her true home and neighborhood? Where, I asked Mariela, would Ruth be able to sleep in the apartment, always so full of guests and their ongoing noise? Mariela, who'd planted her flag in Ruth's old bedroom in Paladero and had possibly brought down Ruth's entire house, said, "I'll give her my room, of course."

On nights when there weren't salons, Hernando and I stayed mostly out on the balcony, and if the power was off, we stood side by side, quiet, watching the whitewash of stars move up high beyond the black bay until one of us yawned and we made our way to the living room couch or to the unmade bed in the tiny ex–servant's room to sleep till late morning. Mariela got to work on her *Shooting Nadies* exhibit and on a new piece commissioned by the Fifth Arte Feria Nacional. She shooed everyone away, kept her studio locked, and when she worked late into the night, no one could talk loudly or play music. She slept in the second bedroom, sometimes alone, sometimes with Oscar when he stayed over. On some mornings, after having fallen asleep on the couch, I'd wake to find Hernando sleeping alone on the cot in the ex–servant's room. The room was white and the small, high window above

Hernando's head showed a patch of sky. "It's like a jail in here," I said, "or a madman's cell."

"Maybe why I like it," he said.

In our togetherness—liaison, romance, I didn't know what to call it—I had freedom to do and say as I pleased. He only disliked clinginess and drama. The second was easier to avoid than the first, as clinginess came close to tenderness, and I was prone to it when drunk. Or maybe I was more prone to it around Hernando than I ever cared to admit. It made me awkward. Sometimes I doubted my gestures and thoughts, and in this way, I kept a part of myself secret. Hernando kept his secrets too. He still ran with his Paladero gang and told me nothing of their doings—and I asked nothing—just as he asked nothing of my feelings for him, which were far from clear to me. I couldn't separate my tenderness from my distrust. I loved him in bed and tried to hold on to those feelings. But I suspected, too, that Hernando hadn't come clean about Oscar's business with Ruth's house; I hadn't pressed him to come clean either. After our fight in Viñales, I knew how it would be to lose him, to live with Mariela alone and have nowhere else to turn. I still wanted to know the truth but was also deathly afraid to hear it.

Laura came over often, and the three of us leaned against the balcony railing high above the city and drank and occasionally smoked Mariela's and Oscar's leftover weed. Laura seemed accustomed to alcohol (her parents drank plenty of wine and rum) and she looked as calm and pensive after drinking as she did when sober. "Wine is like water in Chile," she said, or I thought she'd said. She corrected me: she'd drunk wine with water, and also pisco, and had eaten *pisco-kekes*. But she abstained when she was writing. In the middle of our conversations on Mariela's balcony, Havana's ruins at our feet, Laura sometimes raised her index finger and paused our talk. She lowered her shiny black hair like a curtain around her notebook pages and scribbled furiously. If the thoughts became poems, she said, they were mostly about Chile, the mountains and earthquakes and the cafés in Santiago, about her lovers (plural and unnamed), and about a condor who flew in and out of her poems and seemed to symbolize something.

She and Hernando called each other *huevon*, especially after we'd smoked some of Mariela's weed. Once, after getting high, Hernando shed tears. The dog, he said, he'd never meant to hurt the dog. "So you're a dog murderer," I told him. By mistake, he said. "I never meant to hurt the dog; I liked the dog." Then he called himself *un barco*, a good-for-nothing ship that sailed nowhere.

Laura told us that when her country would fully free itself from the fascists and bring them to trial and lock them up forever, she'd go back to Chile on a ship and live on Isla Negra, where The Poet had spent his last days.

In one of our foggy conversations on the balcony, Laura asked about my aunt.

"She's touched," Hernando said. "Jehovah fanatic. Got caught with black-market butter."

"She gets out in a few days, we have the letter," I said to Laura. She looked up at me and didn't scribble. I said, "Sometimes I don't know what I'm doing sitting here in this apartment."

Laura said, "Sometimes I think that my real life goes on back in Chile. I go to my school in Santiago and eat and talk with my friends. It's my body that sits here waiting. Sometimes I dream about my real life in Santiago. Then I wake up and see I have no real life. I've been robbed."

"That's what Mariela says, that she's been robbed of the life she was supposed to have." I told Laura that Mariela claimed to be my sister, that she insisted my mother had her in secret, and then Ruth sent her off to *la yuma* as a four-year-old, to live in orphanages.

Laura thought this over, raised her finger, and wrote for a while in her notebook. Then she said, "Mariela has no real home. That's how you two are sisters. But Mariela is not a Marxist and you are."

Hernando smiled. "Yuri likes *jama* and liquor too much to be a Marxist." Of course, each floor of El Focsa was stuffed with Marxists, their bellies full of both.

"You're for the underdog," Laura said to me. "So you side with your regressive aunt and not with the rich yankee. The thing is, you must take action. I'm a Marxist, but I'm not blind. Your aunt should be released. Believing Jehovah nonsense is stupid but not a crime, and buying on the black market to feed her family shouldn't be a crime either. Stealing babies—that's different. The Nazis did it, and the Argentinian *esbirros*, and in Chile the fascists took babies from mothers who had no money and sold the babies or gave them away to other fascists and told the mothers their babies had died in childbirth."

"So Mariela is right. Ruth is her kidnapper."

Laura paused. "Your aunt took a baby no one really wanted, sent her away, then lied to her. Maybe she should go to jail for that. But for those crimes, people are often their own prosecutors. Or the children do it for them. I, for one, don't forgive my mother for being a lazy, pill-addled bourgeois bitch and she knows it. But in my poems, I understand her, I understand everyone."

ON JULY 30, the day of Ruth's scheduled release, I woke early. I swept and washed the dishes. Mariela's bedroom and her studio were locked. I tapped on the door—no answer. Mariela had stayed out all night, I figured; she did this occasionally. I wouldn't have worried except that on this day, she needed to be home to welcome Ruth.

I sat on the balcony waiting for Mariela or for Ruth, whoever arrived first. I watched the specks of ships pass in and out of the bay and imagined that Mariela was somewhere buying food for Ruth's homecoming. I imagined Ruth standing next to me on the balcony, astonished at the view. I saw myself offering her one of Mariela's sandwiches in the kitchen, then showing her Mariela's bedroom—Ruth's new room. Then I worried that Mariela hadn't made the bed or changed the sheets, and this thought and Mariela's continued absence seemed signs of a larger carelessness that frightened me.

I went inside and sat on the gray couch beneath the five shiny spiral plates. I watched the front door. I got up for a glass of water, dried the pots, sat again. Hernando frowned at me. He got to work on radio parts on the dining room table while I pushed the curtains aside and opened the balcony doors to make the room bright and to freshen it with the salt air from the bay. Then I checked the stairs, the balcony, the phone in its cradle. No word of Mariela. No word of Ruth.

Around four in the afternoon, footsteps sounded at the top of the stairwell. I jumped up. Hernando stopped his fiddling with the radio parts. But instead of Mariela or Ruth or any official escort, I found Don Juanito gasping for air on the dark landing. His sweaty guayabera was stuck to his belly and he dragged a small bundle past me into the apartment, then collapsed into the rocking chair. He looked fatter, an accomplishment in the Special Period, and wore sunglasses as shiny as his shoes. He coughed hard and long into his handkerchief. I brought him a glass of water, and after he calmed down, he surveyed the apartment. He said, "You've reached the top of the world, *niña*. The rest of us sit at your feet."

Hernando went back to tinkering with the disemboweled radio, his head sideways on the table, looking into the hollowed-out carcass, poking at it with a screwdriver, pointedly ignoring the old man.

"For you." Juan nudged the bag toward me with his shiny shoe. "I salvaged what I could. Locusts cleaned out the rest."

Inside the bag were some of Mariela's and my clothes and underwear. Nothing of Ruth's. "But she comes home today," I said to him. "I thought you were Mariela just now. I thought Mariela had Ruth with her. Ruth will need her clothes today."

The old man looked at me, blank.

"What did you do with Ruth's things?" I said, panicked. "You sold them?"

"*Niña*," he crossed himself. "Ruth was my friend of forty years."

"Was?" My eyes smarted.

"*Niña*, calm yourself. As far as I know Ruth is in good

health. I make arrangements for her to eat in that place. It's not easy."

My own thoughtlessness shone before me. I had collected nothing of Ruth's from the wrecked house; her long Frida Kahlo skirts and her white blouses were probably scattered all over Havana, folded in someone's drawers or worn now by some stranger as she walked home from work. A pair of Ruth's double-soled shoes, which no one but Ruth could have worn, was lost somewhere, useless. I'd left it to Don Juanito, to Cuevas to gather Ruth's things, clean them, and keep them till Ruth could put them on again. They didn't love Ruth.

"What will she *wear?*" I said to Juan's fat, old baby face. "She comes home today, should have been here by now."

"I didn't know she was getting out today. May it be so." Don Juanito put his hands together as if in prayer. Part of a purplish bruise showed under the old man's left eye, below his dark glasses.

"We have the official letter," I said. "Ruth should be here any minute. She'll want to see a friend when she comes, when they bring her . . ." The more I repeated Mariela's description of how Ruth would arrive at El Focsa, the more far-fetched it sounded. Why would any militia, as Mariela had promised, drive a newly freed prisoner to a Central Committee–favored high-rise during a blackout and then carry her in his arms up eleven flights of stairs?

Don Juanito finished his glass of water, lifted his hat from his knee, and set it on his head. His going felt like a dreadful omen. His presence had kept me from crying; I was relieved that he was sitting in our white living room as the sun started its long descent into the bay. To keep him in his seat, I asked after Tere.

"She's well," Don Juanito said, "Happy. A blessing to be happy always."

I made myself ask about Ruth's house. Was it secure? Did it get fixed up?

"Arrangements are being made. Ask your sister. Materials are being gathered, though it might take some time." Juan said this quietly, without conviction. He'd made up his mind to end his visit and answered without details. To stall him again I took off a nickel-plated bracelet that Mariela had bought me in a shop in Viñales. "Give this to Tere. Tell her that I'll come see her before school starts."

I doubted Doña Barbara would let me near Tere, but Don Juanito nodded, took the bracelet, and put it in his shirt pocket. He coughed into his handkerchief and stood. I asked about Rosario.

He looked at me, surprised. Then Don Juanito glanced at Hernando, and I realized that Hernando knew something about the Prietos and hadn't told me. "The microwave," Juan said, "it blew up a couple of circuits and the lights went out on the whole street for about three days. Antonieta and the rest of them packed up after that and left for their in-laws' place in the countryside for a few weeks." He drew a breath, gathering strength for his long descent down the narrow, back-and-forth stairwell. "I always say, don't call attention to yourself, don't be flashy."

I followed him out into the dim hallway and shut the door behind me. It was nearly 5:00 p.m. and Ruth had not come. Neither had Mariela. I was terrified to go back to waiting inside the apartment. I said to Juan, "Please say hello to Julio."

Don Juanito said, "That boy must be crossing the Atlantic by now, no?" He saw my confusion at this too, and added gently, "Julio married an Italian woman last week and he's gone off to live in Naples."

"A woman? An older woman?"

"A nice girl. They met at the beach, love at first sight and all that. Plans were made quickly. She was able to claim him, you know, as spouse, and his exit papers came just like that. Cuevas will fly the coop soon too, even if he's CDR president. When the visa comes with an Italian stamp, he'll wave such a fast arrivederci none of us will need a fan against this heat."

I'd left Paladero for only a few weeks and that world had tilted and then blown away. I hadn't thought of Julio since I'd started going with Hernando, but the sudden news of his absence made my chest hurt. I wanted to go back to the neighborhood right then, live with Don Juanito if he'd have me, iron his shirts and clean his floors and help him shine his ridiculous pointy shoes. Don Juanito took out his handkerchief and coughed into it again.

"When Ruth gets here," I said, surprised at my own words, "she and I may need a place to stay for a little while."

The old man leaned over the railing as if measuring the long distance down. "Think of your luck," he said finally. "Many would give anything to have what you have up here."

My worried face, distorted in the old man's dark glasses, stared back at me. I saw the bruise again below his eye, and I took off his glasses suddenly, the way Mamá said I'd done to her friends when I was a toddler. The old man's face was puffy; black and purple bruises underlined both eyes.

"What happened to you?" I said. He took the glasses from me and put them back on. "Gaffs of the trade, *niña*," he said. "Don't worry yourself. We'll help poor Ruth when she gets out. We'll lend a hand."

"She's supposed to be here right now. Today. But it's too late." All government offices would have closed for the day.

"How can she live here," I said, "with these people?"

These people. I'd said it. I'd come to this thought without knowing it. Don Juanito gave only a slight nod. "Stay good," he said, and went slowly down the long staircase, his hand on the railing. I watched him appear and disappear at the turn of each floor. I stood there, unable to move forward or backward, having declared my aversion toward the people I lived with and having run out of ways to stop Juan from leaving me with them.

Hernando didn't look up when I came back into the apartment. "Bad news about your boyfriend?" He peered into the shell of the gutted radio on the table. He must have figured that the old man had told me about Julio's lucky wedding, which meant that Hernando himself had known about it all along.

I said, "Ruth isn't coming out today, is she?" I hoped Hernando would contradict me. He scraped his chair backward and the screws on the table jiggled. He looked at me. "Who says? The old coot?"

"Tell me the Truth." I pronounced the word with a capital *T*, as if he and I were sitting in Ruth's Kingdom Hall with the congregation. *Are you in the Truth, brother, sister, are you still in the Truth?* "Ruth is not getting out today, right?"

Hernando set down his screwdriver. While I was in the stairwell talking to Don Juanito, he must have been phrasing in his mind what he'd say now. He turned serious. "Let's go north, Yuri. You and me. It's time. I got a contact; we can leave on a boat. I'll help Ma from *la yuma*. You help Ruth. Suppose it's just you and me. Fresh start, eat well. Tell the truth like you say."

The wise-guy mockery had gone from his eyes, and his face was as solemn and handsome as in that early morning in Viñales after our fight when we'd driven without aim on the quiet streets of the town. It struck me that this was the best of him and the most he'd offer anyone.

"And your gang?" I asked.

"No gang." He took my hand. "The truth, right? We'll live that way."

"First Ruth gets out."

Hernando's face turned dark. I had agreed to leave the country with him and live in the truth, and yet he saw that I still cared more about my almost-dead aunt and about Mariela's revenge on her than about his "just us." He was quiet for a moment, then let go of my hand and walked calmly to Mariela's bedroom with the screwdriver he'd used to gut the radio. With a few strokes of the wrist, he pried the lock open.

The usual scramble of Mariela's clothes, paints, papers, scissors, and jewelry lay scattered across the unmade bed. Hernando opened Mariela's drawers and rummaged through her shirts, panties, and bras, and finally found what he was looking for: a small metal box tucked away in the back of the bottom drawer. I didn't know how Hernando knew of the box and I never asked him. It was sealed with a small lock. Hernando held the box in his hand as if it were a large, delicate egg, then hurled it to the floor against the tiles and stomped on it with the controlled violence of a gang leader. It didn't budge. He lifted a pair of tweezers from the mess on the bed and picked up the misshapen box and worked the tweezers into a crack. Like a magician drawing scarves from a sleeve, he pulled out a twenty-dollar bill, then another one, and bill after bill followed through the small opening. He handed me the money; it was more than two hundred *fula*. He kept three twenties for himself.

"This must be all of Mariela's money," I said.

"She won't be happy about it. And it's probably not all of her money." Hernando put the three twenties in his pocket. "Go see the old man. He'll help you now. Take Laura with you—he'll be nicer to you if I'm not there." Hernando said he knew someone who'd arrange for two spots for us on a boat to *la yuma*. He'd set up the deal and catch up with me in the park later that night. A golden ring lay in the mess on Mariela's bed. "We might need it," Hernando said, and I put it in my pocket.

A TALL, BURLY middle-aged man swept Laura and me onto the front steps of the 18 bus to Paladero. The folding doors tried squeaking closed, but all the packed bodies—some arms and legs bulging out—kept them open. I worried about slipping back and tumbling down onto the street, but the burly man's flanks pressed against the back of my legs as the bus gathered speed, his breath across the back of my neck. Young men had stuffed themselves in at the rear door too, pushing against the other passengers. Laura, a step above me, clutched her little notebook; my chest pressed against her lower back. At each stop, passengers screamed to be let off, but our driver, like other bus drivers in Havana, probably scared of taking in more people than wanted out and maybe flipping over altogether, ignored the screams and curses and pushed the gas pedal instead.

The burly man's groin pressed against me with every bump in the street. I couldn't move backward or forward. His erection poked against my butt whenever the bus jolted over another pothole. All the while the man hummed in my ear. There wasn't enough room to swing a kick or land a jab with my elbow, and any agitated motion from me would probably encourage him. I made myself small, tried to shrink away, but there was nowhere to go. I held on to Laura, who clutched her notebook in one hand and the greasy silver pole in the other. The burly man hummed on.

The bus hurried down the wide Calzada del Cerro, and an air of exhausted resignation fell over the passengers. Hardly anyone screamed or cursed the driver over the missed stops anymore. All seemed lost, and the trick was only to endure, get out in one piece, try one's luck again on another bus or on a different day.

The driver finally stopped at Paladero, the end of the route. Everyone got off. The burly man who'd pressed his erection against me stepped to the street and offered his hand to help me down. I dodged him and stepped quickly to the curb, Laura tumbled out behind me, and she and I rushed past the man down Dimas Street. When we were far down the block, I glanced back. Some passengers, stranded far from their destinations, had crossed the street to wait for another bus headed back in the direction from which they'd just come. The burly man stood back in the bus fumes, still looking in our direction as if puzzled—he'd meant to be courteous by offering his hand (no hard feelings, girls?). It struck me then how rarely I'd endured the horrors of public transportation. Mamá, a Party member, had taken me on foot to the better stores in the city center and later Ruth, clomping her bad leg, often got on these buses herself to scavenge for our food. And after Ruth's arrest, Mariela had dropped ready-made meals into my lap.

Laura and I walked across the park toward Don Juanito's house. Paladero Park was "pretty," Laura said, but she didn't take out her notebook to write nature-inspired verses. I imagined she'd seen much better—the peaks of the Andes, its forests and valleys. Till my visit to the Viñales mogotes, Paladero Park with its orange *flamboyan* flowers covering the cement paths to the Milo statue each summer had been the greenest place I'd known. I pointed out Lucho's weedy grave under the ceiba tree. "We set off the rockets here."

"They wouldn't arrest your aunt for that," Laura said.

I saw now, with her eyes, how absurd the idea had been—Ruth arrested over a few homemade rockets, or even more absurd, over a slab of black-market butter. But Ruth that day, one hand on the car roof and the other on the opened door, had lowered herself into the police car. She had arranged her bad leg into the back seat without protest, as if she had understood the nature of her offense which, I realized then, might have had no more to do with rockets or butter than with the occasional envious look Hernando gave Julio, or the distasteful look Compañero Oscar sometimes gave Don Juanito, or whether Dr. Cuevas had enjoyed his coffee that morning, or the arresting officer a good night's sleep. Unlike the perched hawk who'd given its prey a warning stare back in the Viñales hills, human objects of hate could remain oblivious to the gaze of their predators and to their own long-standing markings as prey. Maybe this cluelessness gives off its own slight scent of hubris—a sudden chemical thrill, and everything's decided—of which the prey remains mostly unaware.

Laura and I crossed the street to Ruth's ruined house. Nothing had been repaired. The front door, unscrewed from the hinges, was gone, along with the porch's metal railing and all the windows. The black-and-white porch tiles were mostly missing or broken—a ragged checkerboard on the ground. Everything that could be dismantled and reused had been hauled away, by strangers or by neighbors, and the husk of the house looked like a snail shell dropped onto a rock by a high-flying bird. Possibly poorer people than Ruth or me would now get to use Ruth's things and give them another life. And still, this violent recycling filled me with grief.

Laura saw my sadness. She said, "Sorrow comes from *maya*. The illusion that solid hammer meets solid nail. Who knows what they've done to my house in Chile? I bet some fascist lives there with his fascist children. They sleep in my bed. I don't think about it."

"But your house still stands."

Laura gave me enough time to take this back. I said I was sorry, and she nodded solemnly and followed me into the ruins of Ruth's parlor. I bent down to the rubble and fished out a doorknob. I couldn't tell which door it had opened. Laura took it from my hand and tossed it back down. "This is a graveyard," she said. "In my country the Mapuche don't keep the things of their dead. They bury them along with the body to keep away evil spirits. Don't take anything from here." But I wasn't a Mapuche and this wasn't Laura's country. I picked up the doorknob again. I decided I'd take it and carry it with me everywhere. I remembered then the box I'd hidden in a high kitchen cabinet. My mother's pictures were in it and her silver pin and her battered *Le Père Goriot*. One look toward the kitchen rubble told me I'd never find it (there were no cabinets, no cabinet doors), so the doorknob in my hand, which opened nothing, could only remind me of what no longer existed. I threw it back into the rubble as Laura had said, and she and I wandered the other rooms and hallways. The low dull sun over the wall-less rooms heightened the feeling of ruin.

Next door, the Prietos' windows were shut. The summer's dance parties, the little lights on the terrace, the Beatles music, the Julio-Rosario courtship, and our three-way kiss seemed as far away as Laura's Mapuche villages. No one answered our knocks; the house sat empty. How much had Julio, now married to someone else and living far way across the Atlantic, cared about Rosario? He must have cared more about fleeing. In this he wasn't like Hernando, I thought, who still wanted to flee with me.

In showing Paladero to Laura, I saw the neighborhood through the eyes of a stranger. Everything about it now struck me as off-kilter, half familiar and half alien. But Tere was home, I told myself. Tere, unlike nearly everyone else on the block, wouldn't have changed. I had a great need to sit with her in her living room for a few minutes before heading to Don Juanito's house to bribe him into helping Ruth—a prospect that frightened me. What if he said no and denounced me instead?

Laura and I headed up the block toward Doña Barbara's apartment. Hernando's boys, Gelson and Reynaldo, perched on a tree branch, watched us from across the street. They kept their eyes on us as we walked past Dr. Cuevas's dull yellow house and turned the corner to Tere's building. What did Doña Barbara think now that Ruth's house was half razed and her possessions scattered?

Doña Barbara opened her door. She frowned when she saw me, then looked at Laura and stepped aside to let us in. Tere burst into the living room, throwing her arms, fat and sticky, around mine, and her hug felt like the truest thing that had happened to me since Ruth had gone to the DSI.

Laura and I sat on the couch, Tere between us, and I said to Doña Barbara, "So many bad things have happened, and I haven't seen either of you."

"We've been here," Doña Barbara said, icy, sitting back in her rocking chair. "I went to help you the very day after Ruth was taken away. Your sister shooed me from the porch."

"I don't think of her as my sister."

"That's good news," Doña Barbara said.

I took Mariela's golden ring out of my pocket and gave it to Tere. She put it on her pinkie and smiled, then thrust her hand toward Doña Barbara, who nodded at the ring as if it were further proof of my badness. I realized then that I'd brought nothing useful for the household—a bit of sugar or a bar of soap—and felt ashamed. "The 18 was bursting," I said as an excuse.

Doña Barbara shrugged. She lamented, just as she and Ruth

had done before Ruth's arrest, the sad state of buses and the disgrace of horse carriages plodding through the city center. "It's the kind of country we live in." Doña Barbara rocked back and forth in her chair. "Someone told me you're living in El Focsa now. It's not that I begrudge prosperity. I begrudge nothing, as long as it's not at the expense of other people."

"I've left El Focsa." I hadn't realized this till I said it out loud. "I'm not going back there."

Doña Barbara's face softened. "Is there word of poor Ruth? Every day I cry for my friend."

"She was supposed to come out today." I felt relieved to say this to Doña Barbara; she might have an insight, an explanation. "Mariela showed me the official letter for Ruth's release. But it didn't happen. All day I waited and now it's almost dark and Ruth never came out."

Doña Barbara leaned forward and touched my hand. She said only, "You must be in need to have come. We were here all this time."

During my conversation with Doña Barbara, Laura scribbled furiously in her pages. Doña Barbara asked her if she was writing a book and Laura looked up and said no, just some thoughts. Doña Barbara said nothing to this and returned to the topic of our country's degeneration, and how such degeneration had led to Ruth's ruin. "Look," she said to me, severe, "nowadays anyone can strip a house, usually an old grand house like Ruth's, and sell the cables, wires, toilets, stove. It happens everywhere, Havana, Holguín, Santiago. 'Destroy to Build,' they call it. They sell the stuff to people who have dollars and want to improve their own houses." Doña Barbara watched the effect of her words on me, as if testing me, the same way that Oscar had tested us in physics class on details he'd never said to study.

"Ruth's house wasn't grand," I said.

Doña Barbara shrugged. She repeated, "Destroy to Build." I saw that this phrase could loop forever: *Destroy to Build, Build to Destroy*. Any house. Anyone. Anywhere.

"Of course, when Ruth's house came down, the whole neighborhood descended on it like buzzards." Doña Barbara sat back, satisfied. All along, her expression seemed to say, she'd been right about the Malanga-heads, Cuevas, Don Juanito—all of them common criminals. Only she and Ruth (and after Ruth's arrest only Doña Barbara herself) could rightly denounce the rabble of the neighborhood. Yet there was also sadness in her voice.

Tere moved the golden ring from finger to finger, holding it up in the air and turning her hand back and forth in admiration. I made myself turn back to Doña Barbara. "I thought Oscar and Mariela were fixing up Ruth's house, the room upstairs, and they made a mistake."

"A huge mistake," Doña Barbara said. "They were taking apart the garage, the Malangón Oscar and his crew, to sell Ruth's bricks and wires and electric parts through Juan, and they must have cut a main beam—Bang!" Doña Barbara smacked her hands together. "Everything comes down on their heads, the imbeciles. Didn't know what they were doing, not like my brother Daniel, who knows construction. They almost killed their own mother."

Doña Barbara, seeing my distress, leaned forward and squeezed my hand in pity, as if all this time she'd thought me smarter. "I reported it to Cuevas, the whole scheme, but it wasn't news to him, you see." She paused. "I thought you knew, love. Everyone knew."

I LEFT DOÑA Barbara's apartment shaken to the core. Laura followed me down the stairs. I couldn't talk about what I'd heard. It was late, Laura said; she had to go home, so I said goodbye to her by the 18 bus stop. I headed to Don Juanito's, sure at last that the "Destroy to Build" scheme Doña Barbara had revealed was the "business" that Julio had hinted at and that Hernando wouldn't come clean about. This "business," according to Doña Barbara, involved not only Oscar, Cuevas, and even Juan, but Mariela and Hernando too. If this was true, I could trust no one from this point forward, only Ruth, and with Ruth still in jail I could only trust myself.

Gelson and Reynaldo were waiting for me on the sidewalk in front of the old man's house. Gelson blocked my way. "Hernando says to take you on our bikes now." He sounded like an American gangster in a 1950s movie, but instead of forcing me into the back of a black sedan, he was going to strap me onto the handlebars of his refurbished Schwinn.

"People are going to the seawall," Gelson said. He grabbed my arm as I moved past him. He whispered, "Hernando's waiting for us. We're going to *la yuma* on a boat. They're coming, the boats from Miami, and we're all going, get it?"

"Genius"—I shook off his arm—"a few weeks back the Coast Guard sank a hijacked boat and some of those people drowned."

"I told you she's a cunt," Reynaldo said to Gelson.

"Tell Hernando to come get me himself. I'm here waiting for him."

I pictured a small boat bobbing on the bay and Hernando's thrill as the two of us boarded it to sail away to *el norte*, Hernando's land of truth. But I wasn't thinking of getaways with Hernando anymore, not after Doña Barbara's pitying looks. I wanted to confront Hernando about the "business" he, his brother, and my "sister" had been running in secret, if I could believe Doña Barbara, tearing apart Ruth's house to sell everything, even the beams and wires, and causing it to crumble to the ground. He'd have to say the truth at last, which he himself held up as the sealing bond between us. Or he'd have to (I still hoped for this) denounce the lies of a neighborhood gossip.

I pushed past the old man's gate into his small garden. When Juan had visited Ruth, he often brought a handful of his white roses. He'd scramble up lines from Martí: "Every day I cultivate a white rose of friendship," adding after the appropriate pause, "for those who tear out my heart." He'd follow the verse with a playful wink in my direction. Ruth would clip the stems and place the flowers in a clear vase. "Martí," Juan would say to us, "never gets old." But Don Juanito and Ruth had both grown old, it seemed, in a short time. And still, here were the roses. Juan's garden reminded me that I was safe on the ground, not boarding a boat to who knew where—hundreds had died that year trying to make the crossing to Florida—and I had to admit that my relief at standing among Juan's spindly flowers was greater than my worry for Hernando. After all, I told myself, Hernando was a thief, a liar, a delinquent. Yet a part of me felt shame as I wondered, in Juan's quiet garden, if I'd ever intended to flee with Hernando at all.

A short woman answered my knock. A boy leaned against her hip and a lanky teenager peered across her shoulder. The woman yelled at Gelson and Reynaldo, still loitering by the gate. "Move it, boys," she said with a high nasal countryside accent. "You lost nothing here."

She waved me into the house. In the living room, Don Juanito lay on the couch, pale, a yellow sheet pulled up to his chin. The furniture was dark, old-fashioned; paintings of gloomy, snow-covered European capitals hung on the walls. The old man watched me come in and lowered the sheet to his chest. He scooted himself half up with difficulty. "Sit, *niña*. I'm under the weather. And your Focsa stairs did me in this afternoon." He turned to the woman, "We'll have water with lemon." The woman did nothing; she stood by the couch like a sentinel. The two boys settled themselves on the floor in front of Juan's Chinese TV.

Don Juanito tipped his head toward the silent woman and said, "This is Sara Suarez. Sara's a nurse. Her husband, Dr. Ramón Suarez, my friend, perished in Angola three years ago, fixing up soldiers in that lost war. And these"—he pointed to the boys fixated on the screen—"are their children."

I sat in a wood-slatted chair across from the old man. He pulled himself up further. I said to him, "You weren't so sick this afternoon."

"Sure I was. I had a terrible cough." His beat-up black eyes, like a sad cartoon panda's, made his face look slightly comical. I felt a little sorry for him. The old man said, "Well? Is it good news, *niña*? Is my poor friend Ruth finally out?"

I wanted to speak to him alone, but Sara stood by the couch, unmovable. "Are you at the Lenin?" she asked me, friendly. "You look like you study. My oldest boy goes. He studies so hard he's rail thin."

Don Juanito tipped his bruised head toward the two boys. "Those two eat like beasts when they're here on weekends while Sara kindly looks after an old man. They watch TV and raze the pantry."

The boys paid no attention; they watched the TV.

"I know what you did," I said. "All of you. You sold Ruth's house piece by piece." Don Juanito looked puzzled, but I didn't wait for his answer. I touched my hand to my chest, to feel the dollar bills folded in my bra, and said, "You get Ruth out of the DSI now. I have money. And you'll do anything for money."

Juan coughed hard into his handkerchief. Sara stepped to the end of the couch, pushed him forward, and pounded his back. She took the handkerchief from him, and when his fit ended, she put the handkerchief in the pocket of her apron. "Bronchitis," she explained.

Don Juanito's wet, blackened eyes and his horrible hacking unnerved me. I worried that Sara Suarez would tell me to leave and stop badgering a sick old man. I kept her in the corner of my eye as I hurried through my rehearsed threats. "Doña Barbara knows about your scam. You helped carve up Ruth's house, the bricks, the wires. You made the house fall and sold the pieces on the black market. Everyone knows. I'll go to the police and denounce you if you don't help me." Don Juanito lifted his purple-spotted hands in bewilderment. Sara walked over to the boys and told them to go play in the yard. They rose reluctantly and

The Tilting House

went out the kitchen door to the backyard. The old man then tried to smile at me, his teeth yellow, his grimace scary.

"My dear, for the love of the Virgin," he said, "Doña Barbara is a gossipy old woman. Her tales are fantasy. With what strength would I pull bricks from a house? With these?" He turned his spotted hands up and down before me.

"I saw you carrying bags out of Ruth's house night after night."

"*Niña*," he sighed. "I was sorting through some things to take to your aunt locked away in that hellish place." He paused and when I said nothing, he scooched himself up taller on the end of the couch and said, "Listen to me. Listen well. When we board the train of life, *niña*, we think we're going in one direction. But then the train switches to some other track, and we can't just get off because we want to. Do you understand?" He took a deep breath and I thought he'd start hacking again, but he continued in his low, con man's voice, "We sit and stare at the view outside, and when the train speeds on, the window goes dark, and we try to shut our eyes. What else can we do? It all passes before us." With this he slumped back against the armrest and pulled the sheet up to his chest. "Don't go around talking about police or money or anything dangerous like that. Don't bring attention to yourself. Look where it got General Acha. Where it got Ruth."

My fury rose at Juan's mention of Ruth's supposed flashiness. "You'll end up in 100 and Aldabó *with* Ruth if you don't fix what happened to her," I said. But my threat sounded hollow. I tried to remember Laura's words—"You must take action." I sat up full length, ready to continue even if I foresaw little more than defeat and ridicule resulting from my efforts.

Don Juanito coughed into his hand, then red-faced, he half shouted, "Your sister's the delinquent here. *She* belongs in prison."

I steadied myself for the truth at last. I wanted (and feared) the truth about Mariela, whose arrival on Ruth's porch had ruined Ruth's life and mine in the span of two months. But Sara switched on the table lamp and told Don Juanito to stop talking. "Time to rest," she said and turned to me. "A lot of police come from the countryside these days."

I didn't know what made her say this, but her comment agitated Juan. "Sara," he pleaded, "you know I'm not well." Sara bent over him and felt his forehead. I could see clearly that despite some gray at her temples Sara Suarez wasn't old. She moved with speed and precision. She turned to me and said that she had a friend on the force, from her town in Villa Clara. A good man. Ate supper with his wife every night. He lived close by, in El Cerro. She could walk to his house if she needed to. Everyone knew that many young men had arrived from the provinces in recent years, hitching rides to the city, slipping into the promised land of the capital as recruits for the army, the police, state security. I couldn't see what this had to do with Ruth or with me.

Don Juanito said, "Sara, please, we're in a tight spot here."

This friend, she continued, would know who to ask about Ruth. She looked at me calmly, then extended her hand. I thought this a consoling gesture and almost embarrassed myself by taking her hand. Then I realized the woman wanted the money I'd offered to Don Juanito.

She kept her eyes on me. There was something mild and

sure in her manner. Don Juanito lay on the couch, the top of the sheet rumpled around his shoulders, his face full of dread. He closed his eyes then, resigned to Sara's will. I reached into my blouse and handed Sara the dollars from inside my bra. Sara stuck the wad in her purse. "I'll be back in an hour, two at the most." She motioned to Don Juanito, who looked terrified at her going. "Don't let him choke on his phlegm."

My chest felt itchy where Mariela's money had been. Music from the left-on TV turned bouncy and loud as Don Juanito stared at the door that Sara had just closed behind her. I realized I'd been left with a sick old man and two children making noise out in the yard. And I'd just given a stranger two hundred *fula* and had only a ten-dollar bill left inside my shoe.

DON JUANITO EVENTUALLY fell asleep, his head on the armrest of the couch. Sara's boys, in from the yard, ate yellow rice out of the pot on the stove. The older boy told me that it was time for Don Juanito's shot and then went back to the pot of rice. Sara had said nothing about a shot. I'd watched Ruth lean over Mamá day after day, jabbing the needle into her arm and depressing the plunger. But I had no idea of the old man's dosage. I pictured him dying on the couch from missing his shot, or me killing him with an overdose. The boys chewed indifferently on their rice, and I started to cry silently at first, then in loud, gushing, embarrassing waves. The older boy looked up from the pot of rice and said to his brother that I was upset because the old man was sick.

After eating, the boys went to bed. I went on crying in the

kitchen, the bathroom, and finally in an armchair by the sleeping old man. His phlegm whistled in his throat as he lay moaning, half waking when my blubbering got louder. I touched his burning forehead and felt sure he'd die on my watch. I cried for him, for Ruth, for my stupidity in giving Mariela's money to a stranger who'd disappeared into the night leaving me with a sick, half-conscious, battered old man. I suspected I'd been fooled again. I didn't know what amount of money, if any, could get someone out of the DSI. I cried too for Hernando, who might have left the island without me and was now somewhere on a crowded boat rising and falling in the choppy water, or maybe worse, who might be waiting in vain to meet me in the park. I should have joined him, left everyone behind. The old man, his eyes shut, gave a loud moan. I wiped my nose on my sleeve, wet a kitchen rag, and pressed it to his forehead.

Late in the night Sara finally returned. By then the old man was less fevered; he breathed through his open mouth. Sara felt his forehead. I said, "I thought he was going to die." Sara went to the kitchen to boil a syringe. She told me not to worry; it was only bronchitis, and anyway, she said, all had gone well with her friend. He thought Ruth wouldn't be kept at the DSI so long; she'd probably been transferred to a common criminals' jail. He'd look into it, Sara said.

She handed me the remaining *fula*. I tucked it uncounted into my bra. "Hang on to it," she said. "We're going to need it."

Sara's *we* made me cry again, this time from relief, possibly hope.

"Crying doesn't help, believe me," Sara said, her dark, efficient eyes on me. She handed me a clean rag to wipe my face.

"Take the old man's bed tonight. He's better off propped up on the couch."

I wiped my eyes. "When Ruth gets out, she can't make it up the stairs where Mariela lives."

Sara nodded. She seemed to think for a minute, then said that "we" were nearly a hospital already, and that Ruth could stay with "us" for a little while. She said she'd need my help with her two patients. I took in a breath but couldn't help myself; I was crying again. Sara took from my hand the rag, turned it over to its dry side, and handed it back. I took it, grateful, knowing full well that Sara, a competent nurse, could have juggled the responsibilities of any sick ward without me.

20

That week at Don Juanito's while Sara and I waited for news of Ruth, an unexpected event shook the island. Rumors had swept the city that boats were coming from Miami to take anyone who wanted to leave to *la yuma*, and a thousand or more young people gathered at the seawall, among them Hernando and his boys. When the boats never came, the crowd turned rowdy and wild, erupting into a rare street revolt. I heard about this the morning after it happened when Gelson washed up in Don Juanito's garden, missing a tooth, his head wrapped in a gauze turban. Gelson had survived and made his way to the neighborhood from what came to be known with grim street humor as El Revolcón del Malecón, the Great Seawall Romp. The German flood that Ruth had predicted would sweep into Havana in '89 had finally come to pass as a brief, unexpected storm—a thousand young men, barely adults, and a few women and children burned trash cans, cried "freedom" from their bicycles, threw rocks at the windows of a dollars-only market, and piled whatever loot they could haul onto their handlebars.

Gelson's head bandages still bled pink in places; his battered face was frightening. But what frightened me more was that he'd made his way back from the seawall alone, without Hernando, and apparently had no idea where Hernando had ended up.

During the riot, police showed up in armored vans and split skulls with metal tubes and shot their guns mostly in the air. By morning the "vagrants" were dispersed or arrested and the street along the seawall closed off. Years later a band would record a song about that day, "We Need More *Revolcones*," but there wouldn't be any more for many years, and the people, frightened, probably weary of revolutions, went back to scrounging for food, toothpaste, soap, and wires to fix old gadgets and cars.

Reynaldo got arrested in the riot. He and Gelson had raced down an empty alley on their bicycles, but when Gelson looked back, Reynaldo's blue bike was on the ground, front tire spinning, and Reynaldo was gone. A plainclothes G-2 grabbed Gelson from behind and smashed his head with a metal truncheon. Gelson slipped from the policeman's grasp, leaving his shirt in the officer's hand, and ran, bleeding, under the porticoes of Prado Street and away from the chaos. Hernando, Reynaldo, and Gelson never met up in the crowd. Gelson said to me, "I was late."

"Because of me," I said.

Gelson shrugged. "You made the right decision." He pointed to his swollen lips and said he was lucky he'd only lost a tooth. "Hernando wanted you to come with us so bad but it's just as well you didn't." He paused. "Maybe he'll make it to *la yuma*, or maybe he's in jail now with Reynaldo."

"Or worse." I pictured Hernando inside a drawer in the coldest morgue in the world.

"They were beating us up mostly," Gelson said, "to clear the streets."

Gelson left and I called El Focsa for news of Hernando. When no one answered, I rushed down the street to the Malangón alleyway. I found Amadora sitting in the small courtyard, tending to two of her grandchildren, a boy and a girl, and picking out small stones and debris from a pot of soaking rice. The courtyard was clean and swept, and Amadora seemed calm. This gave me hope. Maybe Hernando was safe, asleep in his childhood bed, or hiding somewhere until the arrests died down.

Amadora had heard from Gelson too, but she didn't believe Hernando was in jail. "Hernandito would slip away," she said to me. "He always told me, 'Ma, I don't get caught.'" She seemed to believe Hernando was one of the few hundreds who'd made it to the sea on flimsy rafts that week, and that he'd appear on the shores of *la yuma* alive. "I'll hear from him soon."

She was cool to me as she spoke, and she looked to the two children. "You and he are not the same. I tried to tell him. You broke his heart."

"I didn't break anyone's heart." I explained that we had planned to meet up in the park, but he never came and went to the seawall without me. I left out that Hernando had sent his boys to fetch me and that I'd refused to go with them.

Amadora stirred the rice water, then said without emotion, "This pain you feel now, with your aunt locked up and you living with strangers—it's nothing. The years'll pass and you'll have your pretty life with your rich sister in *la yuma*—we both know neither of you are staying here—and in a while my son's absence, you'll feel it everywhere you go. You'll breathe it in like the air. It'll make your nerves burn and your head hurt day and night, and you'll be lost in every direction you turn. You think now is the worst? Your aunt, your bad sister, your mother? Nothing." The granddaughter walked over and leaned on Amadora's knee, and Amadora untucked a handkerchief from her skirt and wiped the girl's nose. "My son's absence will come down on you then and you'll be old."

The little girl went back to her brother, and Amadora turned back to the rice as if I weren't there. I smiled a little at her dramatic omen; it sounded like one of Ruth's end-of-the-world predictions that had never come to pass. And just then Amadora raised her head from her rice and pebbles. "Laugh for now," she said. "And tell the old pervert nobody thinks he's got bronchitis. We know what he's got and tell him he deserves it."

21

It took a few more days for Sara's policeman friend (I never learned his name) to confirm that Ruth was alive. She'd been transferred to a women's prison west of the city, he reported, her charges still unknown. He predicted that following the seawall riot, nonviolent prisoners like Ruth would be released to make room in the jails. Hernando possibly in jail, Ruth possibly out—was this some secret, perverse balance the world kept so as not to tilt too far one way or the other?

During long weeks, I waited for news of Ruth and Hernando. I helped with the chores, following Sara around like an apprentice. I went to bed each night exhausted, as much from the work as from trying to keep Ruth and Hernando out of my thoughts.

Don Juanito mostly slept now and ate little more than a few spoonfuls of clear broth at a time. The blue-black swelling beneath his eyes had given way to pink, sunken half circles; his cheeks had collapsed, his mouth turned pasty with thrush so that Sara and I took turns wiping his lips with a moist sponge.

Asleep on the couch, Juan sometimes looked peaceful, as if an innocent child had made his way to the surface of his suffering face. I knew that look. "We should take him to the hospital," I told Sara. She said no. "Juan stays in his own house. If he goes to the hospital," she said, "they'll send him to one of those camps where they keep the sick men."

It took me a moment to understand that Sara meant the "quarantine camps" everyone spoke of. A terrible new illness had swept across the island, and hundreds of men were now held in camps, according to the news, to avoid "contamination." I'd never imagined that Juan had this awful disease or that we were breaking the law by keeping him home.

"But what if he dies here?" I asked.

"Better here than there," Sara said.

I wondered what evil the old man could have done to Amadora for her to wish this sickness upon him, or for Hernando to dislike him so much over the years. Don Juanito's love for men couldn't possibly be the cause—yet sometimes the pettier the reason, the stronger the hate.

That same week, Laura visited us from El Focsa. She brought a new issue of *Juventud Rebelde*; Mariela smiled on the cover, circled by school children. Inside the magazine a full-blown article featured Mariela's new exhibit. She had become, as she'd aimed to, a full member of the revolution she'd been wrenched from. "I had a right to it," Mariela declared in the magazine's interview. "My birthright and my duty were to fight alongside my people."

Laura reported that Mariela's Focsa apartment was busy at all hours, lit up night after night. I thought of the Prietos' bright house after Cousin Sonia had arrived with her pockets full of dollars. The new racket in Mariela's apartment had caused Laura's mother to file a request to swap apartments with someone on a lower floor, but so far no neighbor had been foolish enough to trade with her.

Laura also said that one night when the electricity was on, she and Mariela had come face-to-face in the stairwell. Mariela half smiled at Laura and said to wish me well and that I shouldn't worry; she wouldn't press charges against me. She declared herself "surprised but not shocked" to discover my theft of two hundred dollars. Just as Mariela hadn't considered what would happen when she took Mrs. Butler's wallet, I'd never considered the actual consequences of my theft. Stealing from a foreigner (and now a slightly famous one) was a serious offense. Mariela could have denounced me and had me locked up in a cell like Ruth's. "She said she'll come see you one of these days," Laura said. "I didn't tell her where you're staying but somehow she knows." Laura had asked Mariela about Hernando, but Mariela knew nothing about him.

"Oscar's not around anymore," Laura said.

"She ditched him?"

Laura shrugged. "The new man on the scene is a guy named Flores. A sharp dresser."

Laura and I sat in the old man's rose garden until she had to catch the last 18 bus back to El Focsa. I said, "The bus may never show up. Let's find you a bicitaxi."

"As a Marxist I can't let a skinny boy haul my ass to Vedado."

"The boy does it for his family. He needs the dollars."

"That's always the excuse of the bourgeoisie," Laura said.

Still, I went to fetch Gelson. Yanked from Hernando's gang, Gelson had started his own business—he'd converted his bike into a one-seat taxi like the dozens of homemade contraptions carting tourists around the capitol. I stuck a dollar in his pocket, but he put it back in my hand. Laura climbed onto the bicitaxi's wood plank behind Gelson and, clutching her small notebook, she kissed my cheek.

Soon after, her family returned to Chile. Laura and I didn't find each other again. I hope she ended up in Isla Negra.

22

At the end of August, without warning, a white car we'd never seen before pulled up to Don Juanito's curb. Sara stopped washing dishes and told the boys to take the old man to his room and to keep quiet. Sara and I went down the flagstones toward the curb, but she motioned me to stay by the gate. A uniformed nurse slipped out through the driver's door and walked to the other side of the car. She and Sara lifted an ancient, slight person from the back seat, her white head rising above the white car's dirty roof.

Ruth looked up to the sky as if surprised it was there above her head. She wore a tentlike gown and gray slippers. The two women, one on each side, held Ruth by the armpits and elbows, and the three of them, like a shuffling animal, made their way past me through the opened gate into Don Juanito's house.

Sara and the nurse sat Ruth on Juan's couch, and Ruth curled herself up and closed her eyes tight, as if a too-bright light shone on her face. Here she was at last, or I should say, here was her scrawny, terrified body. So little of Ruth seemed to be left in it. I knelt down to her ear and whispered, "*Tia*, it's me." Ruth kept her eyes shut. Her legs were thin and goose-bumpy. I wanted to cover them, but the sheets were in the old man's bedroom. The nurse stood by the front window, breathing hard after helping Ruth into the house.

Don Juanito coughed inside the bedroom and Sara said to the nurse, "My uncle has the grippe."

"Nasty grippe," the nurse said from her spot by the window. Sara nodded to me. I got some dollar bills from the kitchen drawer and placed them in the hand of the nurse, hoping it was enough. The nurse closed her fingers around the money and put it in her pocket. She seemed pleased and wished us luck, then headed out to the dirty white car.

I ran to Ruth and leaned my head against her bony shoulder. Her gown smelled of old sweat and lye.

IN THE BATHTUB, Sara lathered Ruth and I poured warm water with a jar, little by little, over Ruth's bony limbs, her back, her hair. An archipelago of reddish marks and bruises ran along Ruth's legs. "Some of it is from fleas," Sara said, "but not this one." She pointed to a centavo-sized hole on Ruth's left hip. "She can't sit or lie on this; we'll have to flip her all the time like an omelet."

We dried Ruth off, patting gently, then dried her thin hair, taking care not to jostle her. We slipped a housedress over her head, then seated her at the kitchen table like a child at feeding time. Ruth's eyes were vacant. Sara put spoonfuls of chicken broth in Ruth's mouth. Ruth swallowed, but her eyes stayed blank as if nothing around her was real—the soup or the spoon, or Sara, or me. I told her who I was. I repeated that this was Don Juanito's house. "Don Juanito, remember?" I got a lost stare.

That night, after the two patients were fed and asleep, Sara and I sat, worn-out, in the kitchen. She poured each of us a half glass of rum. "Give her time," Sara said. "She'll get her strength back."

"And her mind?"

"Maybe. Little by little."

Sara drank another shot and nodded to where Juan was sleeping in the bedroom. "My husband died of the same thing, in Angola. But the old man dies in his own house." She said this with determination, even with a bit of pride. I was afraid to ask anything. Sara said, "They were good friends once." She leaned on the word *friends* and sipped her drink. Seeing my surprise she said, "I grew up on a farm, *mi niña*. I'm a nurse. Believe me, everything horrible and wonderful comes down to the body's goop going back and forth. Sticky stuff in the barnyard. Sticky stuff on the sheets. But the love is real. The love is serious. The rest, people make too much of. Don't let anybody tell you different."

I said that people told me all kinds of things and I spent half of my waking hours trying to sort them out and the other half doubting my conclusions. "Why was Juan beat up the day I got here?"

"Juan's no saint. He thought he could hold his own but got ahead of himself. And he was already sick."

The Tilting House

I sat still in my chair, afraid of my next question. "Did Hernando beat him up?"

Sara leaned. "I don't think that boy did it." She smiled a little at my relief. Then she said, "Yuri, you have to call your sister. Your aunt needs fresh milk and soft foods. Her gums are bad. She needs eggs and chicken broth and puddings and root vegetables. Even if I use up the old man's pesos, I can't find the stuff. Your sister can buy food at the dollars-only stores."

In the morning I called El Focsa. No one answered. I wondered if Mariela had moved to a more exclusive residence. I also wondered whether, after my theft of her money, she'd do anything to help us. But for Ruth's sake I kept calling.

Finally, late at night, someone picked up. Loud music played in the background. A woman's voice, someone I'd never heard before, got Mariela to come to the receiver.

"It's me," I said to Mariela.

Silence.

I said, "Ruth is here."

Mariela yelled at someone to keep it down.

"Ruth got out of jail," I said. "We're at Don Juanito's."

Silence. Then, "I'll see you tomorrow."

"The thing is, Ruth needs food and we need—"

"I can't hear you. I'll come tomorrow."

23

Early the next day, the kitchen was dark and there was no breakfast. I found Sara sitting by the old man's bed, his face covered with the same yellow sheet he'd held up to his chin when I'd first arrived at the house. His sparse, combed-over hair was visible at the top of the sheet. Sara had apparently washed him; the sheet, wet in places, clung here and there to his body.

"He mumbled all night. Gibberish," Sara said. Her eyes were red from lack of sleep. Sara uncovered his face. "He's at peace." Mamá's waxlike face in her casket, drained of expression, had the same quality of goneness and strangeness as the old man's. Sara took my hand. Hers was warm and rough, and I felt lucky to touch what her hands had touched, even the old man's cold skin. Her hand made it easier to look at his rigid white face.

Sara said, "You asked me last night about that boy, Hernando. I thought about it. You know what my husband told me once?" I shook my head, and Sara said, "One afternoon, years ago, Juan's mother—Juan called her Maman Martine—she served Juan a piece of her guava tart and a cup of *café con leche*. The two were eating at the table when two Malangones, young Oscar and his father, knocked on the door. This Maman Martine set down her cup, let them in, then went into her bedroom and shut the door behind her. Oscar and his father pulled Juan into the backyard and roughed him up good. Juan had made the mistake of tutoring that boy Hernando a few times, and the Malangones made him pay for it. *Maricón, pervertido, degenerate*. All through the beating Juan's Maman sat in the bedroom, listening. She sat on a chair—no one was allowed to sit on the beds once they were made in the morning—and after a while she got up, went into the backyard, and stopped the beating by giving the Malangones an aquamarine necklace of real stones from her birth town in Guadeloupe. The Malangones left, and she nursed Juan with kindness and love. But she must have felt that her necklace was wasted because months passed and Juan didn't change his ways and kept chasing men. And here's the thing"—Sara pressed her lips together in consideration—"sometimes I wonder if it was jealousy of that boy that made her do it, not Juan's chasing men instead of women. This Maman Martine, eaten up by jealousy of this boy that Don Juanito loved like a son." Sara looked very sad. She shook her head once, then said, "Even after the Malangones' little visit, Juan kept tutoring Hernando here and there for a few years until the boy hit puberty, gave up his lessons, and started running up and down the block with his older brother and the neighborhood thugs, pissing in the street in daylight, and keeping his mouth shut when his family spread their Malangón lies about Juan."

I pictured Hernando and Don Juanito reading side by side, the fuming Maman Martine pouring them coffee, watching the two of them from over the top of her magazine. I wondered if Hernando had ever defended Juan. Or had Hernando, little by little, given in, closed the old man's books and pretended to hate the lessons, and to hate the old man too? Maybe it was Don Juanito who'd advised Hernando not to turn himself into a commodity, and from then on Hernando couldn't look at Juan, who was walking proof of Hernando's cowardice when it came to standing up to his family and their taunts and threats. Was this also why Hernando longed to go abroad and start over and live in the truth?

I didn't know. And where was he now? I thought of Ruth's law: Jehovah gives and takes away, which made life and death sound like simple arithmetic. But Ruth's presence didn't make up for Hernando's absence or for Don Juanito's death. There was no equity in anything.

Sara left the house to make the arrangements for Juan, and when Ruth woke, I fed her broth and half a boiled egg, brushed her teeth, combed her white hair back from her forehead, and splashed her with the old man's cologne. Her eyes were more focused, and for the first time she said more than "Leave it be," a phrase she used whenever she found her soup too thick or too salty. At other times, even if she liked the food, she whispered, "Time will tell"—not a word of thanks to Jehovah or to anyone. Before the DSI, Ruth would've bowed her head and prayed in gratitude to Jehovah before each meal.

This time after eating, Ruth looked up at me with mild recognition and thanked me. Then she asked for her Bible.

"It's not here," I said, thrilled at her lucidity and ashamed that I'd never tried to recover her Bible from the fallen house.

Ruth frowned. "What kind of house doesn't have a Bible?"

"We'll get you a Bible."

"I want mine," she said, "the red one on top of the nightstand. Bring it here." She scrunched up her face and her eyebrows rose, as if her mind were struggling to get back to the time and place before her arrest. She almost seemed to reach that place, but then her expression dulled again.

Ruth and I were still at the table, me trying to get her to recall more things and people—Juan, Doña Barbara, maybe even call me by my name—when the sound of a car came from the street. A bright-blue Lada had pulled up to the curb. Mariela emerged from the driver's side, her hair bunned up like Audrey Hepburn's. She looked radiant and gave off the air of what Doña Barbara had called "prosperity." Seeing Mariela again, I had to admit that against my better judgment, I'd missed her a little.

I went out and opened the front gate. Mariela said, "Finally I see you." She turned back and waved to another Lada, yellow and white, parked a few houses down the block. "Pablo and Ramón. State security," she said to me. "Go ahead, wave to them." I waved to the two dark silhouettes behind the windshield and the dark silhouettes seemed to wave back.

"They keep tabs on you?" I asked.

"They keep an eye out *for* me."

We went into Juan's garden, and I wondered if Mariela understood that she had led two security officers to the home of a dead, gay black marketeer, and to a Jehovah's Witness ex-jailbird. Mariela stood by the old man's roses, shading her eyes from the sun with her hand. I told her I had bad news: Don Juanito had died in the night, and Sara had gone to make the arrangements.

Mariela looked at the house. "He's in there?"

"We haven't told Ruth about it," I said.

"Before we go in," Mariela said, stopping at the door, "I need you to know something. I've let go of what happened between us. It was a fight between sisters, okay? You took my money and had no use for me until you needed something. Still, here I am."

I nodded, for peace's sake. In any case, I was glad she'd come.

Inside, Ruth looked up at Mariela from her chair and then smiled almost painfully. Her eyes immediately filled with tears, as did, to my surprise, Mariela's. Mariela walked quickly to Ruth and bent down and kissed Ruth's cheek.

"I knew you'd come one day," Ruth said. Mariela sat on the edge of a chair next to Ruth's and rested her head on Ruth's shoulder. Mariela's expression was kind, forbearing.

"You know who she is?" I asked Ruth. I suddenly burned with Maman Martine's searing jealousy.

Ruth took Mariela's face in her hands and Mariela smiled at Ruth. "My baby," Ruth said. "Such a long time." She pulled Mariela down and kissed the top of her head. "You're exactly as I dreamed."

"Most nights she has nightmares," I said, bitter.

"Is that right," Mariela said.

Mariela didn't stay long. She glanced at what she guessed was Don Juanito's bedroom and raised her eyebrows to me as if to ask, In there? I nodded, and Mariela nodded back solemnly. Soon she motioned to go, and Ruth, like a well-behaved child who accepts arrivals and departures, didn't protest. She kissed Mariela and for the first time spoke of Jehovah, who made all things right in the end.

Mariela and I went to the curb. She opened her car door and waved to the two men in the yellow Lada parked down the block.

"This is the best she's been so far," I said. I had to admit it; Ruth hadn't been half as alert in the days she'd been out of jail as during the previous few minutes with her "baby."

"Now that we got her out of that place," Mariela said, "she can mend. I'll help her." She put her hand on my arm.

"Sara got her out."

"With my money, I guess," Mariela said casually, and she brushed back some strands of hair that had escaped her Audrey Hepburn bun.

"Since you got Ruth arrested in the first place and her house destroyed and you profited from the sale of her things, one could say it was Ruth's money."

Mariela pushed the opened car door shut behind her. "So this is what you've been storing up. And I didn't even press charges when you broke into my bedroom and stole from me."

"I was trying to get Ruth out of jail. You never did."

"How do you know what I did or didn't do?" Mariela spoke without raising her voice, maybe to keep the security boys out of it, but her coolness, as usual, unnerved me. "Let's get some things straight once and for all," she said. Her voice was low but there was heat in it. "Because of that woman I lived in orphanages all my life. I never saw my real mother or my country. Never knew about *you*. And you never knew about *me*." She half whispered and half hissed, "I didn't put that woman in jail. *I* fed her. That old witch would have died in that hellhole without me. She would be as dead as Don Juanito is now. And you would have starved out here."

"What did you do to Ruth's house?"

Mariela drew a breath. "The house fell, Yuri. How many times do I have to say it? It was an accident. We were fixing it up for Ruth, and Oscar and his friends botched the job. What do I know about house repairs?" She placed her palm across her forehead and said, "The neighbors grabbed Ruth's things afterward. It's ugly, but it's not my fault." Finally, as if she'd spent herself having to yell at me without raising her voice, she leaned back against the car and looked toward the security boys in their Lada. "I don't know what you want. The facts are the same: Ruth is not well, you're a minor, and I'm all you've got. When you called for help, I came. But nothing is good enough for you."

She opened the car door and slid into the driver's seat. If she drove away furious in her blue Lada, followed by Pablo and Ramón, I had no idea how Ruth would eat. I'd have to tell Sara I'd screwed up everything for Ruth, first with Mariela's secret rockets, and now with my thoughtless rage.

Mariela said through the open car window, "I came here to tell you that my projects are getting notice. That I'd get Ruth what she needs in this country." Mariela looked away through the windshield. She rested her forearm in the frame of the open window. "And I came to tell you that I've thought about you this whole time. I've thought how you might want something different. Something more than this kind of life." I saw her disdain for the kind of life she'd claimed in her magazine interview that she'd been robbed of. She looked up at me and I braced myself. She said, "How much can you do for Ruth here? You and I can do more for her if we live abroad. In New York. That's what I've thought about."

It was nearly the same offer Hernando had made me, to go to *la yuma* and send help to those left behind. It was also the prediction Amadora had made in her courtyard, that Mariela and I would leave this place for *el norte* and not look back. With Hernando, if we'd made it there alive, I would have crossed the ocean on a crowded stolen boat or on a flimsy raft as part of an "us," he and I huddled with other refugees in a sort of continuation of all we'd known, the neighborhood and people, dead and living, the familiar accents, the jokes, and the foods that had nourished us all our lives. But going to *la yuma* with Mariela, I suddenly understood, would let me leave myself behind. Despite her cries about her stolen country, Mariela had none of this country deep in her bones. With her I'd start from nowhere, become a stranger to all and maybe to myself. There was something to this thought that felt sweeping and radical and brilliantly painful. I didn't recoil from it.

Sunlight made flickers of brightness on the Lada's windshield. And I thought I saw my own temptation there, a small, shiny, almost reachable thing. I wasn't afraid. Mariela tucked her hair behind an ear and said, "We'll earn more in New York. And send more. Here you're a burden to Ruth."

"So you're not staying here with your people?"

Mariela ignored my sarcasm. "The kind of work I have to do now is in New York. I have a show scheduled there, lots of footage for exhibits—videos and such. You can help with that work and we'll both send money and supplies to Ruth and Sara. And we'll let everyone know the truth about this place, its rivers and valleys, its schools, its support for artists. North Americans know nothing of life here."

I thought Mariela could save her patriotic speeches for *Juventud Rebelde* journalists who ate them up. Her new plan, the two of us in *la yuma* as ambassadors of goodwill among nations, was as absurd and grandiose as her other projects. Yet I couldn't deny that she'd gone through with them all. Maybe there was something about the world that she understood and I didn't. I wanted to know what that something was. Of course, Mariela had left in her wake a number of "accidents"—Lucho's life, Ruth's house, Ruth's mind—and this was a charitable way of saying it, because the terrible question in my gut was still whether some of these hadn't been accidents at all. Yet some part of me, a reckless, wicked part, suddenly wanted to get in her blue Lada and go back with her to El Focsa, followed by Pablo and Ramón in their yellow Lada, and then keep going, through the sky to New York City.

Mariela must have sensed my change of heart. Or maybe she was peering with me over Ruth's precipitous drop, admiring the chasm as a rich panorama. "I've told you," she said, warmer, "*she* would have wanted us together."

"Mamá never told us about each other. That's how much she wanted us together." But I realized that I hadn't said "my mother."

The Tilting House

Mariela shrugged. "A friend of mine has an apartment in New York. You can study, learn English." She paused. "Think of it as a vacation. You can come back here if you don't like it."

"If I get a permanent exit permit I won't be allowed to come back to live here. I'll just be a visitor like you—if they let me."

Mariela looked through the windshield to the potholed street and said coolly, "I guess you'd be a kind of visitor, here and everywhere you go from that point on. Like me." She depressed the clutch and turned the key in the Lada. "But aren't you a visitor now, you and Ruth, in a stranger's home?" I wanted to ask whose fault that was, but Mariela turned to me, weary, and I felt her leaving me and Ruth for good. "There are worse things than being a visitor. You can stay in this house that isn't yours and never live out your fate. Ruth is old. Sara will take care of her for a fee, and we will pay it." She shifted gears in the car. "I'm done talking. You're realistic. You see what I'm offering. Take it or not." She pulled out into the street and in a moment Ramón and Pablo passed me in their yellow Lada. Ramón (or Pablo) waved.

A few days later, I took her offer. I told myself I'd send for Ruth as soon as I had a place in *la yuma*.

24

My three-month visitor's permit for New York felt like a small miracle. On November 13, after waiting in long lines at different offices in the city center, I got my passport, but only a temporary visa—Mariela couldn't prove that she was my blood sister, a family connection needed for a permanent exit.

I was immensely lucky. During the Special Period, very few Cubans received visas to go abroad, even for a short time. Many thousands took to the sea in those years on homemade rafts bound for South Florida. Many thousands never made it. Hundreds were picked up half dead in open waters by the U.S. Coast Guard; others washed up in the middle of the night on some black shore or in broad daylight, at the feet of bewildered sunbathers. Yet here I was with my brand-new visa, a strangely privileged traveler from a socialist state bound for New York City. Mariela was right; I went on taking from her, benefiting from her resources and contacts even as I deeply mistrusted her ways. I rejected the hand that fed me while I kept on filling my belly. Was this all I was, a body greedy for sustenance, comfort, escape? In New York, I'd seek asylum and send for Ruth; this was all I knew. And if Hernando had made it to *la yuma*, I might be able to find him, or maybe he could find me.

Back at Don Juanito's house that November afternoon, my visa and passport in hand, I found Ruth sitting in the garden's soft light. She had gotten stronger over the past few weeks. As she sat placidly among the tall plants, looking through advertisements for long-vanished Jell-O and Hellmann's mayonnaise in a wrinkly copy of *Ladies' Home Journal* that Sara had pulled from Maman Martine's old trunk, I wondered if, with time, she'd come to believe the old man's house was hers, and Mariela and I might disappear from her mind—a blessing maybe. I wondered if this would happen to me too. Would I forget everyone—Ruth, Mamá, Tere, Sara, Hernando—after I landed in *la yuma*? There was still no word of Hernando. I had promised to flee with him on a crowded boat or flimsy raft and live in the truth, but instead I'd decided to fly away on an airplane and live with the sister who was no real sister of mine. I tried not to think of my betrayal too often, or of Amadora's curse, but all of it lodged inside me, and part of me wondered what kind of person I really was.

"I'm going away for a while," I said to Ruth in Juan's garden.

She looked up from her *Ladies' Home Journal*. "You're going to school?"

"Yes."

"Don't believe everything they tell you there."

"I'm not going to the Lenin," I said. "I'm going to school in *la yuma*, in New York. To learn English."

Ruth looked up, delighted. "Make sure you visit the Empire State Building."

I promised to send pictures. Ruth said yes. Then she said, "Tell your mother to smile right. She never smiles right for the camera."

"I'm going to live with your daughter," I said.

"My daughter." Ruth beamed. "Please tell her that I can't go see her in the north yet. When I get better. Ask her to send for me."

DAYS LATER, AS the airplane took off and I watched the island shrink and then disappear outside the small window, it came to me, the kind of person I was. I realized with a shudder that I'd probably never send for Ruth, and that like many others buckled in their seats around me, I'd just traded something precious for something shinier. It also struck me—and I shook inside as I thought this—that I might not be too lonely or confused in the new place, as many like me were also doing the same heartless thing—leaving their old lives and making their way—and that I had Mariela in the north to help me.

25

Winter settled into Manhattan soon after I arrived. Mariela borrowed an old coat and a pair of gloves from an artist friend, and with them on, I roamed up and down Broadway, then east and west between the rivers.

Everything in the city appeared as enormous and fast as it had in the few black-and-white movies of New York I'd seen in Havana. I learned to walk faster and to fix my face with a neutral expression; I didn't want to show the astonishment I felt at the sight of skyscrapers, and at the men's bright loops of scarves, the women's shiny, tall boots, the older ladies' fur-collared coats and their dogs also wrapped in lavish sweaters. At all hours the fierce bustling went on, for work, for money, to get somewhere, then somewhere else, and I tried to keep up as best I could.

Bob Sands's Alphabet City walk-up was tiny and cramped, cluttered to the ceiling with papers and books and boxes. There was no corner in the apartment in which to hide or to be left alone. My bed was a foldout in the living room–kitchenette, and

I couldn't sleep much, as Bob and Mariela were up late, lounging on the couch and watching the TV. The "bathtub," a plastic contraption that slid out of a kitchen cabinet, got filled from a rubber hose running from the sink. Bob was tall, balding, older than Mariela by a couple of decades—she'd been his student in a philosophy course—and their drinking, fights, loud sex in the tiny bedroom, and the occasional party of Mariela's artist friends and Bob's students went on through the winter. Each night I stayed out as late as I could.

Some mornings, while Bob got ready for work, Mariela took a few dollars from his wallet and gave them to me; she'd circled a few spots on the subway map and off I went. I didn't visit the Empire State Building or the Statue of Liberty as Ruth had urged. Instead, I looked at pictures of these landmarks in yellowed books under the cathedral ceiling of the Forty-Second Street Library. Sometimes, following a bad night, I'd lay my head down on the library's mahogany table and nap between the pools of lamplight. All day I read books in Spanish and tried to teach myself English from children's picture books and grade school history texts. From those history books I learned about the Brooklyn Bridge and, as my reading improved and I could decipher passages with a dictionary, I learned from other books about Manhattan and Wall Street's "wall," erected to keep out bewildered natives and later used as backdrop for a slave market on the corner of Pearl Street. The world was walls and money, I thought. And I was my own kind of wall, too, reading without aim in the silence of the library, in the wood and stone shadows, under the arching pink clouds of the ceiling.

At 8:45 p.m. the library lights flashed three times, and I'd have to walk out with the others, mostly loners, homeless, or the insane, down the broad marble steps between the white sentinel lions. I'd make my way to a cheap restaurant on St. Mark's Place and order steaming chicken soup and try to puzzle out words in my borrowed book (Mariela had given me her library card) or, as I'd done in El Focsa, eavesdrop on conversations at the tables beside me. I still had hopes of becoming a journalist, but those hopes seemed far off now that I had to learn new words as if I were a toddler. I tried to match the sounds I heard around me with the words I'd read in the library, and when it got late and my head hurt from my efforts, I rode the subway to my stop, walked the few icy blocks to Bob's walk-up and slipped into my foldout bed, having hardly said a word to anyone all day.

It struck me after a month in New York that I was living a different version of my old dream, wandering alone in a sort of urban *manigüa*, studying, speaking little—though, as usual, not how I'd pictured it—and like all dreamed existences, this one felt weightless, distressing, but ultimately left no imprint. I felt as if everything important in my life had already happened, and whatever I was doing now or would do afterward would leave little mark. I was floating, untethered, living up to my astronaut name as Hernando might say. I read nonstop in the library to keep myself from panicking at my weightlessness (once I'd felt it I couldn't stop feeling it) and to distract my mind from Hernando, but nearly everything I read or saw in the city sooner or later reminded me of him.

Despite my floating, dreamed-up life, the hard ground was there beneath my feet. One afternoon I practically kissed it when I stepped from a curb and twisted my foot badly on Fifth Avenue and Thirty-Sixth Street. I fell diagonally onto the street, and a sharp pain shot up my leg. People's shoes went by my head until a man bent toward me and helped me up, the tip of his blue tie brushing my eyes. "You okay?" he asked. I said no, but when the man asked me again, I realized I had to say yes, and then he nodded, smiled kindly, and headed down the street. I limped to the train and back to Bob's apartment. Mariela happened to be home. She frowned at my swollen ankle. "Let's not tell Bob about this," she said. Her hair was pulled back tight; I could tell she hadn't washed it for days. "He can't afford it." She put a bag of frozen vegetables on my ankle and turned back to the loud TV. On the screen a blond woman pointed to a map of the United States. Above the Eastern Seaboard a smiling sun shone down on the cities of the coast, though far away in Texas it would rain; lightning zigzagged from a purple cloud over the middle of the state.

"Bob paid for your trip to Cuba, right?" I poked the bag of frozen vegetables and felt my swollen ankle throb beneath it. "And for my plane ticket here?"

"Bob helped a little and now wants to lord it over me."

In New York, Mariela had become nervous and morose. The queenly coolness by which she'd moved events in Havana had disappeared, and she complained regularly about people who hadn't kept promises or returned phone calls. Apparently, the city hadn't stopped to admire Mariela's videos of her Taino and Afro-Cuban Nadies bleeding paint from gunshots and plaster wounds. "No place is more closed-minded than New York," Mariela said to me once after she'd been on the phone for hours yelling and cajoling into the receiver. When she and Bob smoked their joints, she sometimes sobbed, and Bob held her. Then they'd gobble cereal straight out of the box.

"Before you go to sleep, put those vegetables back in the freezer." Mariela turned off the TV. "Here we *will* starve."

"Maybe we should go back."

"Back where?" She looked astonished, then grabbed the remote and switched on the TV again.

ONE FROZEN MORNING, a bundled-up man on Madison Avenue, woolly flaps over his ears, said to a woman from behind his steamy pretzel cart, "You want mustard with that?" and I made out clearly his five separate words. Then, a few days later, in an incident that could never have happened in Havana, I got to test my grasp of English again in real time. I'd left the library early (Mariela wanted me to help with a dinner for Bob's friends) and I spotted a kid, no older than me, stranded halfway up a tall glass-paneled building on Park Avenue and Forty-Eighth Street. A spotlight from below circled him. The kid wore suction cups on his hands and feet. I stood with the crowd behind a perimeter of yellow tape and a round rescue net as the police officer spoke calmly into a megaphone, urging the small figure to come down. The boy, after many minutes, stuck on what must have been the fifteenth floor, glanced up to the stories above him, then down to us gathered below. He kept still for a moment, then, making his mind up perched above a few dozen puzzled and entertained gawkers, he suctioned his way down the windows. I held my breath with the crowd. When he reached the bottom, all of us cheered, and the policeman handcuffed him and put him in the police car.

That night the spectacle was replayed on the ten o'clock news. I told Mariela, sitting beside me on Bob's couch, what the cop had said. I was proud to have understood him as I stood on the street half frozen with the crowd. "You could have killed yourself if those windows got wet," the cop had said. "Next time check the weather, kid." For an instant my upward-staring face appeared on the screen beside the upward-staring faces of other New Yorkers and for the first time I felt I was a kind of New Yorker too.

"That's a stupid stunt," Mariela said about the suction-cup boy, and her voice sounded as harsh and judgmental as Ruth's. Had she forgotten her own smoking rockets flying above Lucho's grave? Or her bullets tearing at the Nadies' clay vulvas and hearts? I wanted to say this to her, but Mariela looked dark in the eyes, and I thought that maybe she already knew this. She, too, was an attention-getter, a performer. The kid had gotten a good-sized crowd to watch, and TV coverage too, and maybe this was what riled her. She went to bed before the news was over.

26

The end of winter brought a rush of hope to the city. In Havana, each season slid unnoticeably into the next, but in the north, one's heart seemed to reset itself when green buds tipped the branches of the dead-looking trees and fat red flowers popped out of planters beneath the brownstones' windows.

With spring, Mariela, too, came back to life. She showed a few photographs of her Cuban works at a gallery and made a small splash. Then a quiet young painter started showing up at the apartment any time Bob was away at a conference, and then whenever he traveled to Pennsylvania to visit his old mother. When Bob came back, his and Mariela's operatic fights resumed.

Now that I halfway understood him, Bob sometimes spoke to me at night at the tiny kitchen table, especially whenever Mariela was out late, possibly with the young painter. Bob grilled me with questions and gave me desperate looks, as if I held the key to Mariela's fickle heart. He asked me, over and over, what Mariela wanted. I didn't know, I said. It exhausted me to answer him evasively in poor English. I shrugged, shook my head, not going so far as to say that I knew her less than he thought, or that in the United States she seemed different. But I tried to be honest when I could and claimed ignorance of the language when I couldn't.

That summer my life with Mariela changed. I had received my residency card in the mail, and Mariela (or Bob—I never found out) paid for my enrollment at Kingsborough Community College. On campus, a steel-girded dome pointed to the sky, and ex-hippie professors in scruffy clothes and natural hair taught English language classes. I studied hard and halfway through the semester, Ms. Emerson, a short lady with colorful earrings and glasses hanging from a chain around her neck, approached me to ask if I would stay at her house on weekends to take care of her cat Lulu while she did field research in New Jersey for her dissertation on computer-assisted instruction to second-language students. Ms. Emerson spoke good Spanish. She said she loved where I came from and had "great respect" for my people. Her car's bumper sticker declared, "I don't believe the CIA." She was a little airy like Mariela, but her house was quiet and full of books, and she never threw late-night parties. For the next seven weekends in her empty house, I sat on her couch with Lulu the cat and parsed out passages from Toni Morrison's *Beloved*. I managed with great effort, with my earmarked English/Spanish dictionary, and sat tortured and terrified and torn open by Morrison's words. In that silent house, I felt almost happy, almost at peace.

I liked Ms. Emerson. She had read countless books, owned intricate gadgets, disparaged those who lived for possessions, and asked me little about my previous life. After one of those cat-sitting weekends, she offered me her spare bedroom to stay in during the school year. "Your little dorm, if you want." She introduced me to her friends as her "Cuban daughter." Like so many others, she assumed I wanted passage into Americanness.

The kindness of American strangers didn't cease to surprise me in those first days. Were Americans, unlike what I'd been told in Havana, simply generous and welcoming? Or were they possibly wishful and romantic, taking my quiet and my books and my polite nodding for docility or honesty or hope, which somehow justified their time and help? I also wondered if (white) Americans supposed that no one, if given a chance, would pass up becoming them.

In any case I felt mostly grateful, and in my outward actions I didn't prove them wrong. I moved my things little by little to Ms. Emerson's room. At about the same time, Mariela moved too, left Bob and went to live in an apartment in Queens, rent-controlled, with two decent bedrooms. The new place belonged to Anton Morrisen, the young painter. He and Mariela soon covered their walls with their art and their friends' art and spent their days working in a small studio Anton rented off Lenox Avenue in East Harlem. Of course, the beauty and order of the apartment rested on Anton's money.

Mariela cut her hair into a pageboy and dyed it pitch-black. When I visited her in the new apartment, she looked glamorous in Anton's bright kitchen, boiling pasta and chopping vegetables on the butcher-block countertop—chores I'd never seen her do. On my first visit she said, "With me, you're free to come and go as you like. As long as you're happy." She then asked me to move in with her and Anton. I said I wanted to stay closer to campus. In truth, I'd had enough of Mariela's late-night parties, her smoking and drinking, and her dramatic claims of sisterhood. Mariela said, "With this Ms. Emerson, I guess." She kept chopping vegetables, making a mound on the counter with the large knife. I told her that I was becoming someone of my own invention. I said this arrogantly; deep down I suspected invention had much less to do with it than mimicry—I imitated what Americans like Ms. Emerson did, their gestures and words, their tone of voice, their attitudes, and I spent considerable time shaping my mouth to the pop songs on the radio. What I accomplished was my own approximate version, to which I added ideas I picked up from books, magazines, newspapers. Mariela said that she'd become someone new too. She was in love with Anton. "Isn't it obvious?" she asked.

The sourness of winter with Bob in his cramped, dingy apartment seemed to have left her, and she wanted me to be happy for her. She opened a bottle of prosecco and brought out glasses. In Anton's white kitchen, her searing grievances about the past had given way to a gentler, more self-mocking nostalgia. She had plans for us. "We'll go to Nebraska when your semester ends. Take a road trip. I want you to see where I grew up, the nuns' school." I should see America's heartland, she said, just as she'd seen the blue mogotes of Cuba's interior. Then she smiled as if amused at her own crazy wish to go back to the land of swaying cornfields and angry farmers and Oliver Twist tables in the orphanage. That I had no such wish to see them never occurred to her, as usual, or that I was now tired of her grim history and of mine.

Her sudden good humor, preferable to her bitterness, drew me to her, but it also unsettled me; I suddenly didn't know my place in her life. Every day in New York I had desperately worked to leave Mariela behind, but now, in Anton's kitchen, I panicked like a child when thinking she'd do the same to me. It didn't occur to me then, or for many years afterward, that Mariela might have seen me as a gift, not as a consolation prize for her stolen childhood. This was my own failure of imagination.

Mariela turned down the stove and went into the bedroom. She came out with an envelope, handed it to me. The handwriting was Sara's, but the words were Ruth's.

My dear daughters,

I love you with all my heart. Jehovah has given me a chance to be in this world for a little longer, and I got your letter and now I know I have done well while on this Earth . . . [I'd written to Sara and Ruth several times from Bob's apartment; Mariela had also signed at the bottom and put the stamped envelopes in the mail, but only Sara had answered, back in the spring—now here was Ruth.] *I help Sara with the boys and they bring me joy. The garden has been fallow, but every day I wait to see if a flower comes and today several white buds appeared and I see your faces there, in Martí's favorite blossom. The two of you stay warm and you keep on studying, Yuri, and learning from your older sister, who will guide you in all things. Life here is the same but I mind nothing because my daughters are where they should be, and I know I made this happen while Jehovah gave me life.*

With all my affection and mother's love,
Ruth

I folded the paper, put it back in the envelope. Mariela watched me put it in my pocket as if it had been addressed to me alone. My grief, reading from the crisp white paper, touching it, almost matched my joy at Ruth's lucidity. I told Mariela something I'd never dared to say, "Do you ever think Ruth might have been in love, like you are now, and got carried away? Claimed you as her daughter because she wanted something of her own?" Mariela waited me out. I said, "Maybe she thought she was doing right when she sent you here as a child."

"Yes," Mariela said, "she thinks she's saved *both* our lives. But you tell me, who's the one paying for *her* life?"

"Ruth has paid too," I said.

"Has she?" Mariela set her drink on the counter. Her expansiveness, the sun-lit Nebraska cornfields, had disappeared. She said, "So you say I'm in love now, I have a sister, I have my art. You say we all make mistakes. We all do wrong when we think we do right." She paused. "This is what you've come up with? Forgive and forget?" Her eyes shone; she gave me a mocking smile. "Are you the forgiver of this family?" She took up her glass as if to toast me, then said, "Not me. In my art I put myself in the moment of grief." She gulped down her glass of prosecco, and I saw her swallow her bitter little pill, that her art was fueled by suffering. She seemed proud of this, the way her bitterness kept her bold, raw, and her projects alive; she might have thought she couldn't do without it. "Our mother must have raised you right," she finally said, going now to the heart of her own grief. "And don't bother forgiving *me*. It makes me irrelevant."

PART FOUR

Return

Havana, 2015

27

For twenty-two years I did all I could to make Mariela irrelevant. I didn't forgive, didn't forget; I simply moved away, hardly saw her, and after a while stopped speaking to her.

Eventually I stopped writing to Ruth and Sara too, and tried not to think of them much or of the old neighborhood and what had happened there in the summer of 1993.

During my college years in New York, while writing an article late at night for the student paper or while deep in conversations that had nothing to do with my old life, I'd sometimes catch a glimpse of Ruth, or Sara, or sometimes both, hovering silently by my side or lingering in the room just within my peripheral vision. Occasionally, I'd catch them glancing at me, their looks grave. But they didn't stay long, didn't berate me, and I'd go on eating dinner or correcting an article or speaking to a friend.

At first, I wrote Ruth and Sara letters, some real and others in my mind, and sometimes, alone in my room, I'd talk to them. I'd say, Now I'm living in this old dorm in Queens with creaky stairs and bad heating and the smell of grease from pizza cartons in the hallways. I read many books in English at the university library. When I first go up the library steps each morning and into the building out of the cold, the quiet of the reading room scares me and I feel like an intruder. And then, slowly, I settle into it, slip into a book away from everything and from myself and from you, and it's a relief, even a joy, and when I come back from the spell it takes a second to remember my name and where I live and who I've become. And at this Ruth interrupts, Get over yourself, *niña*, be grateful, what's wrong with greasy pizza, it's delicious, I wish I could live in a place that smells of pizza and not of hunger. And Sara nods, and then Ruth, the old Ruth who could tear me apart with a glance says, What's wrong with marble steps or with the crushing pain of having left everyone? Get over yourself. You left your own mother's grave and turned away and went on breathing. You think you're the only one who cries at night, the only one who betrays? Get over yourself. Write us and say you miss us and love us—that's all we ask. But I say no to Ruth. Sometimes I'm glad, I say, endlessly happy to be free from everyone and from you. Disappearance was what I wanted. I'm not going to cover up my badness with letters and food packages. Like my deadbeat father, and like you, I choose to make my badness complete. I want my abandonment, in the long line of Vilar abandonments, to stand out in heartlessness and, I'm almost proud to say, in self-pity. It's my own devised punishment.

With time I saw Ruth and Sara less out of the corner of my eye. And finally, sometime after college graduation, they didn't come back. I suppose even ghosts have dignity.

THEN IN 2015, a historic event promised to change life on the island, and despite my long fight to stay away, I found myself back in Havana.

The U.S. Embassy was reopening in the city after fifty-four years, and my assignment for Reuters was to cover the last of Havana "before it changes," according to my editor. She meant before the city's crumbling fin-de-siècle art-nouveau architecture sprouted, as she said, "golden arches."

That week I made the short flight from Miami to José Martí Airport. Then, from the back seat of a 1957 Chevy taxi, speeding along the bay toward El Telegrafo Hotel in Central Havana, I saw the seawall again, deserted in the late July rain. The sky was gray and silver, the ocean the color of the sky. No one strolled along the normally busy walkway, no one sat on the miles-long brick wall facing the ocean. Groups of men and women bunched themselves up against the weather under the street porticos, waiting for the sun to come out.

Over the previous ten years on assignments for Reuters–Latin America, I'd often arrived in drizzly, developing capitals with their garbage heaps and squalor and touristy pockets of prosperity. In this, Havana seemed no different. But the city's familiar, dilapidated beauty pressed down on me hard, and I felt myself slip down into the Chevy's back seat as the gray people under the porticos disappeared and appeared in the wash of the windshield. By the time I stepped out of the car onto the wet curb of El Telegrafo I felt again the confused, aggrieved yearning of a sixteen-year-old and a sixteen-year-old's shame at feeling such yearning.

IN THE HOTEL's upscale lobby, the young woman in uniform at the counter looked over my American passport and explained the room rates. Back during the Special Period, Hernando and I had sometimes walked past El Telegrafo's dark, boarded-up doors, but now the polished lobby hummed with well-dressed guests from abroad. A bright mid-century chandelier hung from the ceiling, and beyond the lobby a thin veil of water cascaded over a tiled recessed wall and made a pleasing burbling sound just below the conversations.

Seated on the leather couch, a Miami Cuban family, parents and two teenage children, chatted in Spanglish; the children tapped at their phones. They were the witnesses—if any bothered to notice—of my first faux pas. When the old bellhop approached for my luggage, I held on to my suitcase and turned down his help with a polite wave of my hand. He and the perky young woman behind the counter exchanged glances; I'd reacted as if the bellhop were a thief. "The elevator," I tried to explain, "makes me a little nervous. I'd rather walk up the stairs with the suitcase," I said and blushed at my excuse. It was partly true; if the electricity died, the rickety Otis could stop between floors, and I dreaded sweating for hours in a hot, dark chute until the power kicked back in. I tipped the bellhop generously and he took my money and nodded, but I knew I'd marked myself as a stuck-up returnee, too good to entrust someone like himself—who'd stayed behind and endured poverty and indignity, and to whom I should hand over everything I'd brought, no questions asked—with my ridiculous suitcase.

Breathless, halfway up El Telegrafo's black marble stairs, I remembered that Havana's elevators ran day and night, now that Venezuelan tankers unloaded a hundred thousand barrels of oil in Havana's shipyards every month before heading back to Caracas filled with Cuban doctors, nurses, teachers, and others required to serve the fatherland for minimal pay in the fields and classrooms and hospitals of someone else's fatherland. Together the two countries had switched on the lights all across Havana. Their deal reminded me of colorful posters I'd seen once in the New York Public Library: earnest Industry shaking hands with plump Capital, whose shiny top hat resembled the smokestacks wafting blue-gray plumes into the sky behind them. Now in Havana, privately owned restaurants, *paladares*, served tourists at all hours, and electric fans whirled day and night in the rented rooms of *casas particulares*.

I set the suitcase on the bed and texted Kiara Johnson, my Reuters editor. She'd sent me here to cover the embassy's reopening and to shed light on the possible flood of U.S. investment. News of renewed Cuba-U.S. relations had excited many in Miami, outraged others, and filled a few like Kiara, who'd never been to Cuba, with funereal concern. "Before it changes, go see your country," she'd said to me in her tiny Miami Beach office.

"It's not my country," I'd answered—the same sort of pouty, teenage dismissal I'd given when anyone had called Mariela my sister.

Below Reuters's second-story office window, groups of my countrymen and women, whom I'd just denied, strolled up and down the open-to-the-sky Lincoln Road Mall. Some of their studied elegance, the men's white starched shirts and sharply creased pants and the women's high heels and maquillage, broke my heart a little. Their careful grooming struck me for the first time as an immigrant's small rebellion—a sign of stubborn disregard toward the careless dress code of our adopted city, its frayed shorts and flip-flops and pastel T-shirts. In our impeccable outfits we, the transplanted, turned our backs a little to the bigger country we lived in and staked our innocent and immodest claim to Miami's hybrid metropolis and its frontier skyline as if we'd raised this city ourselves out of the swamps of the receding Everglades.

"All right," I'd said to Kiara, extending my wrists as if for handcuffs, "book me."

On her computer screen, CNN streamed breaking news: the orange-faced developer from New York had just launched his presidential campaign. "I know how you feel," Kiara said, her eyes fixed on the screen. "My country's not my country either."

Kiara opened a new tab and booked my flight, and four days later, I stood with other Cuban American returnees at Miami International, each of their allotted forty pounds of luggage mummified in plastic. They'd soon hand their wrapped-up goods to their families in Havana, or maybe sell the shampoo, vitamins, toothpaste, aspirin, Sazón Completa packets, batteries, and other cargo to budding entrepreneurs on the island who, in turn, would use or resell them to a cousin of a cousin of a cousin. Standing in the bustle of one of MIA's long passageways, I felt useless; my small suitcase would help no one on the island. It carried only a few outfits, a change of shoes, and a handful of Mariela's ashes inside a plastic baggie.

The Tilting House

PALADERO PARK, SO grand in my childhood, had shrunk to human size. The white benches were painted a dark brown. The swing where the Prietos' visitor pumped her legs back and forth had disappeared, along with the large ceiba tree by Lucho's grave. I could see from one end of the park to the other. Much of the park's greenery had been razed.

"Hurricane Wilma," Chino, my driver, explained. "Then Ernesto."

A coral, flat-roofed, two-story building brighter than the weathered houses around it occupied the ground where Ruth's house had been. I'd seen Ruth's house fall and crumble, and still somehow I pictured not the rubble but the old Vilar home sitting on its spot as it always had, untouched. The new square building didn't fit the block or the neighborhood. I stepped from the car, fished my phone from my purse, and took pictures from various angles. Then suddenly on the phone screen, a gray-haired Dr. Cuevas rushed toward me, his arms open, his face astonished and gleeful.

"I look out the window," he said, hugging me on the park's sidewalk, "and there you are standing by that bench like when you were a kid." He beamed.

We talked of the recent changes to the park, then of the new, square building across the street. He said, "For so many years that lot sat empty, you know? Stray cats and dogs and kids roaming around garbage piles. It wasn't right." The neighborhood eyesore—and the site of Ruth's disgrace and Mariela's dissolute gatherings of long ago—had finally been redeemed in Dr. Cuevas's eyes. Who'd brought down Ruth's mighty house? Not Cuevas, his innocent look seemed to say.

He led me across the street. "Come, I'll show you," he said, seemingly proud. "Three years ago we got permission to build a house and a *paladar.*"

We.

The building's front door opened onto a long room of wooden tables; on each sat a thin vase sprouting plastic flowers. Around each table were four wooden chairs—a homey restaurant probably meant to serve locals or the few tourists who might wander this far from the city center. Behind the tables ran a counter with stools, and a small TV sat high on a shelf against the wall. To my astonishment, Sara Suarez, not the ghostly one I had imagined conversations with in my college years but the small, plump woman I loved, walked into the dining room with her quick, purposeful steps, untying a yellow apron from her waist.

Sara's hair shone white against her dark skin. She pulled me to her chest, and I smelled the scents of the old house, Don Juanito's house, where she'd taken me in when I'd had nowhere else to go. I rested my head in the curve of her shoulder and closed my eyes. Sara said, "I always figured one of these days you'd come back to us." She directed Dr. Cuevas and Chino to sit by the counter as she pulled me with her toward the bright kitchen. "Have a beer, boys," she said. "There's *beisbol* on the TV."

A thick stove, stolid like the building and built for serious cooking, sat against the back wall of the kitchen beside a large refrigerator. Sara poured us coffee and filled me in: She and Cuevas lived here together—I recalled her predilection for doctors—and the two of them, apparently Cuevas's "we," managed the small restaurant and the rooms for rent on the upper floor. They slept in one of the rooms. Her older boy now lived with his wife and children in Don Juanito's old house, and the younger boy served in the army in the provinces. Sara, to my surprise, knew of my job with Reuters and of my divorce; Mariela, it turned out, wrote her over the years, and my shame for not writing Sara was almost as great as my relief at not having to recount details of my life.

Then without preamble—I wanted to be done with it—I informed Sara that Mariela had died while driving too fast to her art show in Arizona. She'd quit both drinking and AA—neither of which had helped her—and was, ironically, sober, according to the police report, when she'd crashed against a semitruck. "She got to be a little famous," I said, as if this would soften the facts of Mariela's death.

Sara lowered her head and wiped her eyes with a dish towel. I told her I'd brought Mariela's ashes to scatter in Viñales according to Mariela's will. Sara nodded, but I could see her shrink from me a little. I knew what she thought: To many Cubans, lugging a loved one's gritty dust in a suitcase was gruesome, an insult to the deceased, and the epitome of bad luck. Dead people belonged underground, not bumping around in a plastic bag next to a person's underwear.

"I'm in charge of her estate," I added.

I didn't describe how things had been between Mariela and me before we stopped speaking. And I said nothing about Mariela's unexpected call from Arizona on the week of her death, when she left me a short, happy phone message about her upcoming art show as if there'd been no break between us and we'd just spoken the previous weekend. She'd said on the message that the bare horizon of the desert gave her "the creeps."

Other than that, she sounded cheerful; she'd try me again on her way back to New York. I couldn't say, then or now, that I'd planned to pick up the phone if she called.

But she never did. Instead, a polite sheriff dialed me from Mohave County. "Are you related to Mariela Vilar, ma'am?" He'd found my name in her wallet. He said quickly that he was sorry, went through the details, said he was sorry again, asked several questions. After a long silence he asked if I was okay. I managed to tell him that I'd be on the next flight out.

Sara poured more coffee. "This building, the restaurant, the rooming house"—she pointed upstairs above our heads—"is named Ruth's Casa Particular and Paladar. Did you know that?" I didn't. "It was what your sister wanted."

The name stunned me. Mariela had apparently named the place after her kidnapper. Was it her idea of reparations? Forgiveness? Or of asking for forgiveness? Was it a wry inside joke like the Canis-starred rockets she'd arranged on Lucho's grave? Why, I asked Sara, of all people, would Mariela get to name the building?

The *paladar*, it turned out, was part of a strange deal I'd also known nothing about. Over the years Mariela had sent money for Ruth's care—this much I knew—but Mariela had also continued sending cash after Ruth's death. The money, Sara said, built the *paladar* and the rooms above it on Ruth's lot, per Mariela's wishes.

"Your sister thought she might come back to live in this house someday," Sara said. "Or you might."

It never occurred to me that Mariela planned to come back to live in Paladero or, crazier, that she planned for the two of us to live here together. Did she see us passing our old age in rocking chairs on the new porch, drifting in and out of our minds like Ruth had at Don Juanito's, long forgetting the razing of Ruth's house and the raising of this new one over the old, Troy on top of Troy?

"I'm grateful for your sister's kindness, Yuri," Sara said.

I didn't know how to answer. I'd never thought of Mariela as kind, exactly. I'd thought of her as mostly faithful, and not so much toward people but toward the strange pledges she'd made to herself because of her stubborn, justice-seeking, and morally slippery dignity. She'd certainly taken me with her to the States and offered me options not available back in the country Mariela had once declared her own, even as she'd ruined my tiny corner of it. Now, sitting across from Sara in Ruth's rebuilt kitchen, I thought there were worse things than being loved like that, worse things than being wanted as Mariela had wanted me. And now Mariela had financed this rooming house and *paladar* without boasting of it. She'd provided for Sara and Cuevas and made them happy in their old age, and in her own sense of rightness, had built for herself (for us?) a house on Ruth's lot as she saw fit.

It wasn't wrong, this sort of restitution, if that was what it was, this effort to make amends. Unlike me, Mariela, by means of this building, helped some of the people we'd left behind.

But I saw too that by inserting herself permanently in the neighborhood Mariela had wiped out every bit of Ruth's old place and of my life before Mariela's arrival. Every step I took now in Sara's new kitchen, I bumped against Mariela's will to "destroy to build" according to her own whim, and I chafed against it and couldn't be at peace.

28

Just as Mariela had hidden her funding of Ruth's *paladar* and rooming house from me, I in turn decided to keep my new name hidden from Sara. I also kept from her the details of the last time I saw Mariela. I told myself that what happened on that visit would never make sense to Sara. It barely made sense to me.

The troubles between Mariela and me got worse in 2001, around the time I changed my name to Julie. "Is this Paolo's idea?" Mariela asked. She'd introduced me to Paolo at one of her after-exhibit parties on Miami Beach, referring to me, sarcastically, as her "mellow little sister." Paolo played bass, had curly hair like Hernando's but not the street-wary look in the eyes. After a round of drinks, I gave him my number and, on a whim, told him my name was Julie. The impulse astounded me at first, but as I drove home that night, it started to amuse me. By the time I parked the car by my curb, it made me quite happy. Paolo called the next day, addressed me as Julie, and I didn't correct him. It felt good to let go of Yuri, a cosmonaut's name smacking of the Cold War and Special Period.

Within a week I went to the courthouse and changed my name officially.

Paolo and I soon moved to a high-rise apartment overlooking downtown Miami. Each evening, we drank wine on the small balcony and watched the sun's white fire-line blaze down the length of the canal and plunge behind the tall buildings downtown. I felt calm, satisfied, glad to live away from seawalls and colonial forts, and away from Mariela. Below our balcony lay a half acre of well-maintained shrubbery and a green swath of grass. A small sign posted on the lawn warned, with red exclamation marks, of alligators swimming up and down the canal. Paolo and I found this amusing. For centuries Cubans had referred to their reptile-shaped island as a caiman, a long, sleepy alligator-like creature ready to pounce, and though I'd never seen one up close, there or here, the warning on the lawn struck me as some cartoon metaphor of a past that couldn't hurt me anymore.

Still, one morning as I gathered the mail, a neighbor rushed into the lobby crying; an actual alligator had snatched her poodle. It clamped onto one of the dog's hind legs with its caiman teeth and dragged it under in a Miami second. "Like a movie," the neighbor said, shaking, "so quick your eyes don't catch up to your heart."

Despite the lightning-fast, fearsome alligators lurking in the dark canal behind the building, I felt safe in the high-rise. My job with Reuters–Latin America kept my mind from its usual brooding and its steady, low-humming grief. I was pulled along lazily, pleasantly by Paolo's lighthearted love. After a few months we exchanged vows in the same downtown courthouse where I'd changed my name.

But the canal's alligators didn't sleep long. On a weekend after Paolo came home from Brazil—he'd made money with a friend in a Rio recording studio and traveled there often—Paolo played new pop and bossa nova for me and we had lovely sex. After our lovemaking, his cell phone rang while he showered. A text flashed: a love message from a certain Evelina. He departed for Brazil again that Monday.

The speed with which I hired a lawyer I'd met at a fundraiser stunned me a little. I said nothing to Paolo. When he returned from Rio, I handed him the divorce papers in the living room. He thought it was a joke, but as he turned over each page and read, his amused, cool smile went slack; his face turned puzzled and sharp. He said, "I thought you were different, Julie. I thought you were free. You know I live for my music." After weeks of wrangling and pleading didn't change my mind, Paolo finally said, "Why are you bringing this sad little lawyer into it? We could understand each other without her petty energy between us."

The day he finally emptied the apartment of his instruments, speakers, and cables, I shut the front door, took a long hot shower, and lay down naked on the bamboo floor of the mostly empty living room. I thought about the woman and her small dog walking along the banks of the canal and the horrific surprise that made her scream. I fell asleep on the cool planks and woke up shivering. My body hurt. I sat up in the hollowed-out room and in a panic, I called Mariela in New York. "Get out of there," she said, "it's depressing. Come up for a few days. Anton's at a conference. How long has it been?" She chided me for my distance, implying again that I only called when I needed her. Mariela was then in her early forties and had just mounted a show after what she called a "fallow period." Stretches without work were dangerous for her, she said on the phone; she'd been going to AA off and on for a year. I looked at the emptied-out apartment again, the gleaming floor and tall windows, the blank walls, and was afraid. I agreed to fly up to see her.

I wondered now if Mariela had written Sara of that last, disastrous visit. If so, I wanted to read that letter, to know what Mariela had thought about me that last time we saw each other.

MARIELA GREETED ME at the door of her Upper West Side loft with a glass of wine—the AA meetings weren't working at the moment, she said, festive; she'd go back soon. We spread out on the bedlike couch, surrounded by Anton's paintings, their books, Mariela's new colorful tapestries. The bohemian busyness of the room soothed me. Snow fell past the window. We finished the bottle of wine and celebrated my "freedom," as she called it; the yards and sidewalks outside lost their borders under the falling snow. I closed my eyes, sleepy from the travel and the wine, but Mariela roused me and out of nowhere said, "Just so you know, last time I went"—she didn't specify when or where—"I paid for ten years' upkeep of their two graves." She meant, of course, Mamá's and Ruth's. Ruth had died peacefully three years earlier; her heart gave out as she slept. Mariela went on, "I thought you'd want the two of them together. Almost got myself a spot too. But then I thought, when the time comes, Yuri will scatter my ashes around Viñales. It's my wish, okay?" She pointed at me, visibly drunk. "I want you to know my wish. Anyway, it'll be good for you to go back. You have to let go of things, Yuri. You can't go on like this."

I looked at her, incredulous. Letting go of things was surely Mariela's specialty.

"My name," I said, "is Julie."

Mariela lowered her head and half smiled. "That poor idiot you married. Did you ever tell him one true thing about yourself?"

THE NEXT EVENING, on our way to her new show, things between us changed again. As our cab made its way over the cleared streets, the lamps came on and whitened the housefronts and the road. Mariela sat, pale and fidgety, in the back seat next to me and tried to light a cigarette with shaky hands. The driver asked her to put it out. She looked frightened, and I thought of the girl put on a train by strangers, speeding backward toward other strangers. I took her hand and she grabbed on to my fingers until we arrived.

If this was the suffering for one's art I'd heard her boast of—the drinking, the shaky tobacco-tinged fingers, the worry and panic, the fights, the money troubles—it hardly seemed worth it. Yet maybe Mariela wasn't that unusual in her drama and strangeness. I knew an old plumber in Paladero who talked to himself loudly while walking down the street with his toolbox, and I recalled also a brilliant classmate in Queens, Martín Nava, who drank in public places until he passed out and at last shot himself in his girlfriend's parents' garage. Up and down Dimas or Forty-Second Street many of us acted out loud or silent dramas. Maybe we didn't write poems or paint pictures about our tortuous lives, never put ourselves in a novel for anyone to read about; if one of us killed ourselves as gruesomely as Julio's mother, no headlines or movies of the week were made from our tragedies. And we didn't make the cover of *Juventud Rebelde*. Yet many of us sought out witnesses to our pain one way or another.

The title of Mariela's show flashed from a digital display on the gallery's lobby wall, *Catharsis—Sins of the Heart(h)*. The *H*s in *hearth* lit up in a sequence that spelled out *earth*, then *heart*, and then back to *hearth*. Below the flashing, changing words, a pixelated Earth also spun, transforming itself from a fiery red heart into a blue planet and so on, back and forth. The lobby shone blue and red and purple from the changing lights of the display, and people's faces turned colors too. Mariela gave me her purse and began to greet the guests in the lobby.

I went past her into the gallery, where a tall oblong plexiglass case stood in the center of the room. I felt a similar wonder as when I'd stood before the rectangular microwave on the Prietos' table and watched its strange magic unfold. Inside Mariela's giant plexiglass case, a black chair was positioned behind a row of six brightly painted fairy-tale houses, as if Rapunzel's and Red Riding Hood's grandmothers had lived on the same block. Each fairy-tale house was a cutaway, and inside the kitchen of one, and the parlor of another, tiny clay versions of Mariela's colorful, large-bellied Nadies were busy at domestic chores—cooking, folding clothes, tucking in the sheets of a miniature bed. I felt the thrill of seeing the Nadies again, but the miniature cutaway scenes sent a shiver up the back of my neck. They were ironic, monstrous. I couldn't look inside them long or I'd have to leave the gallery and walk outside for air.

Mariela stood before the gallery crowd. She paused until everyone in the room hushed and paid attention. When they did, Mariela turned her gaze to the plexiglass box and the strange, fairy-tale neighborhood and large black chair. She raised her right hand, held it in the air, and when the silence of the room became unbearable, she pressed the tip of a penlike tool with her thumb. Inside the box, the tiny roofs and miniature doors and fairy-tale walls of the houses exploded, one by one like fireworks. Multicolored clay pieces and splinters of wood clattered against the smoke-filled glass box and fell to rubble on the smoky floor, and the audience flinched back reflexively from the hurtling debris and clatter inside the glass.

When the racket subsided, Mariela lowered her hand and walked to the side of the oblong case and entered through a door. She lowered herself into the black chair behind the row of ruined houses and Nadies and looked straight ahead in the dust and smoke. She sat fixed in her chair, half hidden in the swirl of smoke settling about her shoulders. Some in the audience clapped. As the rest recovered from the shock, all but me joined in the applause.

Mariela kept her sphinx stare. She didn't acknowledge the applause. Maybe she sat in her black chair all night. I couldn't say. I slipped out to the street as soon as the applause started to thunder. Mariela had brought me to witness another of her demolitions; she'd had me watch her triumphant, hollow gaze over the debris.

I still had Mariela's purse. I hailed a cab to her place, paid the driver to wait, and let myself in with her key. I grabbed my things, and at JFK around two in the morning I caught a flight back to Miami. I didn't answer my beeper, and I didn't speak to her again.

29

After dinner in Ruth's Paladar, Sara, Cuevas, and I sat at the kitchen table drinking coffee. Cuevas served me another cup and said, smiling, "Take, we have plenty." I told him if I drank any more I wouldn't sleep all night. He shook his head, amused. "Ruth used to give you milk and coffee every night before bedtime."

"That's why I never slept much."

"But you did," Cuevas said. "You slept long, even in the worst times."

I got up my courage and asked if he had news of old neighbors, Oscar, for example, or Hernando. (During my second year in New York I'd heard from Mariela that Hernando had made it out of the Seawall Riot alive; he'd been arrested and kept inside for months. By the time he was released, I'd already left for New York. Soon afterward Hernando got someone from El Cerro pregnant and married her. I stopped asking about him after that.)

Cuevas frowned at my question. "The younger Malanga-head? He's in some jail, last I heard." He shrugged as if it'd been inevitable. "Didn't he steal your grandfather's car?"

"No," I said. "Hernando never stole our car."

"Bags of shit, both of them," Cuevas continued. "I had to go along with the Malangón crooks in those days. I was like a matador before those beasts." He shook an imaginary cape before a bull. "But I'm no longer CDR president, you understand. It's been years."

"Hernando is in jail now?"

Cuevas shrugged. "It's what they say."

"And Oscar?" I thought Oscar might be able to tell me where Hernando was now. Or at least give me some proof that Amadora's omen had been wrong and that whatever bad luck Hernando shouldered his way into had nothing to do with me.

"Oscar was a bum," Cuevas said. "A delinquent like the rest of the family. After the wife let him make her three bellies, she kicked him to the street as he deserved." The old man looked at me fiery, happy to renounce Compañero Malanga-head and offer this as proof that he, CDR president, had been an honorable and reasonable man in those hard years, mediating the demands of an unreasonable system, doing his best to protect his neighbors in bad times. This new Cuevas in Ruth's rebuilt kitchen now distanced himself from all his past connections, his handwritten CDR reports during the Special Period, and the threat his very presence had posed to his neighbors in those years. I saw him as he used to be: neighborhood boss, occasional snitch, Oscar's go-to, dispenser of official and unofficial policies, wise judge, and sad widower.

"What about the Prietos?"

"They left the neighborhood years ago," Sara said. She took the cups and saucers to the sink.

"On account of the microwave?" I asked.

"It was a health hazard," Dr. Cuevas answered softly. His tone suggested that Cuevas, who'd sipped coffee each night in the Prietos' parlor, might have fulfilled the required duties of his CDR office after the microwave allegedly overloaded some neighborhood circuits, and his actions might have led to its impounding and to the Prietos' "relocation" to the countryside.

Sara said to Cuevas, "Outside this island everyone has microwaves, old man."

"That's no way to cook food. It's dangerous," Cuevas said.

Sara turned to me, conciliatory. "We don't know where the Prietos went, Yuri. A young couple lives next door. I take care of their boy sometimes." Her calm manner suggested forgiving and forgetting, those qualities Mariela had sarcastically assigned to me in Anton's apartment. Sara's tone seemed to imply that none of us—Cuevas, Oscar, Juan, Hernando, Mariela, the Prietos, Sara herself, or I—could be guilty of anything outrageous. We'd been defrauded and betrayed, like everyone else, and in turn our petty schemes and thieveries and betrayals couldn't be worse than anyone else's and were unavoidable from time to time—first world or second or third. All this had happened in the past, the terrible past of the Special Period, and who could ever understand the past?

But the absolution in Sara's voice didn't account for a different kind of offense that I'd witnessed in the city since returning, an offense for which, unlike bicycle thievery or microwave usage, there was no forbidding statute—and that was the hard stopping of time. In 2015, decades after the Special Period, '57 Chevys were still held together as if with *chicles* and string as they drove up and down along the seawall (their quaint backwardness attracting tourists), and buildings still flaked and tottered, and the black market thrived while the rationing bodegas sat mostly empty. Some blamed the failed policies of a cruel dictatorship, others the United States' cruel sixty-year blockade. Some blamed both, and others neither. But with the stopping of time came a cruel stopping of thought—the stale, decades-old attacks, insults, bromides, still endlessly recycled and presented as new. And the people on the worn-out island went on making do, busying themselves with small triumphs like the acquisition of a chicken for a dinner with friends, or the sudden return of electricity seconds before a favorite TV program started.

Time had also stalled for many of us who'd fled and now lived north of the strip of ocean that separated the two countries. In Miami's Little Havana, an industry of aged Cubans brought out wares of nostalgia to sell to tourists or to other aged Cubans on Social Fridays. Grizzled men bent over their dominoes or hawked cheap memorabilia from card tables: refrigerator magnets in the shape of the lost fatherland, Chinese-made key chains of the Cuban flag, carved wooden replicas of the tocororo in its nest, or of a palm tree invoking a lost Cuba that some still believed they'd return to one day, as if they could step into the same Florida Straits twice and travel back to Oriente or Camagüey and find their homes and towns and relatives as they'd left them.

And now, having just crossed back over those straits to the actual Havana and sitting across from Cuevas and Sara in this well-lit kitchen paid for by Mariela, on the spot where Ruth's own kitchen had stood, I still tried, with my stale teenage rage, to parse out the past and to apportion everyone's share of blame. But I also knew that I was searching for enough evidence to absolve me and all of us—some clue, for example, to debunk Doña Barbara's long-ago story that Mariela and Oscar, and maybe even Hernando, Juan, and Cuevas, had, back in 1993, dismantled Ruth's house for money. In short, I was a foolish, bothersome child seeking justice and some absolute answer that would settle all questions.

What was worse, I wouldn't stop. I proceeded to ask the aged ex–CDR president turned entrepreneur what exactly had brought down Ruth's house in the summer of 1993.

Cuevas sighed at my question as if he'd expected it all along and seemed almost relieved to be done with it. "That wasn't meant to happen," he said, shaking his head slightly. "It was one of Oscar's bright schemes in those days. He was crazy about your sister." Sara touched Cuevas's arm gently, reassuringly. Cuevas continued, "You know that your aunt's house was particularly valuable in some respects. Your grandfather did well in the thirties. He fixed up the house with fancy stuff, Spanish tiles, expensive cedarwood, even in the garage where no one saw it but himself whenever he parked his Chevy."

Abuelo Alberto's Chevy had nearly filled the garage like some hibernating beast until Hernando had fixed the engine and woke it back up, and he and I took it for our drive that night to the Ciudad Deportiva Stadium. As a child, I'd sat in the front seat of the stranded car, windows rolled down, and in the fuzzy dark of Ruth's garage, I turned switches and pressed dashboard buttons and held on to the steering wheel, pretending to drive along the seawall.

Now Cuevas had confirmed that the garage, the kitchen, and much of the house had come down, not because of an innocent mistake while renovating rooms for Ruth's return, as Mariela had always claimed, but because of a malevolent plan to rob Ruth of her tiles and beams and sell them for profit. "Oscar's scheme was a crime," I said. "And dismantling a house and selling the goods on the black market was illegal."

"Of course." Cuevas shook his head again. "It was a bad plan. A stupid plan. Oscar thought he'd sell the original beams and tiles to some high muck-a-muck and replace them with cheaper wood, rebrick around things. The house wasn't meant to fall down. But he was a fool. He took it too far. Your sister needed funds in those days. Her source in *la yuma* had dried up, that's what Oscar said—that your sister needed funds for her art, or whatever it was she did back then." Cuevas paused, then shrugged. "Oscar thought she'd be famous, and I guess he thought he'd get famous through her."

"Mariela knew what Oscar was up to? It was *her* idea to dismantle Ruth's house?"

"It was Oscar's idea. He was crazy about your sister," Cuevas repeated. "Anyway, it took a while. Juan wanted nothing to do with the scheme from the start, but he was—how can I say—vulnerable to official pressures like Oscar's and had helped sell some of the stuff on the black market. But other officials who'd been left out of the profits snitched on them both. Juan was not well by that time—he went, you know, before State Security showed up for any of this. But Oscar—they cooked his goose.

Property damage, theft, contraband, illegal sale of materials. They caught them, Hernando and Oscar both."

"They caught Hernando?"

"Grabbed him on the street. He had some of the money on him—a wad of dollars."

My heart sank. About this, Cuevas was wrong. Hernando had often wrangled a few dollars for a stolen bicycle or two in those days, but he'd never had a "wad," not until the afternoon he broke into Mariela's metal box to help me with Ruth's release. His possession of Mariela's dollars that day must have compounded his seawall riot offenses, as did his attempt to leave the country illegally. His arrest would have been violent, as Amadora said; Hernando wouldn't have let himself be caught easily. Any hope I'd had for absolution had vanished.

But despite my part in causing Hernando's misery, I plowed ahead like General Acha's cartoonish prosecutor. "So Hernando took part in dismantling Ruth's house?"

Cuevas adjusted his glasses as if to gauge, just as Julio and Doña Barbara had years before, the degree of my stupidity. He took a breath and said, "Oscar and Hernando were both the same. Oscar went to your sister after the Security people came around. He sought protection, but your sister's fancy art friends didn't want to get involved. Still, someone high up must have helped Oscar, because in the end he only lost his job at the school. He was lucky. His brother already had an arrest record and did hard time. And your sister—well, her case was important then, you know. Some people wanted more artists and their dollars from abroad. They thought your sister would mean something." He shook his head in disgust but also in wonder.

"She got through the mess unscathed," he said, his eyes focused on me.

Of course, Mariela had gotten through very little in her life unscathed. *In my art I put myself in the moment of grief.* But there was no point in saying this to Cuevas. His account confirmed what Doña Barbara implied all those years ago, that Mariela was at least partly to blame for the debacle of Ruth's house. Yet it explained very little. Even after Mariela's smug satisfaction at blowing up her fairy-tale houses in the New York gallery, I'd never believed that she had ruined Ruth's house only for money, or even for revenge. Cuevas's indignant face now struck me as a kind of pose. And it came to me.

"It was you," I said.

Cuevas didn't flinch.

Whatever fury had simmered in me all those years far from the neighborhood and from Ruth's ghost house now found focus. "You told State Security about Oscar, Hernando, Juan, all of them," I said. "To save yourself. And you accused the *yuma* foreigner too. But it had all been your idea, hadn't it? You were the mastermind of the whole scheme. It was you who'd surveyed the house; you knew what was in it and what it was worth. You'd done your inventory."

Cuevas shot to his feet, and his chair toppled behind him. He raised his voice for the first time. "I was in terrible shape. Didn't leave my house for months." He leaned across the table. "It was the Special Period. Do you remember anything?" He swept an angry, dismissive hand. "Of course you don't remember. What do you know of privation and struggle? You two, you and your fancy sister, left us here to clean up your mess."

Clearly, it wasn't all our mess; he'd just confirmed as much. But he was probably right in one regard—what did I know about any of it? Hernando served time in prison, Oscar lost his job and position, Juan died, and Cuevas carried out the unpleasant duties of his office and did what had to be done. He'd stepped down afterward as CDR president, most likely in disgrace or maybe in shame, and all the while Mariela and I went on to plentiful lives in *la yuma*, just as Amadora predicted. We'd abandoned them, yet the full story was complicated, because leaving was also at times an act of compassion toward those who stayed. It had been for Ruth, as Mariela helped support her from New York, and it must have been for Cuevas himself, who in his own life had sacrificed to care for Julio following his wife's gruesome death. Now, as the framed picture on the *paladar*'s mantel proved, Julio lived happily with his blond wife and children in the snowy mountains of Europe, and the prosperity of his son, along with Sara's presence in his life, could at last give Cuevas some peace.

Who was I to disturb it? He'd been glad to see me when I'd pulled up to the park, but now he stared back at me with rage. Only Sara's presence prevented him from pushing me out the door. Her hand lay on his, steady. I wondered if she thought this airing of old hurts was something like the medicine Mamá once said the country needed. *Bitter but good for you. Go on, Yuri. How else do we make progress? How else do we get on?* Dr. Cuevas picked up the fallen chair and sat again, exhausted now, his eyes half shut. Sara squeezed his hand and said to me, "You can't judge what's past, Yuri. You can't come here and judge what a person does in a moment of desperation . . ." Surely, her sadness suggested, I wouldn't begrudge the two of them this late happiness; surely, I saw who was actually dispossessed around this table. On this simple matter, Mariela had never wavered. She'd always professed her loyalty, self-deluding or not, to third world peoples as she'd called them. She hadn't sat in judgment except of Ruth.

I said, ashamed and bitter, "Things are better now. You both own Ruth's Paladar."

"The *State* owns this building," Cuevas said, red in the face again, offended to the core. "I didn't profit from Oscar's stupid scheme against your aunt. Understand? Never touched it. I wouldn't do that to a person."

"You were in charge. You did nothing to stop it until it suited you."

"I've never been in charge of a damn thing." He paused, then pointed at me. "And what about you?"

"I was a child."

"You were a young woman as I recall. Doing what a young woman does as I recall." At this Sara's face squeezed tight as if she might cry. Cuevas pointed at me again. "That scum was your boyfriend. You saw what you wanted to see."

What I saw: Abuelo Alberto's dirty tools strewn on the back patio, Don Juanito's mysterious bags, Amadora and sometimes Hernando sleeping on the cot, minor repairs around the garage in the days before the house came down. I saw me at sixteen roaming the hallways, often drunk, afraid, aggrieved, and without understanding. The "Destroy to Build" operation had gone on under my blindness and deafness while I'd lived in the house with the culprits, some of them my friends, the people I loved. And now after coming back, I seemed to have taken refuge in Sara and Cuevas calling me Yuri, my childhood name, as if this might speak to the possibility of my innocence. But would a guiltless person have flown a thousand miles away from her birthplace and changed her name?

Sara put her arm around Cuevas's shoulders. The two looked older to me now, frail.

I said as softly as I could, "I'm sorry for all this. I really am." I felt ugly, petty, supremely wrong. "I want to know why Ruth got arrested in the first place and that is all."

Cuevas took off his glasses and rubbed his eyes. He put them back on and said, "Ruth broke the law with those rockets, and the police arrested her."

"Mariela and I made the rockets, not Ruth. We lit them, not Ruth."

"Well, you shouldn't have," he said, louder than he'd probably intended. "I warned all of you to go home that day." He paused. "But I didn't call the police. Oscar did. But even he didn't know Ruth would be sent to the DSI. He thought she'd be out of the house for a day or two and they could raid her pantry and take some of her valuables, pillage the garage. Small-time stuff. They had no grand plan at first. Anyway, Ruth wouldn't have been sent to the DSI on Oscar's word alone. He was a little rattled when she wasn't released." Oscar had never seemed rattled except around his mother. But looking back now I saw that he'd mostly puffed out his chest and blustered his way through situations that made him feel insecure.

Cuevas went on, "Ruth might have had previous offenses, black-market transactions, or maybe her religion—maybe they wanted to make an example of her. How do we know what's in the minds of people who work for State Security? That's why we should never come close enough to any of them to find out." He paused. "Who knows why Ruth, why me, why you, why anybody."

"Ruth had no mind afterward," I said.

Cuevas pursed his lips. "It was a tragedy. About Ruth's illness I am very sorry."

Sara said, "Your aunt lived peacefully afterward, Yuri. You helped us with that."

"Not me," I said. "Mariela helped with that. And you took care of Ruth. I went away, didn't write, didn't help with Ruth, didn't send for her."

Cuevas looked down and said, "You were young. Young people are selfish."

There was enough kindness in his answer that I almost forgave him, and in the moment I almost forgave myself.

Sara added, "Nobody's to blame, Yuri."

Was this true? Could each of us, if pressed, justify our actions by pointing upward: I to Cuevas, Cuevas to Mariela and Oscar, Oscar to the State Security agent who held Ruth at the DSI, the DSI agent to his superior, and up and up and up and then, sooner or later, to the bearded man in fatigues who'd woken each morning for fifty-six years to rant at the mirror about the machinations waged against him by the most powerful country on Earth up above him on the map, and who, after reading reports from State Security, ordered the "necessary" arrests and executions of those below?

Up and up and down and down, first, second, third world.

The Tilting House

Two days earlier, as I'd sat on the runway in Miami waiting for my flight to leave for Havana, a news item appeared on my iPhone. In China, factory workers labored for over sixty hours per week, often in twelve-hour shifts, on behalf of Apple, soldering tiny pieces of metal to tinier pieces as they stared through large magnifying glasses mounted on rows and rows of worktables. They earned about two dollars per hour and relieved themselves only during scheduled breaks, and when any one of them could no longer take it, they jumped from a high window. Plant managers addressed the work conditions by placing nets outside the windows. Everyone around the world knew this had happened.

In the city where I'd once marveled at Mariela's perfumed sanitary pads strewn on her bed, and where no spectacular gadgets were yet produced for corporations through semi-slave labor, I sat in a bright kitchen with my iPhone in my purse and insisted that Cuevas and Sara think of me as one of them and answer my questions as dutifully as they might for someone who still lived in the neighborhood.

LATER THAT NIGHT, Sara showed me to my room upstairs, and from the hallway I caught a glimpse of Ruth's painting of the ugly baby, now hanging in Sara and Cuevas's bedroom—the same painting positioned nearly where it had been in Ruth's house, only a floor higher now, looking past the bed and straight out the door at me. Someone (Dr. Cuevas?) had snatched it from Ruth's rubble.

Was the painting a valuable commodity, a true Portocarrero

as Ruth had boasted, staring out from its new wall? Sara asked if I wanted to take the painting back with me to the States. No, I said, it belonged here in Ruth's Paladar. She smiled and kissed me good night. But the truth was that the baby's accusatory look disturbed me. What kind of baby, I thought, is born with a look like that? What had made her catch on so quickly?

I sat on the strange bed and opened my notepad, and instead of jotting down notes for my Reuters story, I wrote of the old house and myself at thirteen hearing for the first time that Ruth planned to send me to my deadbeat father. I stayed up most of the night scribbling, getting down the events that had led to my interrogation of Dr. Cuevas in Sara's kitchen.

But earlier that night, before coming up the stairs to bed, I had asked Cuevas two more questions: Did Doña Barbara still live in the neighborhood?

"The biggest gossip in Paladero, may she rest in peace," Cuevas said, worn out but trying to sound neutral.

Then, despite fearing the name of the institution I'd have to visit, I asked about Tere.

"She's still there, in the apartment," Cuevas said. "She got married, I think. Anyway, a man takes care of her. I don't see them much. They keep to themselves."

30

I didn't follow Mariela's instructions to scatter her ashes in the Viñales *manigüa* among fossils of the Guanahatabey people and ghosts of escaped African slaves, or at the feet of her ruined Nadies (if any were left). I wouldn't go back to Viñales, wouldn't retrace the trails that Hernando and I had traipsed along on top of that terrifying black horse. Instead I took a bus to Varadero, to the touristy beach resort Mariela had dismissed in 1993.

Varadero's famous turquoise ocean was actually as turquoise and serene as advertised. Visitors from Canada, South America, and Europe strolled up and down the sand wearing white wristbands like the ones assigned to newborn babies after a good scrub. A few children splashed wildly in the surf and adults, shiny with lotions, laid themselves in the sun on hotel towels and chaise lounges. Someone had left a beach chair at the water's edge. I sat in it and stared at the horizon, then watched the mild waves slide into the shore as the undertow dragged sand from around my feet back into the sea. The motion made me a little dizzy. I closed my eyes and breathed in the salt air and listened to the come-and-go of the surf.

A cloud shadow lodged itself over my head. I opened my eyes and a policeman stood beside me in the sand, blocking the sun. He pointed to my bare wrist. "No wristband, no chair," he said, and before I could hand him my Reuters credentials, which had protected me from harassment in the past, he asked to see my bag. He poked inside it with one hand, shifting my keys and wallet about in the jumble, then pulled out the plastic pouch filled with Mariela's ashes and asked, "What is this?"

"Ashes."

Surely, he knew that such rough gray powder couldn't be drugs. Still, this sharp-faced policeman whose chest blocked out the sun unzipped the baggie, dipped his hand inside, and stirred a finger into the chunky powder. His eyebrows rose then. I wondered if he'd lift his finger and put it into his mouth as if tasting a treat. "What is in here?" he said, louder. He held the bag out at the full length of his arm.

"Ashes," I said again.

The policeman, flustered now, realized that he was holding half a pound of human remains, and whether from shock or pure disgust, he opened his hand and let go of the baggie. "Those are my sister's ashes," I said and tried to go after the bag. But the policeman's dopey confusion had turned to fury, and he seized my arm and demanded my passport. The press credentials inside alarmed him more. I was to follow him to his patrol car immediately. The open baggie with the handful of Mariela's gray remains bobbed unsteadily, then filled with Varadero's sparkling turquoise water and sank below the mild waves.

TWO *JINETERA* WOMEN made space for me on the wood bench of the twelve-by-twelve-foot holding cell. I shook between them, cold, scared, but the two women, their arrests probably routine, looked mostly bored and sleepy and this helped calm me down. To my left, the older woman introduced herself as Mercedes. A large tattoo of a snake wound up her thick leg and disappeared beneath her skirt. She made small talk and broke a crumbly set of four soda crackers into two and handed me half. "*Dále,*" she said, "these *cabrones* always take a long time." I chewed, swallowed; the few dry bites made me hungrier.

Mercedes's tattooed snake led to a small flask tied with a thick ribbon around her upper thigh, apparently undetected or ignored by a guard's careless search. She untied the flask, took a sip, then held out the flask to me. I didn't want to drink from it but felt too unnerved to refuse her kindness. I took the flask from her hand and tipped it into my mouth. Aguardiente. The familiar taste burned my throat, my eyes watered, and I returned the flask. She laughed. "Feel warmer now?" I nodded. Mercedes then handed the flask to the pretty woman with bleached hair sitting to my right.

I sat quiet and desolate. Mercedes's plump arm sometimes rubbed against mine. Her skin was smooth and warm. I pressed against her in those few seconds, for the comfort of it. She didn't seem to notice or to mind. We sat silent and she fell asleep leaning against the wall behind us. When Reuters got me out a few hours later, the guard's voice woke Mercedes, and she nodded a sleepy approval. "*Dále*," she said. I kissed her cheek.

Sara and Cuevas picked me up in a borrowed 1950s Oldsmobile. Sara took my belongings—all scrupulously returned by the police except, of course, Mariela's ashes, now lost forever. We headed to Havana in the dark. I couldn't bring myself to tell Sara about the ashes. On the road Sara turned from the front seat and said to me as if speaking to a troublesome teenager, "You should have been more careful. You should have consulted us. You don't know how things are here. You don't remember." Dr. Cuevas drove on, silent. I apologized for my thoughtlessness, my idiocy; I could see that this had been, as Mariela had said years earlier about the suction-cup climber in Manhattan, a useless, dangerous stunt.

THE NEXT MORNING, I felt terribly sore and low. Sara served me toast and strong coffee. "You're lucky your job got you out." She dried a few plates from the dish rack. She seemed serious, even a little stern. Soon enough I realized she was actually worried, as if she had moved beyond my stunt into more pressing problems. She put the dishes in the cabinet and said, "The restaurant needs spices and supplies." Her tone wasn't forbearing anymore. "Ingredients we can't get here. We haven't been doing too well as you can see." The *paladar* was empty even now, close to lunchtime, and the rental rooms on the second floor also sat vacant. I felt desperately sad for Sara and Dr. Cuevas, old and tired, who wanted only to get along quietly with the rest of their lives. I wondered, too, if Mariela's brainchild, this coral *paladar* in this small faraway suburb, wasn't ultimately, even if well-intentioned, another sort of foolish stunt. In the few days I'd spent in the neighborhood, the *paladar* had only hosted five or six people, elbows on a table, having a few sandwiches and cold beers.

"I'm not sure how much the estate can expect—" Sara said.

"What estate?"

She looked at me steadily. "I gave your sister twenty percent of the business we did here, which, as you can see, has never been much."

"Mariela charged you a percentage?"

Sara said nothing to this. "Ruth's Paladar isn't near rich tourists in Central Havana. We're out here in Paladero. We serve the neighborhood, people who are just getting by, who need discounts."

"I'll send you what you need," I said. "Please don't worry, I don't want any percentage."

Sara thanked me, but I also saw that she squinted at my promise. I wondered if my generosity struck her as squeamishness. She said, "The thing about your sister was, she cared about this place." I realized that Sara wanted a solid partnership with me, not a one-time charity I could walk away from at any time without much thought or, as she'd just implied, without much feeling. Maybe Sara feared that while in Havana I loved her, but that soon I'd flee as I'd done before, and I'd go back to the life I'd been living for the last twenty-two years, to my job and my friends in swampy South Florida, and I'd be done with this place and with her.

I tried to put her at ease, made pledges of support, did my best, and then, little by little, I lost heart. Sara had seen that I'd come back to this place mostly to be through with it. And I couldn't, in the end, convince her, or myself, that she was wrong.

31

The small Malanga-head courtyard was deserted in the midday heat except for a woman hanging clothes on the line by the water tank. She had the square build of Amadora, who'd cursed me on that very spot for deserting her son, and I froze at the sight of her there pinning up a wet shirt, her back to me. Then I remembered that Amadora would have to be ninety years old, and she wouldn't be out in the sun, bending and lifting and shaking wet, heavy clothes onto a line. The woman turned then and nodded in greeting, and I saw that she was in her fifties and looked nothing like Amadora.

I knocked on the Malanga-heads' door and waited. Oscar finally opened it, squinting against the glare. Then he settled on my face, as if trying to reconcile my features with his memory. His hair was brownish gray; he was still as thin as when he was young.

"Yuri," I said to him. "*Soy* Yuri."

He gave me a wry smile and ushered me into the small, dark apartment. Oscar's eyes, behind his glasses, were like his brother's.

He gestured for me to sit at the small table. "About the last person I expected to see today," he said. He tried to sound friendly, but he looked startled and his tone was wary. He turned to the stove and poured two cups of coffee. The small living room–kitchen–dining room was tidy, the sink free of dishes; a folded towel lay on the clean counter beside shakers of salt and pepper. Maybe a woman lived with Oscar, and my relief at the thought of a wife surprised me. Maybe time hadn't stalled in Oscar's small apartment. To have found him middle-aged and alone would have sapped my courage, and I needed courage to get through the visit.

Oscar set the cups of coffee on the table and sat down across from me. I said, "I've been visiting people in the neighborhood. People I knew as a child."

He nodded and kept his eyes on me, then said, almost casually, "I take it you've seen the neighborhood's new establishment."

I was surprised that he'd mentioned Ruth's Paladar right away. But my presence must have brought back to mind the disaster of Ruth's house and its aftermath, and with them, the end of his career and ambitions and his good standing in the Party. He had walked away from that public humiliation and maybe hid here in his childhood home after his divorce, working at any job he could find. And here I was now, nearly a *yuma* tourist among Havana's other tourists, wearing shiny shoes and carrying a shiny purse and sleeping in the new *paladar* as any tourist would. It had to rankle him, how the few yankee dollars the *paladar* generated went, not into his pockets, but into the pockets of others who'd surpassed his old ambitions and prospered now, half entrepreneurs, half patriots, full citizens of the twenty-first century.

"How," I asked, "is the family?" I named no one in particular. Oscar didn't take his eyes from me. His look was less friendly. All were well, he said. "And Amadora?" I asked. Died several years before, he said. He asked nothing about my life. He sat silent, studying me, and I said at last, "How is Hernando? I was hoping to send a letter to him. A package."

Oscar half grinned. "Hernando is not on this island, but on the next." He watched me, and when he saw enough panic in my eyes, he laughed. "The Isle of Youth. Like your Alcatraz. Way out in the water." He meant the small island thirty miles off Cuba's southern coast, serving mostly as a warehouse for prisoners sent from the mainland. Oscar said, "Nobody's young on the Isle of Youth, you know? Nobody," and I saw in Oscar's lined face the face of his imprisoned brother, no doubt more lined than Oscar's, harder, more beaten down, made old by the Isle of Youth's terrible sun.

Oscar took a breath and said with the old confidence of the youth leader and physics teacher, "But I'll take Hernando your package."

He sat back then, satisfied. He said more warmly, "I am glad to see you well." He seemed to mean it. "Stay for dinner. Tonight, when my wife comes, stay and meet her." I wondered if Oscar had married one of my childhood friends, someone whose face I could still recognize. But I didn't ask.

Out in the courtyard, the water tank woman yelled someone's name. Someone screamed back. Oscar paid no attention.

Through the kitchen window, I watched the woman fling a towel into the basket and rush inside an apartment.

The everydayness of the small commotion outside, the call and return of voices, drained some of the tension between us, and Oscar regarded me from his chair, not unkindly, but simply trying to make sense of my presence in his kitchen. I gathered my strength and spoke. "I was hoping you'd have an address for Hernando. I haven't brought the package with me now," I lied.

Oscar said, "Sure. Try this. 'Hernando Pita. Isle of Youth. Prison.'" He looked at me with bitter amusement, then laughed again.

All at once I saw my colossal mistake. I'd get nothing out of Oscar. And why should I? Twice in the last forty-eight hours I'd demanded gifts from people who themselves needed far more urgent gifts from me. I fumbled for my bag and thought of handing him the present I'd brought, a box of valuable shampoo and perfumed soaps. But something—shame, maybe sorrow—wouldn't let me do it. I pulled my purse up my shoulder and stood. "It was good to see you."

He rose too and set his hand gently on my arm. "Please don't go. Have a seat, I didn't mean anything." He looked contrite and I felt too weak to walk out the door. I sat again, and as a small gesture of reconciliation, he offered the name of the prison where Hernando was held. I wrote it down in my journalist's pad. "How long has he been there?"

Oscar shrugged. "Years. Most of his shit life."

I could see that he wasn't finished and braced myself. "Hernando got caught trying to leave again on a raft some years ago. They said he was dealing drugs, weed mostly, and he got twenty years. They don't care about weed, you understand, what Hernando did was nothing. But they need young men like him for free labor. They need people like us, people who don't matter." He breathed in and started again. He couldn't help it; he'd been gnawing on this for twenty-two years. "The thing is, we're just fodder, right? We were fodder, too, for you people," he said in a low voice. "My brother went to prison for you that time. He stole for you. You put ideas in his head. And now you come back here polished like silver. You look finished." He took another breath, then added, "Someone finished you." It seemed to please him to say this, and it also seemed to make him a little sad. He cleared his throat. Some of the tension in his face eased and he half smiled and asked again that I stay for dinner. "The least you can do. And bring your sister." I realized then that the whole time he'd been working up to a mention of Mariela.

"Mariela died."

Oscar looked at me, his bitterness replaced by deep confusion. He let out a low, whistling breath. He said, "I knew it." And then, "I knew it, I knew it, I knew it." He seemed to forget about me. He put his hands on the table and lowered his head between his arms. He drew in a breath, seemed to hold it, then started to sob. "Where will I go?" he asked, low.

THE SKY HAD turned thick with dark, low-hanging clouds and the woman in the courtyard was taking down the clothes she'd finished hanging up a few minutes earlier. I left Oscar hunched at the table, wiping his face with the back of his hand.

The Tilting House

His pure, bright grief shook me. I realized I envied it. I'd never cried so fully and openly as he had—gulping for air, head down between the arms—not at Mamá's funeral, not when I left Ruth and my country behind, not after Hernando disappeared, not after the breakup of my marriage, and not after the officer's phone call from Arizona about Mariela's accident or after her ashes were tossed into the sea by the wrong hand. Nothing had come up from my chest the way that Oscar's grief poured out of him. Impacted grief (adding sadness and bafflement to it each year) was a slow-growing poison, I knew that. But now I saw, as I left the Malanga-head courtyard, that Amadora hadn't cursed me with some omen those years before; she'd simply made a reasonable prediction. By turning my back on her son's offer and fleeing to the north without him, I'd thought that I'd embraced the future. But I'd done the opposite. Now I saw that Hernando's thuggish will might have pulled me into an ordinary present where I would have exchanged vows sincerely with others, broken them sincerely, and exhausted myself in real time with a real name.

A visit to Hernando's prison cell, even if I could arrange for the connections and bribes to make it happen, would only compound my mistake. I'd show myself as I am now, with my journalist's pass and my shiny purse and shoes, finished, polished like silver—the way Mariela had appeared to me in 1993. Hernando would receive me as a fraud, a foreigner, and he would stomp on my care package the way he'd stomped on Mariela's secret box of cash because, of the two of us, he was the braver one who'd always meant to live in the truth.

32

The couch and chairs and old lamps with their yellowed lampshades in Tere's living room stood in the same spot as on the afternoon Doña Barbara had told her "Destroy to Build" tale. Tere and I sat on the same couch, and she laid her head on my shoulder and repeated my old name. In a while the afternoon downpour stopped, and she and I went out to the balcony to feed the pigeons. One pigeon, then another, landed on the end of the railing and made their comical way to Tere's trail of sunflower seeds. After eating they flew back to their branches or eaves. Tere and I had fed pigeons this way when we were children.

Without Doña Barbara's wrathful presence, the attractiveness of the apartment and the beauty of Tere's face, her smooth skin, her clear eyes, shone through easily. Mundo, a distant cousin, lived with Tere now. A large man with glasses and close-cropped hair, he kept her from being sent to an institution and then from losing her vacated home to the government. He brought to us on the balcony a tray of doughy croquettes and glasses of watermelon juice. Tere swallowed hers in a blink. I took my time, dislodging each bite of the croquettes from between my teeth, savoring their familiar blandness.

A passerby walked hurriedly in the street below. Tere greeted her and the sunflower hulls scattered from the rail. She called the woman's name and introduced me, shouting, "My friend is here. Yuri." The startled woman waved. Tere said to her, "She's from Miami. She's my friend." The woman nodded. I wondered if I should explain what sort of friend I was. A friend from childhood? From the neighborhood? A friend who hadn't spoken to Tere in two decades?

The woman smiled up at us. I offered a polite wave, and she waved goodbye to the two of us and walked on toward the bus stop. The sun was dropping out of view, but the heat lingered. Tere and I sat on the balcony's chairs. We stared at the sky, the fronds, the trunks of the palm trees. I had nowhere I had to be. The tumult of Doña Barbara's and Ruth's reigns had passed—they and Don Juanito and Mariela were gone—and Tere and I sat together in peace, our arms touching.

The sun was almost down when Mundo, who'd apparently finished his caretaking duties for the day, came out to the balcony. He wanted to settle Tere in for the night. He said to me, "If she gets too excited, she can't sleep. And if she can't sleep, she keeps everybody else up."

By the front door Tere hugged me with her sticky, fat arms. I headed down the stairs to the street. From the balcony she called out to me just as she'd called out to the passing neighbor. She repeated my name, and I thought, when she was almost out of view, that she made it sound like a question.

33

Dr. Cuevas and Sara drove me to the José Martí Airport in the same Oldsmobile they'd borrowed to pick me up from jail, and after hugs and kisses and Sara's tears and mine and Cuevas's cool goodbye, I moved into the corridor among hurrying passengers. I showed my ticket and boarded my flight to Miami.

The plane waited to taxi on the hot tarmac. I checked the time on my iPhone; there was some delay. After some chitchat, the young man in the seat next to me asked if he could practice his English with me. For his future, he said. He said he was a video producer traveling with a Cuban *fútbol* team to Dallas through Miami. I must have seemed to him as if I came from that place called the future.

He asked what I did. I told him I worked for Reuters, and he said, "What does one need to do to work for Google?" I said I didn't quite know, and he protested in halting English, "But you're a journalist." Like many on the island, he thought that a journalist from *la yuma* should be a trove of information as vast as Google.

A voice from the speakers said to buckle our seat belts. I asked the young man, as a journalist, wasn't he concerned about Google or some multinational or some American or Cuban American billionaire swooping in and buying the people on the island for cheap?

Apparently, I was the wrong messenger for twenty-first-century neocolonialist doom. He switched to Spanish. "You eat steak every day, right?"

"I'm a pescatarian."

He smiled, a little amused. He said, "With all respect, whatever you eat you look well fed to me." He kept his smile friendly. "Look, we, the people my age, don't care that much about politics. We don't care where we get our *jama* from, as long as we get it."

I'd seen this young man's enterprising attitude all over Havana's center. Gathering quotes for my Reuters article, my driver, Chino, and I had stopped at various stores. One young woman on Galiano Street confessed that she'd opened her small shop with profits from sex work (I was to change her name for the story). Three mannequins, like white geysers gushing from the ground, shone resplendent in her store window. The gowns had come from Miami. Later Chino and I ate at a fancy *paladar* in Central Havana, owned and operated at least partly, Chino told me, by Cubans. People lined up outside the restaurant's entrance waiting patiently for a woman in a white shirt and black bow tie to come out into the heat of the busy walkway and read someone's lucky name from a clipboard.

In the airplane's stuffy cabin—we still waited on the tarmac—the young man beside me sat up and tried his English again. He would interview me—"Okay?" And he asked a question that apparently filled him with wonder: "Your president lives with his mother-in-law?"

I nodded. He shook his head and said in near-perfect English, "Above my pay grade." Then he shook his head again, this time in frustration. He lived with his wife's grandparents. "Who," he asked me, "do you live with?"

He wasn't flirting; he seemed truly curious. "No one," I said, and I saw myself in his eyes: a rich, not-so-young single woman who didn't have to live with anyone at all.

"Look," he lowered his voice, "I'll tell you something about politics. With the revolution, they"—his parents, grandparents, in-laws—"felt they had a cause, had pride. But that's pretty much over."

"Who do you blame?" I asked.

"Blame?" He sounded a little surprised. He shrugged. "Plenty to go around."

The young man asked to look at my iPhone and asked about various apps and the phone's memory. He turned it over in his hands several times, thanked me, and passed it back. Then he rolled up his sweater, wedged it behind his neck, and closed his eyes as the airplane started rolling forward on the tarmac.

I put the phone back into my purse, and a thought, like a voice from long ago, came, *The people got your gadget.* I'd said this to Mariela in the park years before, and she'd smiled at me with her benign indifference. That was the day Hernando kicked Lucho, lifted him off the ground with his swift dancer's foot, then took Mariela's expensive camera and ran off with his two friends across the park's dusty expanse beyond the Milo statue. Mariela had stayed put beside Lucho as he bled from his side onto the rocks. She patted the whimpering dog, but her eyes followed the running boys and the camera Hernando had snatched from her hand. And then, *in a twinkling*, as Ruth might have said, Mariela took off after the boys. She gained on them across the open field. A gray dust cloud swirled in the air behind her as she flew across the dry field while a real cloud in the sky floated in the opposite direction, toward me, Tere, and Lucho, and I looked up from the ground by the dying dog and felt my stomach slip from its place, just as I felt it slipping now as the ground sped by the window and the plane finally gathered momentum and started to lift. It was probably the same feeling Mariela had—she'd told us about it once—when someone had seated her backward in a large seat and the train started, many years before, for Lincoln, Nebraska. The moving train had rumbled up through her feet, and then, she'd said, the station and the people were sucked backward, slow at first, then very fast.

The plane gained speed and height, and I counted, "One Mississippi, two Mississippi . . ." My heart beat fast. The young man beside me was curled in his seat, his eyes shut; I could hear him breathing. The strange artificial air inside the cabin grew bright as the sun poured through the small window and the plane banked and set its course. Soon, below, the ocean would appear.

But for now, the streets on the ground were disappearing, changing into mottled shapes of grays and greens. My heart beat faster. Somewhere in those tiny streets below (and though I knew it was impossible, I squinted and stared) was the small apartment on Misión Street where Mamá and I had lived. This was the one place I hadn't bothered to visit during my return, the one house my sister, who had lived in many houses, had searched for her entire life. I had not visited that apartment—and never would—so as not to lose it again. All this time I'd thought that no matter where I went or what I did, I could go on living in that nowhere house with the woman who'd died there with a loaded gun under her bed.

The young man shifted in his seat beside me. I wiped my face quickly with my hands. He opened his eyes, and it must have come back to him—the *yuma* stranger in the seat next to him, the nice rich woman who seemed too naïve to be a real journalist. "Hello again," he said to me in his thick English. "Are you feeling well?"

I nodded, wiped my face again.

"Don't be sad," he said to me, putting on his charm. "We sit together now. We talk," he said. "It's not easy, believe me, I know." His seriousness moved me, and I smiled a little. The flight attendant brought snacks and he unwrapped his, then made a face at the salted peanuts scattered on his tray. "You eat like birds in *la yuma*, no?" he said in Spanish. He ate several peanuts, then said quietly, serious again, "It is my beginning when this plane lands. Do you understand?" He paused.

I understood. He meant to defect on the ground, leave behind whoever he needed to, and stay in *la yuma*.

"Help me please," he said.

We were over the ocean now, the earthly blue that Gagarin had seen from outer space, which must have convinced him of an up and a down.

"Yes," I said. "Yes. We start now."

Acknowledgments

This book would not exist without the help and encouragement of family, friends, fellow writers, mentors, teachers, agent, editors, and many others. My heartfelt thanks to my grandparents, godparents, and extended family, and to Mamá for the stories, even if I can't remember. To lifelong friends Cary Castro, Virginia Fuillerat, Cecilia Rodriguez Milanés, Carolina Hospital, Victor Calderin, Kelly Kennedy, Esther Perez, Larry Apple, and many others for your care and faith in me. To my brother, Gabriel Lamazares, and his husband, Terry Milner, for being part of my life. To Josh Fernandez for the author website, and to Lisa Saldaña for our life-changing work together. To MAWLs Gigi Marino and Nina Adel for our supportive writing community, and to Lisa Roney for years of creative and nurturing phone calls; without your advice I'd still be revising page 3. To my chosen family, Pat Leitch, Sara Mirabal, and Julian Mirabal, for your ongoing kindness, and to Elena Perez, my sister and best friend, *juntitas siempre*; no words can say what you mean to me.

Acknowledgments

I can't thank the Counterpoint Press team enough, especially my brilliant, insightful editor Dan López; thank you for understanding the history in this book and all that I meant to say. My deep gratitude to Dan Smetanka, Laura Berry, Rachel Fershleiser, Megan Fishmann, Vanessa Genao, Ashley Kiedrowski, Jaya Miceli, Lily Philpott, Luis Francisco Pizarro Ruiz, Yukiko Tominaga, Miriam Vance, and the entire Counterpoint team for a fulfilling and collaborative publication experience.

A huge thank-you to Mitchell Kaplan for thirty-plus years of book celebration, friendship, and invaluable support. And especially to Gail Hochman, my agent of many years; thank you for your abiding generosity and faith, for the multiple readings and encouraging advice, and for directing me to Counterpoint Press.

My biggest thanks to my daughter, Sophie Juliet Kronen, for being my inspiration and joy, and for giving me your enthusiastic support at every step; it lifted me every time and helped me believe. And to my beloved Steve Kronen, thank you for three-plus decades of love, poetry, and creativity; no words can express what you have done for this novel and what you do for me every day; without you I wouldn't have written a single word.

© Elena Perez

IVONNE LAMAZARES was born in Havana. She left Cuba at the age of thirteen and settled in Florida. Her first novel, *The Sugar Island*, was translated into seven languages. Her short fiction and nonfiction have appeared in *Latina* magazine, *The Southern Review*, *Michigan Quarterly Review*, *The Florida Review*, and elsewhere. Lamazares is the recipient of a National Endowment for the Arts Fellowship and three Florida Individual Artist Fellowships. She lives in Miami. Find out more at ivonnelamazares.com.